FOG CITY

FOG CITY

A FOG CITY NOIR MYSTERY

CLAIRE M. JOHNSON

First published by Level Best Books/Historia 2024

Copyright © 2024 by Claire M. Johnson

All rights reserved. No part of this publication may be reproduced, stored or transmitted in any form or by any means, electronic, mechanical, photocopying, recording, scanning, or otherwise without written permission from the publisher. It is illegal to copy this book, post it to a website, or distribute it by any other means without permission.

This novel is entirely a work of fiction. The names, characters and incidents portrayed in it are the work of the author's imagination. Any resemblance to actual persons, living or dead, events or localities is entirely coincidental.

Claire M. Johnson asserts the moral right to be identified as the author of this work.

Author Photo Credit: Nancy Warner

First edition

ISBN: 978-1-68512-680-3

Cover art by Level Best Designs

This book was professionally typeset on Reedsy.
Find out more at reedsy.com

I would like to dedicate this book to all those secretaries out there who would gladly take an axe to their typewriters or keyboards. You are ma soeurs.

Praise for Fog City

"Claire Johnson has stepped right into the footwear of the Thirties, with her smart-mouthed secretary-turned-gumshoe taking over her boss's investigations and poking a well-powdered nose into all kinds of San Francisco chicanery. *Fog City* is a delight! I hope we see much more of Mags Laurent—oh, and that trouble-making boss of hers, Nick Moore."—Laurie R. King, *NYT* bestselling author of the Russell & Holmes series, The Kate Martinelli series, *Back to the Garden*, and others

"Claire M. Johnson's *Fog City* is the dark, dangerous, and delicious San Francisco of classic noir, a city of smoke-filled speakeasies and jazz singers with secrets to keep, of scheming families who built their fortunes on crime and the corrupt officials who cover for them. The twists come hard and fast in this one, and Maggie Laurent is a welcome addition to the city's rich history of private eyes."—Margaret Dumas, author of the Movie Palace mystery series, *Speak Now, How To Succeed in Murder*, and *The Balance Thing*

"A snazzy, snappy, delightful romp through early '30s San Francisco!"—Kelli Stanley, Macavity-winning author of *City of Dragons*

"When her P.I. boss goes on an extended bender, Maggie Laurent decides she can handle a simple case to keep the firm solvent. As in any great noir tale, the case turns out to be twisty, but Maggie's a quick learner who is happy to add the occasional rosary prayer to her innate smarts and willingness to ask for help from some intriguing characters. She's brave, shrewd, and a bit cynical. Perfect for this fog-drenched San Francisco noir. I loved *Fog City* and Maggie!"—Susan Shea, author of *Murder Visits a French Village* (March

'23), *Murder and the Missing Dog* (March 2024), and the Dani O'Rourke Mysteries

Chapter One

On a windy day in November, the leads of an American flag hammered against the aluminum pole in a haphazard banging as the flag twisted in the harsh wind. The pants of the prison guards flapped against their legs, and the force of the wind flattened their shirt fronts against their chests. They put the rope around Eileen Taylor's neck, placing her in the center of the trapdoor. We stood there, watching two guards tugging on the rope to make sure it wouldn't fray, and then they stepped back. Eileen Taylor caught Nick's eye right before a third guard pulled the lever to the trapdoor. Up until that moment, I never believed in evil. It was too abstract, worse than sin, but how worse, I didn't know. I forced myself to watch the drop. It was then that I knew the difference between evil and sin.

Every Sunday, Father O'Flaherty lectures us about sin. He touches on God's grace for a second or two, and then it's right onto the main feature: our sins over the last week. We sit in the pews, trying not to blush, as we mentally make a list for confession. Based on the line for the confessional box every week, it's easy to sin. That time I stole money out of my mother's purse to buy a packet of gum? It qualifies. In the greater scheme of things, this seems like chump change, but I'd confessed it.

Father talks about evil almost as much, but he has a harder time pinning it down. The good father had little sympathy for lying—worth a couple of rosaries for sure—but I don't think your garden-variety lying is evil. Coveting your neighbor's wife is sinful, but evil? There are always a few sermons a year devoted to Satan, the embodiment of evil. Even though I could count on one hand the number of times I'd missed a Sunday mass, I still had a hard time envisioning what makes evil different from common-place sin.

Then I met Eileen Taylor. And I learned that evil wasn't a dancing figure with horns and a red trident in his hand. No, siree. It was a blue-eyed, raven-haired beauty who'd shoot you point-blank three times and then step over your bleeding carcass on her way out the door, indifferent to your moans of agony and prayers for help.

Chapter Two

Fourteen months earlier

I loved almost everything about being Nick Moore's secretary. The only thing I didn't love was making excuses for him when he got tired of the skirt of the month. His yen for dumb-as-dirt blondes whose curves make men chase sin always backfires on him. Sooner rather than later, he walks, leaving me to field their sob-filled telephone calls when he dumps them. As he always does.

Mildred was his latest bottle blonde with the nicest pair of gams you ever saw. Unfortunately, when she opened her mouth, her voice resembled nails on a blackboard. I held the phone at least a foot away from my ear, and I could still hear her screeching, begging me to tell her where he was.

"On a job in Los Angeles, Miss Roberts. Like I told you. Special request by the mayor. I don't know how long he'll be away."

Since I'd started working for Nick, it never failed to amuse him at what a good liar I was. That's what the nuns used to say about me, too. Nick was lounging against the doorframe, chewing on a toothpick, and listening to me make excuses for him. He threw the toothpick in the trashcan and snorted in response to my comment.

I put my hand over the mouthpiece. "Will you be quiet! If I have to lie on your behalf, then the least you can do is keep a lid on the commentary."

Mildred cried some more. When she stopped, I told her I'd give Nick the message that she'd called and hung up.

"Why do you bother with them, Nick? That last one? Mildred? Okay, pretty, sort of, and I admit she has great legs, but dumb. Rocks are smarter."

He shrugged. "When you're a little older, you'll understand."

I threw my pencil at him. Which he caught like he was anticipating I was going to throw it at him.

"Don't be so patronizing. I'm twenty-four and not a child." I belied that statement by stamping my foot. "And if you'd done any detecting, Mr. Detective, you'd have known that Mildred Roberts is just a floozy looking for a ring."

"How do you know I didn't know that?" he jeered, and for a second, his face lost its usual hardness.

The San Francisco newspapers always described him as a hard man, his resting face resolute and determined, with gray eyes that didn't flinch at much. Nick had come home from the Second Battle of the Somme over ten years ago with a cough he couldn't shake and speaking French like a native. He never talked about the Great War, but when it was mentioned, he'd throw his shoulders back just a little, like he was waiting for someone to hit him. He gave the impression of having seen too much and not liking what he'd seen.

He wasn't traditionally handsome. His chin was too pointy, with his lips often pursed in a grimace. In his mid-thirties, he looked older most days, and the blond of his hair now going gray. Even though he wasn't much of a looker, he wore his suits with a panache that made you think they were more expensive than they were. And no one wore a hat better than he did, at a jaunty angle that softened his chin. He was someone you noticed at a party. His easy grace when he moved would catch your eye, and the more you watched him, the more captivating he became. I guess you'd call it charm. He could lay it on thick when he wanted to, but kept it straight with me and didn't play me. I liked that. He treated me like his kid sister, albeit one who had to lie for him now and then. A lot of nows and thens.

"Someday, you'll meet someone, and it will be kapow, buster, right between the eyes." I pointed a finger at him. "And you'll be crying on my shoulder."

"Sure, sweetheart, sure," he said with a roll of his eyes and threw the pencil

CHAPTER TWO

on my desk. As he moseyed back to his office behind me, I heard the strike of a match and the acrid scent of his cigarette as the flame hit the tobacco. How many did he go through in a day, I wondered?

The phone rang again, and I braced myself for a repeat of Mildred's sob story. But it wasn't Mildred. A voice, soft with the faintest hint of a Southern accent, told me the caller was educated and had a bit of class. Her name was Eileen Taylor. She wanted to know if the Moore Detective Agency did divorce work because she was convinced her husband was cheating on her. I told her our going rates. She'd stop by in an hour if that was convenient. Money was always convenient.

She walked into our office with eyes the color of cornflowers, her black hair cut in a Louise-Brooks style bob, and a body so lush it had me blushing. Within five minutes of hearing her story, I was ready to strangle her wife-beating, cheating husband myself. It took Nick a little longer. Like seven minutes.

Her husband beat her constantly. He was jealous to the point of insanity. Oh, help me, Mr. Moore. Will you find evidence, anything, so I can file for divorce before he kills me? she pleaded. When she handed over the money for the job, her sleeve slid up from her wrist, and we saw a bruise the size of a plum climbing up her arm, which hinted at bruises everywhere else.

As it turned out, her entire story was hooey. Her husband was a successful doctor. She'd been his secretary, and within six months of him hiring her, she'd elbowed out wife number one, and within nine months, she'd become Mrs. Doctor with a rock on her fourth finger as proof. Plus a plan to murder him for insurance money. Three weeks after crossing the threshold of our office, she shot the husband. In self-defense, she sobbed.

I asked Nick once why she roped him into her scheme.

"Oldest trick in the book. She didn't want wife number one to hire me to investigate her ex-husband's death, so she came to me first. That put me out of the running. Because most men had fallen for her act, she assumed I'd be her latest chump."

"That was stupid on her part," I sneered. "You don't have the reputation for being the best detective in this city for nothing."

He didn't respond.

I'd never seen Nick that dizzy over a woman. She just, I don't know, dazzled him. Still, her kisses weren't hungry enough to stop him from finding out about the insurance policy she took out on the husband, her signature barely dry before she shot him. No matter how much she cried on his shoulder and bent her body into his, Nick refused to turn a blind eye to her murdering an innocent man for fifty thousand smacks.

Too bad for her that Nick was a detective first and a sucker second.

We sat at the back of the courtroom during her trial, those oak benches as unforgiving as a judge. It was his evidence that was going to sink her. He knew it. She knew it. And it did.

Eileen had been in prison for a little over a year when she turned those big blue eyes on an eighteen-year-old prison guard who'd been on the job for only two weeks. He tried to help her escape, but they were caught. The guards pumped eighteen bullets into his gut. Before his body had even hit the ground, she'd grabbed his gun and killed three other guards. She didn't stop shooting until they took out her knee.

A month later, they hanged her.

Nick and I had a big fight about me driving up with him to San Quentin. Hammer and tongs for hours. He'd insisted on seeing her to say goodbye.

"You aren't going with me, Mags, and that's final."

"Nuts to that, Nick Moore. I'm going with you, and you can shout and scream all you want, but I'm going to be there."

We didn't speak the whole drive.

Although the summers are hot across the Bay, the winters are brutal, with temps down in the twenties. Already, the newly planted palm trees were bent over in a painful arc in deference to the nearly constant wind as it rushed in from the Pacific Ocean, past the Farallon Islands, and whipped through the wide bowl that constitutes San Francisco Bay. Peering through the grime of the car window, I wondered how many winters it would take before they died. The hem of my skirt lashed my calves, and I had to hold onto my hat to stop it from blowing away. I caught Nick's hat as it threatened to sail into the water. He never noticed.

CHAPTER TWO

I stood next to him as we watched Eileen hobble up to the scaffold, leaning on a guard for support. Even at that moment, her beauty made me gasp in surprise, and I put a strong hand under Nick's elbow to keep him upright. As they put the rope around her neck, she caught his eye and mouthed, "Fuck you, Nick," right before the door dropped open.

When we finally emerged from the prison gates, he staggered the whole way to the car, a flask in one hand and the bulge of another weighing down his coat pocket. Without a word, he got in the passenger side of the car. Once we had closed the doors, the smell of bourbon hit me in the face. It had splashed down the front of his shirt, which told me he hadn't bothered to be nice about his drinking. He wanted to get drunk and fast.

My brother, Al, had been giving me driving lessons, and I knew enough not to crash the hire. Nick slumped in his seat, finished one flask, and then began to work on the other. On the drive up, it had taken three hours to load the car onto the Sausalito car ferry at the Hyde Street Pier and then drive to San Quentin. I floored it on the way back, and it only took two, even considering the ferry ride.

I half-dragged him up to his apartment on Post Street, dumped him on the bed, and then took off his shoes. It wasn't until I reached the door that he uttered the first words I'd heard from him in three hours. "She fooled both of us, Sweetheart. " I had nothing to say to that. I left him there alone to nurse his drunk and heartache. She broke a heart I thought was untouchable, but she made me feel like a fool. A real chump.

I didn't see him again until two weeks later when he came back to the office, his face a sickly gray courtesy of the sort of long bender where you go to bed drunk and wake up still drunk, never quite sober.

A year went by and it was spring. The stock market had crashed the previous October. Six months later I was walking past men slumped up against building fronts trying to sleep or with grimy hands cupped in front of their shirts in the hope someone would take pity so they could eat that day. The lines for soup kitchens were now around the block.

Nick looked pretty rough most mornings, but he made it to the office by ten. The divorce trade was brisk. I don't know why people bother getting married, to be honest.

To everyone else, Nick was Nick.

To my eyes, not even close.

Then I bought a blue hat, and that was that.

I'd seen it in the window of I. Magnin's, composed of the most beautiful shade of cobalt blue velvet with a matching veil that swept down in a graceful arc. I'd been eyeing that hat for months and had skipped lunch for weeks to pay for it. The second I put it on, I felt older, sophisticated even. I looked swell. And the first day I wore it to work, I poked my head around his door to say good morning. He leaped up from his desk, ran out of his office, and tore the hat off my head, only to throw it in the garbage. To make sure it was good and destroyed, he stomped on it several times with an angry foot. Too late, I realized it was the exact color of Eileen Taylor's eyes. He apologized later—"Sorry, darling, I'll buy you a new one"—but that was the beginning of the serious boozing. The times between when Nick was sober and when he wasn't disappeared until he was soused morning, noon, and night.

People always asked me why a nice girl like me was working for a detective. Couldn't I get a nice job in a doctor's office? I didn't want a job in a doctor's office. Sure, I did the menial stuff like typing letters and answering the phones, but Nick and I were partners in a way. I was on a first-name basis with all the bail bondsmen in town, gathered tidbits of gossip from Dickie Vance, the local society page editor for *The Examiner*, and could put a name to a face with most of the cops in town. On every job, Nick would ask my opinion. On the make? A good Joe? A grifter? Before Eileen Taylor came into our lives, he said I had the best instincts in the business save for one person. "Oh, who's that?" "Me, precious, me. How about lunch at the Pig 'n Whistle? My treat."

He'd squire various women around the high-class restaurants and speakeasies in town, women who were nearly as beautiful as Eileen, but this one woman, this blue-eyed Circe with a smile that knocked you over, had KO'd him. You can't be a detective's secretary and not see a few things. But I'd so believed in her, just like Nick, and I bet countless others. She had this unholy knack for projecting helplessness and innocence. And once she got

CHAPTER TWO

her hooks in, you fell into those blue eyes and then couldn't see straight. She wasn't a floozy or even bad, because if you're bad, I think it means you've fallen from grace somehow. I don't think she had any grace to fall from. After her final look of pure hatred directed at Nick before the rope pulled tight, I'd crossed myself. Evil incarnate. I did not doubt that she'd gone straight to hell.

Chapter Three

Helen Washington knocked on the office door on a cold day in late July. Mark Twain once said, "The coldest winter I ever spent was a summer in San Francisco." Brother, did he know it.

It was the kind of day when the fog hangs around the lampposts and never leaves. When car tires squeal and there are collisions at every other corner. When children huddle under the covers, ignoring their mother's call to get out of bed. When the wet ink on the newspapers leaves the newsie's hands black and shiny. When the damp creeps under the sleeves of your shirt and then wraps around your throat like a noose. When you can't seem to stop shivering. When the foghorns moan all day, singing to the ships, *Beware, beware*.

I was late for work. Ma had overslept, too. The first batch of oatmeal had burnt the bottom of the pan, and the milk for my tea had turned.

Nick hadn't worked in weeks, choosing to sleep off the previous night's hangover on the floor behind his desk most mornings. Like this morning. His apartment wasn't far away, but I guess, in a twisted, alcohol-fueled logic, he was at work. In a fashion. When I was feeling generous, I'd let him use my coat as a pillow. It was too cold this morning, and I wasn't feeling generous. The Moore Detective Agency was going to fold if he didn't sober up.

I was circling adverts in *The Call Bulletin* for secretarial positions when someone knocked on the office door. Probably the landlord wondering why the rent was late.

I yelled, "Come in!"

A woman just shy of forty opened the door and walked in. She looked

CHAPTER THREE

around and half-turned to walk right out again. I admit we didn't make a good first impression, but then the majority of the people who hire us usually can't afford to be too choosy. Unfortunately, the door to Nick's office stood ajar. I moved my chair to make sure she couldn't see him laid out on the floor of his office with his feet sticking out from behind his desk.

"May I help you?" I said above the bang of the radiators. About time. Every week I complain to the maintenance people about them stinting us on the heat. I get the same response. "It's summer, Lady." I managed to put my shivers on hold and gave this woman my best smile.

She hesitated. I sized her up. Her eyes flicked back and forth between being green or hazel, depending on the way the light hit her face. Her hennaed hair, corralled in a tight bun at the base of her neck, probably wasn't that auburn originally, but her hairdresser knew her stuff, as did her dressmaker. She was definitely a cut above our usual clientele. Topped with a fur tippet, her custom navy suit cinched her waist with just the right amount of cinch. She must have been a real beauty when young, and even though she was edging toward middle age, she had nothing to complain about. To flaunt her good looks, she'd ditched the usual cloche so in vogue and had opted for a small hat the size of a saucer with only a satin ribbon for decoration. Perched on her head in a gravity-defying slant, it matched the color of her suit. No veil. No gloves. No necklace. No earrings. No bracelet. But she had a narrow gold band swallowed up by a gigantic emerald surrounded by a bunch of diamonds weighing down her ring finger. Explained why she wasn't wearing gloves. How would you fit a glove over that hunk of green ice? The stone was big enough that I wondered if it was real.

All in all, she looked the very picture of your extremely well-to-do San Franciscan matron who shopped at the City of Paris four times a week and the White House the other three days. The only off-note was a white silk blouse peeking out from the V of her suit jacket that had one too many buttons undone. I saw a whisper of cleavage, and I doubt I was the only one.

"Please, have a seat." I gestured to the chair opposite my desk. "I'm Margaret Laurent, Mr. Moore's secretary. How may I help you?"

She sat on the very edge of her chair, ready to run out the door if she didn't hear what she liked.

"Is Mr. Moore in?"

"He's on a job at the moment," I replied, which this morning consisted solely of sleeping off last night's drunk. "What can I do for you?"

"Mr. Halston Smith recommended Mr. Moore."

That case. Halston Smith had fallen for a frail who'd pretended to be a French countess. Smith's mother, Constance Smith, hired Nick to save her son from yet another foolhardy engagement. Mother knows best. Comtesse de Vigonné, fiancée number seven, didn't speak a word of French. Nothing more than a streetwise hustler born in Hackensack, New Jersey, with a rap sheet as long as my arm for the same scam in ten different states, she'd conned Smith out of twenty thousand smacks and a diamond engagement ring with a rock the size of a dime. If Smith had resented Nick's discovering her true identity, his bank account was grateful. So was his mother.

"Yes, how is Mr. Smith?"

"Halston is getting married next month." The tiniest remnant of a British accent hovered, but it was there.

Eighth time a charm? I jotted down on a notepad: "Call Constance Smith."

Having established our credentials, I waited.

"It's Philip, you see."

I didn't know who Philip was, so I waited some more. She was a ring-turner. If I had that emerald on my fourth finger, I'd be advertising it, too. Made a nice green flash when it caught the light.

"Oh, silly me. You don't have any idea who Philip is, do you?"

There was nothing silly about this woman, so I didn't know what the coy act was about, but men probably ate that up like it was manna from heaven. Didn't impress me much. Her clothes, poise, and obvious wealth told me she was all business. I smiled. And waited some more. I wriggled my toes to warm them up. I'd put a piece of cardboard in each shoe to keep out the wet and the cold, but it hadn't worked. These shoes needed to be resoled, but I preferred eating.

"My name is Mrs. Harold Washington." She didn't offer me her hand but paused, waiting for me to exclaim or grovel at her feet; I wasn't sure

CHAPTER THREE

which. When I didn't do either, she continued. "My husband's family owns Commerce Bank."

That explained the rock; it was real.

"My husband and I haven't been married very long. Only a couple of years. I'm his second wife. Both widowers, some friends set us up, and there you are."

Imagine that.

"My husband, Harold, has a son from his first marriage."

"His name?"

"I told you. It's Philip."

That was a little on the arrogant side, but I let it pass.

"And Philip is…" I left the question open.

"Well, missing. No, that's not the right word. He and his father had a terrible row last week, and Philip walked out, vowing never to return."

He'd return when he ran out of money, but I didn't say that.

"What was the fight about?" I asked.

"Harold fired him. For some trivial reason, something about his accounts not balancing."

I imagine missing a few hundred sawbucks out of the till every day might irk most banks, nor would they consider it trivial. My impression of the stepson took a nosedive.

"I couldn't follow it all. I'm not very good with money," she admitted and blushed a delicate pink that traveled across her cheekbones to the edge of her hairline, highlighting the color of her eyes. I bet she got a lot of mileage out of that blush. Eileen had blushed exactly like that, and for a brief second, the hair on the back of my neck stood up.

"Few of us are," I commiserated and wondered how much it would cost to get my shoes resoled.

"Anyway, this wasn't the first time Harold had fired him, but Harold insisted it would be the last."

"Do you have a picture of your stepson?"

She opened her handbag slowly as if debating the wisdom of handing over the photograph.

"Here."

With obvious reluctance, she handed me one of those over-shadowed photos that professional photographers specialize in, the ones that added chins that nature had omitted and carved out cheekbones in faces as flat as an ironing board.

Philip Washington didn't need that expertise. He had the flashy, confident smile of a young man who knows he's good-looking. Those kinds of men are attractive at twenty but turn porcine at forty. He had ten good years ahead of him before he gained weight, and that toothy grin would start to sour. I didn't trust men like him. The city was full of these scions of wealthy fathers who were shocked that, at some point, people expected them to grow up. Or at least not fund their nights on the town with money from the cash box. The confidence in that smile didn't quite hide the cruelty around the edges. It sounded like Pop Washington was made of good stuff, with a mug for a son and a silly woman for his wife.

"Good-looking fella. May I keep this?"

She looked reluctant but nodded.

"It would be helpful if I...I mean, if Mr. Moore could talk to your husband. Just to—"

"No." She didn't shout at me, but close enough. "Harold mustn't know I've seen you. He's forgotten what it's like to be young. He's got old-fashioned ideas and expects Philip to be as mature as he is."

Like Harold Washington, I saw a lot of sunlight between maturity and thievery, but I didn't pursue it.

"Age? Hair? Eyes? Height? Build? Any distinguishing marks?"

"Twenty-eight. Blond, with gray eyes, slender, a little over six feet tall. A chipped front tooth from where he fell off a bike when he was ten."

I kept my face smooth and wrote this all down. Fell off a bike. Hah! He probably fell off a barstool and smacked his mouth against the foot rail.

"The last time this happened, Philip found work down at the waterfront. If Mr. Moore could see if he's working there again and persuade him to come home? It's so dangerous. There are accidents every week. My husband has a bit of a temper. I'm sure Harold didn't mean to fire him. Just put a scare

CHAPTER THREE

into him."

The ring was getting a real workout.

I scanned the photograph again. If that guy had done more than ten minutes of manual labor in his entire life, I'd eat this photograph for lunch.

"It's so dangerous," she repeated.

I couldn't argue that point. The two dockworker unions were fighting with each other, and the shipping magnates wanted their goods unloaded, rough seas or not. At the best of times, waltzing down to the waterfront and asking questions was a surefire way to get a load of timber dropped on your head.

A snore came from the direction of Nick's office. I pretended to cough. It was on the tip of my tongue to tell Mrs. Washington we couldn't possibly help her with our current workload. It seemed pointless. Even if the father relented and hired his son back, this guy would start stealing money again, and the cycle would repeat. Then I scraped my foot along the cardboard lining my shoe.

"We'll find your stepson, Mrs. Washington. We can't guarantee he'll return home, but at very least Mr. Moore will find his new address for you. Our fee is three hundred dollars. If we can't find him in two weeks, then we can negotiate if you want us to keep looking."

Our initial fee wasn't even close to that, but who was going to tell her differently? She didn't even blink. I tried not to stare as she hunted around in her handbag for a few seconds before pulling out a wad of bills as thick as my wrist. She extracted three hundred dollars in fifty-dollar increments from the stack and threw them on my blotter, as casual as you please.

That would cover two months of rent for this office, my salary, the rent for Nick's apartment, and some groceries. The last time I opened his refrigerator, it contained three bottles of bathtub gin and nothing else. We had a one-month reprieve.

I added, "If this case involves any travel outside of San Francisco, it will cost you extra. Mr. Moore will contact you soon."

"You mustn't call my home. I'll call by the end of the week to see if you've made any progress."

I smiled as I wrote her a receipt, signed it with my name, and then swept the bills into the drawer of my desk. Nick would be sober by then. I hoped.

Chapter Four

Once the elevator had clanged and banged its way down to the first floor, I entered Nick's office and stood over his prone body. The room smelled like cheap bourbon.

"Nice job on the dough," he muttered.

"Thanks. I'm paying the bills and buying you a few groceries. I'll put what's left over in the safe."

I didn't wait for an answer. I was halfway out the door when he mumbled, "Dickie Vance will have the dirt on Washington." Then he went back to sleep. Or at least pretended to. Or passed out again.

Infamous in society circles for his love of food and his chartreuse shirts paired with fire-engine-red bow ties, Richard Vance lived with his mother in the penthouse of the Mark Hopkins Hotel, located at the top of Nob Hill. His mother's ancestry harkened back to the Mayflower, his father's to Confederate generals. Although his detractors made snide remarks about him being as queer as a three-dollar bill, in Nick's opinion, Dickie would prefer a grilled rib-eye or a custom suit over a man or a woman any day. If Nick Moore traveled in the seedy underworld of San Francisco, his high-society counterpart, Dickie Vance, was the doyen of the elite underworld. These two worlds often overlapped.

Dickie wrote the society page for *The Examiner*. Rumors were that his salary topped the publisher's, but I doubt Dickie ever saw a cent of it. With every maid, janitor, gardener, and cook in this city on his private payroll, he knew who was getting a divorce before the offended party did. Independently wealthy, he refused to be used for political gain and never printed what he considered lies, which made him asbestos. In his way, he was as powerful as the mayor.

Dickie held court Monday through Friday at his own table at John's Grill, the only one in the joint with a booth, which he'd paid for after he broke four of their chairs. He ate the same lunch five days a week: grilled sole with French fries, creamed spinach, and a double slice of pecan pie with two scoops of vanilla ice cream, washed down with his secret stash of French Champagne kept in their cellar. He drank it out of a coffee cup. Like many heavy men, he moved with a peculiar grace when he walked. With his overly plump cheeks and puffy hands, his age was an open question.

I waited until nearly two before arriving at the restaurant so I could catch him on the tail end of his meal.

"Mr. Vance, if you please. Would you tell him that Margaret Laurent would like to speak to him," I said to a waiter at the podium, who was a thousand years old and wore a spotless white apron so long that it touched the tops of his perfectly polished brogues.

"Buying or selling, Miss Laurent?"

Depending on your business, Dickie would have a coffee cup filled with fine bourbon or nothing more than coffee waiting for you when you sat down.

"Neither. I'm just a friend." I paused, wondering what that meant in Dickie's world.

The waiter led me to the back of the room, where Dickie was smoking a post-meal cigarillo. The moment he saw me, he stood up and stubbed out his cigar. His manners were impeccable. He'd sooner cut off his right arm than smoke in front of me as he knew I didn't smoke. I hid a smile when I got a gander at his attire: the usual loud shirt with an even louder bow tie.

"The delightful Miss Laurent. How are you, my dear?" Out of the side of his mouth, he said to a second waiter hovering next to the table, "The lady will have her usual: a tea, black. There's my good man. Now shoo."

We kissed French style, one cheek first, then the other, never touching skin. The elderly waiter pulled out my chair. The lunch crowd had already disappeared, and the dinner crowd had yet to materialize. A couple of men

CHAPTER FOUR

sat at the bar drinking their lunch, but Dickie's table was at the back, away from prying ears. Before I could open my mouth, the waiter put a small pot of tea in front of me. The kitchen must have begun my tea the second they saw me standing at the podium.

With his standard graciousness, he said, "How is that dastardly Nicholas Moore treating you these days? Say the word, and I'll hire you yesterday."

We both knew he ran a one-man operation, but I ate up the flattery with a very large spoon and blushed in appreciation of the compliment.

"I've heard through the grapevine that our dear Nicholas is not well these days." He dipped his three chins to give me a look.

"He's fine," I said. "The grapevine is wrong."

A nod of his head and a slight smile told me he appreciated my lie.

We got down to business.

"Harold Washington. Helen Washington. Philip Washington."

"Ah." Dickie took another sip of Champagne to delay answering so he could craft the appropriate response, or he just wanted another sip of the bubbly.

"*Père* Washington has barely kept that bank of his above water. The crash last year nearly did him in, and it is debatable whether he'll be in business next year. Shame. I quite like him, but he is not the sharpest knife in the drawer. A bit of a skirt chaser, as most men are." He shuddered at the thought—of men or skirts, I wasn't sure. "Interestingly, he's very good at bridge. Less good at banking."

"Mrs. Washington?"

"The first one? Delightful woman!"

"His second?"

"Less delightful."

"She seemed jake to me. Checked all the boxes at least."

"I might admit," he said with emphasis on the word "might," "that she suffers from being compared with the truly lovely woman who died far too soon, but there's something predatory about her that I can't put my finger on. Mrs. Washington Number One was barely cold in her grave when Mrs. Washington Number Two married Harold. A bit unseemly, that. What did she want with Nicholas's services?"

"The stepson is missing. He's probably holed up in a speakeasy, guzzling his ill-gotten gains. Pop fired him from the bank for misappropriation of funds. Not for the first time, apparently. Sounds like a mug."

"Stay away from him." Dickie's voice had lost all of its flirty flamboyance. "Washington *fils* is a bad egg. I cannot imagine why Helen needs to find him. They are better off without him. Harold has given that waster a hundred chances to do right. He's got a, ahem, a woman—I use that term loosely—in the Fillmore that he cohabitates with on and off. She's a torch singer at the Ship. Very, very good, but an addict like him. At a certain point, the drug owns you. He reached that point years ago. No one can go through that much money in such a short time unless someone is a gambler or clutching that opium pipe day and night. He suffers from both afflictions."

"The ship? Is this an actual ship?"

"Oh, *ma petite*. It is truly refreshing to witness such innocence." He patted my cheek. "It is a speakeasy down near Pier 29 on Chestnut and Sansome, with the grimiest storefront you've ever seen. I think it says ABC Shipping on the front door. I've only been there once, but it is something like that. I took Mother last spring, but she found it too noisy."

"Does it get raided a lot?"

I had trouble seeing Dickie and his *grande dame* of a mother being hustled into a paddy wagon.

He roared.

"As if! Both the police chief and the mayor have a table reserved for them every night of the week. They haven't paid for a drop of liquor in two years."

Sounds about right. Prohibition was nothing more than a headache in California. It didn't stop anyone from drinking. The Board of Supervisors was so incensed at the Feds for implementing the law, that they repealed two ordinances against illegal saloons. Drinking establishments in town did nothing more than put up blackout curtains or require membership cards or passwords to get in. The liquor still flowed like always. Being on the coast meant we could get decent booze from Canada. The shipping companies had to be sneaky about it, but it was an open secret. According

CHAPTER FOUR

to Nick, the current mayor, Smiling Tim Stephens, has been voted in year in and year out, largely due to his stance on Prohibition, which is to say, he turns a *very* blind eye. Six months after Prohibition went into effect, the Democratic Convention was held in San Francisco, and he gave out free bottles of whiskey to every delegate in town. And he's a Republican.

"If I wanted to go there, can I just walk in?"

Some speaks had passwords or even membership cards.

"Don't be ridiculous. It's for members only. You will need a membership card. Nicholas has one, I believe. Use his. The shades will be pulled down, and the office will look deserted. Knock. If they let you in, you go down a set of stairs at the back of the office, which I swear hasn't been swept in twenty years, and then *voilà*. Very la-di-dah. It's more of a nightclub. And they serve real booze, not bathtub gin. I have heard on good authority that they sell other items, which might explain why young Washington has a bit of a habit. He's something of a regular."

"Mrs. Washington didn't say anything about his drug use," I countered. "But how's he paying for it? It sounds like Pop keeps Junior on a short leash."

"Not short enough. Another tea, my dear?" At my shake of the head, he continued. "His mother left him a trust fund when he turned twenty-four, large enough that it left me green with envy. Gone in four years. The rumor floating around town is that he is now in need of funds."

That face in the photograph didn't look like a hophead. I pulled it out of my handbag.

"Is this him?" I remembered Nick's first rule: ninety-nine percent of what a client tells you is a lie. Dickie nodded. There's my one percent.

"Yes. He used to be quite fetching if you like that sort of thing," Dickie sneered. "Note the emphasis on the past tense. Four years of smoking opium, and you'd be hard-pressed to pick him out of a line-up based on that photograph. If you're that desperate to find him, ask his sister. She must know where he's living."

"What sister?"

"Helen didn't tell you he had a sister? Not surprising, I suppose. They don't speak. The sister and Helen, I mean. Catherine is Philip's twin. They aren't identical twins, obviously, but close enough in looks that in dark light, it's hard to tell them apart. She lives on a boat or a yacht or some sort of sea-going vessel down at the St. Francis Yacht Club. The *Aurora*, I think. To each their own. I loathe water."

Dickie's world was limited to catching the cable car at Powell Street up to Nob Hill and back and cab rides to cocktail parties in Pacific Heights. I doubt he'd ventured south below Front Street or east beyond Market Street more than three times in his entire life.

"Tell Catherine I sent you. She might talk to you. A bit of a prickly pear, that one."

"Thanks, Dickie. I appreciate it." I began to stand up.

He wrapped a gentle, doughy hand around my wrist, forcing me to stay in my seat.

"I'm worried about Nicholas. One hears things."

I bet one does. I didn't say anything.

"If he needs my help, say a loan,"—he coughed around the last phrase—"have him contact me." Before letting go of my hand, he gave it a little pat. "My dear, do not go alone to the Ship. I'll be quite frank. If you go unescorted, you will be considered a lady of the night plying her…shall we say, wares? Darling, one more thing? Please stay away from young Mr. Washington. He's poison."

Chapter Five

The next day was no warmer than the previous one. Since I was going down to the waterfront, I wore trousers, with long underwear underneath my blouse and pants. After lacing up my walking oxfords, I brought my winter coat out of mothballs. I left my hat on the dresser and reached for a scarf to tie under my chin. Windy enough at my house on 9th Avenue that wearing a hat was out of the question meant it would be blowing a gale near Fort Point. Before I caught the streetcar, I dropped off my pumps at the cobblers to get them resoled.

Despite all my efforts, I was shivering by the time we passed Gough Street and didn't stop until I got off the streetcar at Crissy Field. The St. Francis Yacht Club had been built only a few years ago, but the newness of the furniture in no way diminished its prestige. Membership by invitation only. I don't own a boat or know how to sail, so I wasn't holding my breath.

The St. Francis Yacht Club is an offshoot of the San Francisco Yacht Club, which is based in Sausalito across the Bay. Don't ask me why. When a fire gutted the building, Nick was hired to determine if it was arson or not. It wasn't, but a fight ensued between those members who insisted that the San Francisco Yacht Club be based in, surprise, San Francisco. Those who lived in Marin County were adamant that the yacht club stay in Sausalito. The city dwellers had what resembles a temper tantrum among the wealthy and, in a snit, took their yachts and opened the St. Francis Yacht Club.

I didn't bother asking the front desk where the *Aurora* was berthed. That would get me thrown out. I slipped in behind an employee as he walked through a gate to the docks. He carried a bucket with a mop canted over his shoulder like a rifle.

"Excuse me. Can you tell me where the *Aurora* is docked? I'm here to see Miss Washington."

He paused for a couple of seconds, as if to question the wisdom of answering my question, and then pointed the mop at a large sailboat moored at the far end of the dock ahead of us.

"She don't like no visitors. Don't say I didn't warn you."

"Oh, she's expecting—" I lied.

He'd walked away before I had a chance to finish my sentence.

I didn't need to see the name on the side of the sailboat to know which boat was hers. Propped up against the wall of the cabin, Catherine Walker was smoking a cigarette while reading a book. Even though I was wearing my winter coat, I still had to stifle the shivers. I doubt she felt even the slightest breeze given that she was wearing a full-length mink coat. Her book obscured most of her face, and round tortoiseshell-frame cheaters with the dark green lenses favored by movie stars obscured the rest. I half expected to see Charlie Chaplin sitting next to her.

I approached the sailboat. "Miss Washington?"

She didn't look up from her book. I cleared my throat and said in a much louder voice, "Miss Washington, may I talk to you for a minute? My name is Maggie Laurent." I hoped using my diminutive would make me appear less threatening.

She still didn't look up. "No, you may not," she said.

"It's about your brother."

She kept reading and said, "Then definitely not."

"Dickie Vance said you'd help me."

Open sesame. She closed the book and looked me over, which gave me the same amount of time to look her over. Dickie was right. A ringer for her brother. Their jawlines and cheekbones were identical. While her brother's mouth had a fleshy quality to it, her mouth was lush and not just a little sexy. Bleached near white from the sun, her hair was cut like a man's, short on the sides and longer on top. She looked older than she should, with the baked-in sunburn of the sailor. Even though half-hidden by the coat collar,

CHAPTER FIVE

her features, sharp and defined, hinted at a slender body underneath all that fur.

Eventually, she said, "I doubt I can help you, but I'll give you five minutes. No more. Climb aboard."

Once I sat down, she offered me a cigarette. I declined, aware that my welcome would only last the length of time it'd take her to smoke one cigarette.

"How's Dickie? I haven't seen him in ages. Still dressed to beat the band?"

"You know it. If his shirt were any brighter, I'd be blind."

She laughed. You can tell a lot about people from the way they laugh. Her laugh sounded like it didn't get much of a workout.

"Anyone who's a friend of Dickie's is a friend of mine. Maybe," she qualified. "How may I help you?"

"I'm looking for your brother. He and your father had, um, a bit of a dust-up, and he's taken a powder. Do you know where I might find him?"

"Knock on the doors of the opium dens in Chinatown. Why are you looking for him?"

I've listened to enough of Nick's conversations with clients to know there's always a point when you lie because it's in your best interest, or you tell the truth. Because it's in your best interest. My instinct told me that lying to this woman would be a big mistake. I might need her help further down the line.

"Your stepmother is worried about him. She hired me to find him. Says he's working down at the docks and is worried he'll get a splinter or two in his pinkie finger. She wants me to plead with him to go home and beg your father for forgiveness. Barring that, at least get his current address so she can plead her case for him to come home."

She blinked a couple of times and then said, "Helen came to see you." Her voice was flat, even hostile, but it didn't feel directed at me.

"Well, not me, exactly. I'm Nick Moore's secretary."

"The detective? I read all about him taking down a bunch of mobsters at Half Moon Bay a few years back. Killed six of them with one shot." She smiled, but her eyes were now wary. I noticed that her smile didn't have any of the latent cruelty of her brother's. But maybe that was the fault of the photographer. Or not.

I couldn't say she moved even a single hair, but her body language changed. Her shoulders firmed up, and when her book fell to the deck, she didn't bother to pick it up. She sized me up again, with more interest this time. This woman had brains. I'd better watch my Ps and Qs.

"So why isn't he here?"

"He's on another job right now." As in visiting his bootlegger over in Potrero Hill. "I'm just doing some routine legwork for him."

She lit another cigarette, inhaled deeply, and then let out the smoke in a rush. "Let me get this straight: Helen's concerned about Philip working down at the port? Have I got that right?"

"Yes. She said that he'd found work down there when he and your father had a previous fight."

She snorted. "News to me. Philip hasn't worked a day in his life. Unless you call filching bills out of the till a day's work."

Like I suspected, Helen Washington had lied to me. Why?

"Dickie says he's got a girlfriend who lives in the Fillmore. She's got a singing gig at a speak down near Pier 29. Do you know her address?"

"His girlfriend." She paused to drag on her cigarette. I wondered how many of those she went through in a day. "I guess that's probably the politest thing you could say about her in mixed company. Dickie is nothing if not polite. No, I don't know where she lives. I'd like to help you, Miss Laurent, but I don't speak to my brother, my stepmother, or my father, so you've wasted your morning, I'm afraid. Now, if you don't—"

"Wait," I blurted out. "Why don't you speak to your brother? I've got an older brother and, gosh, he's aces. My dad died when I was twelve, and Al... Why, I can't imagine what we would have done without him. Me and Ma, that is."

"Lucky you," she muttered under her breath.

We didn't say anything for a while. She studied me some more while I listened to the ropes bang against the mast. The fog pouring in through the entrance to the Bay was so thick that I couldn't even see Fort Point.

CHAPTER FIVE

"You're tan for a secretary. Do you sail?"

"No. I play golf every chance I get. At Lincoln Park. I also like to swim. I'm a bit of a tomboy."

"Me, too," said Catherine. "Did you know the golf course at Lincoln Park used to be a cemetery?"

"Really?" My eyes widened at the thought of stepping on all those dead bodies.

"Relax. They've moved the bodies somewhere else. You can tee off without feeling guilty."

At my sigh of relief, she laughed.

"Look, you seem on the up and up, so here's the story. I don't speak to my brother because he tried to cheat me out of my inheritance, claiming my mother was sick when she drafted her will and, therefore, cuckoo." She circled her finger around her ear a couple of times. "I don't speak to Helen because I think she's a phony. She and my father tied the knot less than three weeks after my mother's death. I don't speak to my father because he's never met a woman yet he didn't try to seduce. He was carrying on with Helen while my mother was dying in some sanatorium in upstate New York. But for me, she would have died alone."

"T.B.?"

She nodded. "Yeah, she was a lunger. Your father?"

"The Spanish flu. He was a doc. Caught it from one of his patients." I tried not to think about those days while he lay in bed, trying to find whatever hint of air he could. Ma was never the same after his death. Al had just started a paper route, or we'd have starved.

"After my mother died, I bought this sailboat and have lived here ever since. You're not supposed to live on your boat, but I give the yacht club so much money, they're not kicking me out anytime soon."

"Was that your mother's coat? It doesn't jibe with this." I swept my hand to indicate the boat. Then I pointed to the book lying on the deck, *The Rise and Fall of the Roman Empire*, and her stocking feet with big holes in the toes. Not exactly the trappings of a society deb.

She nodded and raised her sunglasses to rest on the top of her head. Her eyes were the color of the fog hovering around Fort Point, light gray but with nothing showing through.

"You're smarter than you let on. I really can't help you, Maggie. My brother's a louse who'd steal the gold from your teeth to feed his habit, my stepmother's a gold digger, and my father's a philanderer. I haven't spoken to them in over two years."

I fished in my coat pocket for one of Nick's cards and handed it to her.

"If you think of anything that might help, please call me."

She narrowed her eyes and the gray darkened. "You weren't lying to me about Dickie, were you?"

"No. I saw him at John's Grill yesterday. He was seated at his usual table wearing a shirt the color of a robin's egg and a yellow bow tie. He said that your brother is a mug and doesn't like your stepmother much but can't say why. He thinks she's on the make. Thought your mother was a 'lovely woman'—I'm quoting—and your father a skirt chaser but a great bridge player."

"And if I had lunch with him today and said that I met a Maggie Laurent who works for Nick Moore, he'd nod and say, 'Oh, yes, dear Miss Washington,' in that lisp of his?"

"Yes, he would."

By the purse of her lips, she wasn't sure if I was a terrific liar, or if I was telling the truth. With a none-too-polite hand, she motioned for me to get off her boat.

I stood up. I'd get nothing more out of her.

"Thank you for your time, Miss Washington. One more thing." I played the only card I had to win her trust. If Washington's bank was going bust within the next twelve months, her brother might not be the only one trying to steal Catherine Washington's inheritance. "If I were you, I'd move your money out of your father's bank. Dickie says it's fifty-fifty whether it will survive another year."

Even as she moved her hand again to usher me off board, I saw a hint of amusement before she lowered her sunglasses again.

"Thanks for the tip. I might not trust you, but I do trust Dickie. My advice?

CHAPTER FIVE

I'd stay away from my brother if I were you. He's poison."

That was the second time in two days that Philip Washington had been called poison by two people who were as different as chalk from cheese. When I turned around to wave goodbye, Catherine Washington hadn't bothered to watch me walk away. She picked up her book and threw Nick's business card into the water before vanishing into the cabin. I could almost hear the click of the lock.

Chapter Six

While munching on an apple for lunch—once I paid Ma for my room and board, I didn't have much left over, and I had to pay to resole my shoes—I spent the next three hours in *The Examiner's* morgue, reading Dickie's columns for the last fifteen years.

Holding onto the banister for dear life, I made my way down a damp and slippery staircase. I walked past a dirty elevator and a wall crisscrossed with a spider's web of rusting water pipes until I reached a pair of metal doors. I knocked twice and then opened the door to face a huge room filled with a sea of gray file cabinets in long rows like someone had planted seeds that grew file cabinets. Six men sat at a long table, clipping articles and photographs and placing them in manila folders, while another two men were seated at typewriters. The only sound in the room was the sharp rat-tat-tat of the typewriter keys. All six men sat in a haze of cigarette smoke and didn't even raise their eyes when I entered the room. Whether the smoke was so thick that it bleached all the color out of the room or they were naturally grey from being holed up here eight hours a day, they gave the impression of being mole people only let out to work, and then they were ushered back into their caves at five o'clock.

"May I help you?" said a thin, reedy older man. He had the pointed face of a mole with a long nose, beady eyes, and a faint mustache that, in the dim light, could be mistaken for whiskers. I had to cough to stifle a bark of laughter.

I sort of lied. Okay, I lied. I told him I was a student at Stanford writing a thesis on the marriage customs of San Francisco's social elite. How many

CHAPTER SIX

debutantes married within five years of their debut, and did these marriages stay within the confines of a certain financial class? This sounded like nonsense to me, but he didn't blink an eye. I imagine it wasn't the goofiest thing he'd heard all week.

He flipped through a gigantic book, jotted down some numbers, and led me down that corridor of endless file cabinets. I had a fleeting thought that maybe I was going to be sacrificed to the mole god, that these file cabinets were merely for show. After walking for what felt like a solid mile, we stopped in front of a file cabinet. He opened it up with a small key and then handed me a stack of envelopes five inches high. That's a lot of marriages. Maybe a lot of divorces, too.

"These envelopes are filed by subject or by a person or business name. If you can't find what you're looking for, it might be listed under a specific name or a business."

"I think I'm good with this. Is there someplace I can—"

"That small table up front next to the table near where all the guys are sitting. When you're done, just leave the envelopes on the table. I'll put them back where they belong."

"Gotcha."

Based on the number of photographs and copy devoted to their comings and goings, the Washingtons were high up in the echelons of San Francisco society. They appeared no less than once a week and more often twice, accompanied by plenty of photographs. Mrs. Washington Number One, née Reade, was quite the dish when she was younger; it was obvious where her kids got their looks. Her wedding to Harold had made the front page of *The Examiner*. Not that Washington was any slouch when he was younger. He looked damn good in a tux, and she gazed up at him like he was the bee's knees of all time. By the time of her daughter's debut, her face already had that weary resignation of a woman for whom the chickens had come home to roost. I'd have to check with Dickie, but I wondered if Aurora Reade brought the real dough into the family. What if Commerce Bank had been her family's, and what if the good-looking son-in-law took hold of the reins when Reade Senior kicked and proceeded to run it into the ground? Dickie would know.

The photograph of Catherine at her debut was definitely pre-sailboat. She didn't strike me as the debutante type, but then it was as if I were looking at a picture of a different girl, not the woman I met living on a yacht. Ten years ago, her hair had been bobbed in the latest fashion, not hacked off by herself with a pair of manicure scissors. Her happy, broad smile seemed genuine, and her shoulders were thrown back with pride as she stood at the top of some mile-high staircase resplendent in white, father and daughter arm-in-arm. Harold's smile was equally broad, ecstatic even, as he ushered his little girl into the whirl of the societal merry-go-round.

What had happened in those ten years? Smiles now seemed hard to come by for Catherine Washington.

Pictures of wife number two, Helen Washington, née Harrison, weren't nearly as plentiful. She'd been on the San Francisco society scene for only a couple of years before snagging Harold. Filled out a cocktail dress the way it should be filled out. According to the copy, she originally hailed from Boston and had been previously married to a stockbroker who died while on a cruise to the Orient. Washington was chump number three. Little was mentioned of her first husband other than he'd been from another banking family based in Boston. She targeted the money men. If I were Harold, I'd be running for the hills and eschewing all cruises.

I didn't hear even a smidgen of a Boston accent when we'd met the other day, only hints of a British one. She was no Brahmin. That's one accent that never dies.

Lie number two.

Philip didn't appear in Dickie's column except for once. No photograph. Dickie announced an engagement between a Miss Lucille Stanford and Mr. Philip Washington, which must have fallen through because there was no follow-up article announcing their marriage. Even I knew that the Stanfords were big stuff. Lucille must have wised up fast that Phil was marrying her solely for her money; her engagement to Washington was short-lived. Druggies don't make good husbands. She married another guy two years later.

CHAPTER SIX

I returned to the office and thought about my next move. Nick had been a Pinkerton for ten years, and all his contacts were ex-Pinkertons. He doesn't talk about those days. It sounded like his job consisted of mostly union-busting and not much detecting. But as a result, Nick had contacts in every state. I dialed the operator, pushing away the thought of the long-distance charges to Boston.

"Mr. Ryan, this is Maggie Laurent from Nick Moore's office. How are you?"

Brendon Ryan was Nick's contact when he needed information from Boston. We'd relied on him in the past. Ryan was a good egg and a damn fine detective.

"Long time, no hear, Maggie. How's Nick? Still putting them away?"

Sure, if you're talking about fifths of bourbon, he was doing a great job.

"That he is," I said with fake jocularity. "Say, would you mind doing some legwork for us? We're trying to track down the marriage history of Helen Washington, née Harrison. Not sure if that's her original name or the name of one of her former chumps. There were a couple of husbands before Washington, but I don't have the name of the first chump. She says she's from Boston, but I can't hear it. It's not like you don't know when someone's from Boston." Ryan's accent was strong enough to churn butter. "There's a trace of an English accent, but she works hard to hide it."

"A dame with a con?"

"Nick didn't think so originally, but things aren't lining up. Some small lies."

"Which means big lies," he said and chuckled as if this were the normal course of things, which they usually were.

"Not sure how big, but it smells fishy for sure," I agreed. "She's got class, I'll give her that. Not your run-of-the-mill twist operating your run-of-the-mill con. If she's dirty, I'm laying bets it's a big-time con. What if she's claiming to hail from Boston because she's steering people away from New York? Can you check there as well?"

"Sure, I'll call Ezra Abramson in Brooklyn and have him sniff around a bit. I'll get back to you with the dope on Boston, and I'll have him call you

33

with the dope on New York. Won't be tomorrow. Maybe the next day, or the day after that. I've got a tail going, and it might take Ezzie some time to track her down if she's smart and dirty, like you say. Same phone number?"

I signed off and thought, what would Nick do? The reality was that I couldn't do what Nick would do. He'd go down to the docks and sock someone's jaw because they were holding out on where Washington was hiding out. Or wasn't. Jaw socking wouldn't be on my menu. Catherine Washington had given me enough info to confirm that Helen Washington was lying about her motives in finding Philip. I didn't think the desperation in Helen's voice was fake, but I didn't buy the reason. Aside from trying to shake down her lies, my next move was to check out the Ship.

I raided the safe for a few bills to pay the taxi and "rent" on a table at the speakeasy. After that, I hoofed it over to Nick's apartment. I banged on the door and yelled, "Nick, I need your card to get into the Ship." I waited. I heard someone stumbling, falling on the floor, some choice curse words, and then a card appeared from under the bottom of the door.

"Don go by yourshelf," came a voice from the other side of the door.

Normally Nick never slurs. He has to be well and truly oiled before he loses his T's and adds H's where they don't belong.

"Taking Al with me." Not that Al knew that yet.

"Goo," he said. There was silence, then more thuds, and then silence again.

Either he'd made it to his bed or had passed out on the floor. I couldn't do anything about it. I left.

Chapter Seven

Luck was with me. Ma would never let me go to a speakeasy, but the Friday night bingo game down at St. Ignatius was sacrosanct. She tried to cajole both of us to join her, but Al was glued to the sports page and grunted out a "Not tonight, Ma," and I fobbed off her invitation to play bingo with some vague reference to a party I wanted to go to. That left me and Al alone in the house. She hadn't even reached the sidewalk before I sat down at the kitchen table across from Al. He had *The Examiner* in one hand and a coffee cup in the other. This would take some work.

"Hey, want to play a round tomorrow?" I asked.

He loved golf as much as I did, but he was so engrossed in the paper that he mumbled a faint "Sure" and kept on reading.

"Al?"

"Hmmm?"

"Do you want to go out?"

He looked up.

"Out? Tonight? Where?"

"The Ship."

He dropped the newspaper.

"Maggie, that's a speakeasy."

He knew that the Ship was a speakeasy. Interesting. Maybe there was a side to my big brother I knew nothing about.

"Yeah, I know. I'm following up on a case, and there's a singer there who might have some information for me."

"You're not going there alone," he insisted. "It's no place for a woman by herself."

"That's why I'm asking you to go with me, dummy." For all his smarts, sometimes Al's got rocks in his head instead of brains.

"They won't let us in."

"I have that covered already. Nick slipped me his entrance card."

"That place is top drawer. We don't have the—"

"I have money. It's a job for Nick."

He fiddled a bit with his now-empty coffee cup before saying, "I should say no."

I stifled the urge to shake him.

"I can't go if you don't take me. And…" I paused, but I had to be honest with him. "I might need some muscle, and you're it."

Tall and thin like me, Al looked about as threatening as a cornstalk. But he was also the winner of San Francisco's amateur boxing tournament three years running. Fast on his feet and faster with the punch, he might not be classic muscle, but he'd make sure no one tried to bother me. When *The Examiner* interviewed one of his opponents, he whined: "I never saw that bastard's fist coming." I'd be in good hands. Literally.

Although too early for the floor show at the Ship, we needed to leave before Ma got home. Before we headed out, I left Ma a note on the kitchen table: *Al and I are going to that party I mentioned. Be back late. Borrowed your velvet cloak and shoes. Love Mags.*

My wardrobe didn't contain the kind of clothes one wore to a high-class speak. My mother's velvet cloak—bought when my father was still alive—was full length on her but only reached my knees. It would have to do. I crammed my feet into a pair of flashy pumps she never wore anymore. They were a size too small, guaranteeing massive blisters by the end of the night. I hoped I wouldn't be doing much walking.

Al had smarted up by wetting his hair down and tried to tame his curls with a severe combing. He'd even put on a fresh shirt and a tie. With some irony, I noted that although not twins, Al and I resembled each other nearly to the same degree as Philip and Catherine Washington. Except that his height, prominent nose with dark eyes, sharp cheekbones, and full mouth

CHAPTER SEVEN

were French in the best way, while none of that worked as well on a woman. My mother keeps telling me I'll grow into my face. I'd better get a move on.

During the cab ride to the waterfront, I filled Al in on current events.

"Why do you think Helen Washington wants to find her stepson?"

I shrugged. "No idea. His sister's jaw hit the floor when I told her that her stepmother wanted to know his whereabouts. I'll have a better idea when Ryan gets back to me."

We pulled up to the door of ABC Shipping. Just like Dickie said, the blinds were drawn, and it looked like no one had crossed the threshold for the last twenty years. Weather-worn newspapers and candy wrappers littered the stoop. A burned-out light fixture above the entrance swung in the wind.

"This is it," said the cabbie and held out his hand.

"Are you sure?" I asked, even as I fumbled with the catch on my handbag.

"Sure, I'm sure. Youse asked for the Ship. This is it."

I handed over a couple of bills, which paid the fare plus a too-generous tip.

"Thanks, sister. Appreciate it."

We got out. I held the membership card in one hand and knocked on the door with the other. Hard. It slid open a peep. A pale hand snaked through the opening and snatched the card out of my outstretched hand. The door closed. It opened again, right away, with just enough room for me and Al to slip through.

The room was empty except for a wooden desk in one corner. There wasn't even a chair to go with the desk. A single bulb in a socket dangled from the ceiling, the only light in the entire room. A heavy-set young man, no more than sixteen, with a newly broken nose and a fat lip, handed us back Nick's card.

"Friends of Nick are friends of ours. How's he doing these days?"

Was there anyone in San Francisco who didn't know that Nick was on a bender?

"Great," I lied.

"Sit anywhere you like," he lisped around his lip.

"When will the singer come on?"

"Thirty mins, give or take." The tone of his voice was doubtful; it was probably more give than take. "Maybe an hour," he qualified. "Down there." He pointed to a dingy, dark staircase. I'd be using the handrail.

When we reached the bottom of the stairs, another man stood at a lectern. If they got by the kid at the door, there was no way they were going to get by this schmo. A head taller than Al and twice as wide, he scanned Nick's membership card with a tiny flashlight. He handed me back the card without any comment but must have pressed a hidden lever because the door behind him opened all by itself, and the sounds of a gigantic party blasted past our ears.

We walked into a large room with at least fifty tables. A small stage sat against the back wall with enough room for a miniature piano and a horn player or two. An enormous bar took up the entire wall to our right, its shelves filled with bottles and backlit in a bright blue light. Dickie hadn't lied when he said this was a high-class joint, so maybe the booze in those bottles was real. In most speakeasies, you'd most likely be drinking today's whiskey that had been nothing more than yesterday's batch of bathtub gin cut with tea, with a matchstick at the bottom of the bottle to give it a "smoky" flavor. It was a nice illusion.

The booze was flowing like water, and there were few empty seats. The chief of police, Bobby O'Sullivan, sat on one side of the room, and the mayor, Smiling Tim Stephens, on the other. Diamonds sparkled on the women's ears, wrists, and necks. Given the size of the rocks on their fingers, it took some effort to raise their glasses of hooch to their be-rouged mouths. Men lit cigarettes with silver lighters. The cloying scent of expensive perfume vied with the sweet aroma of pomade and the tangy smell of the ocean. Nick had some serious cachet if he was rubbing elbows with this crowd. He never talked about his family, but after working for him for a while, I gathered he grew up in this type of milieu: privilege with a generous helping of money. He might have willingly turned his back on his background, but he wasn't above exploiting it when he needed to.

Talk about being out of our league. I pulled my cloak around me so they couldn't see my years-old dress, and Al tugged on the knot on his tie. These

CHAPTER SEVEN

people lived in Pacific Heights, Nob Hill, and Park Presidio, not in the Avenues like me and Al.

I could see a couple of empty seats to the left of me and made my way along a narrow path between the tables. At a table farthest from the stage sat a woman with a jet-black bob, a slash of lipstick across her mouth in a red so bright it had no counterpart in nature, and a mink coat slung over her shoulders.

As we approached the table, she said, "Miss Laurent, as I live and breathe. Have a seat."

Chapter Eight

"Good evening, Miss Washington. This is my brother, Albert."

"How do you do?" She held out a hand, gloved up to her elbow. The bracelet on her wrist slid back along her arm, and she raised her hand to meet his. Talk about sparkle.

He stammered back, "A p-pleasure, I'm s-sure," and shook her hand. I could tell he didn't want to let go.

"Come on, Al. Sit down before you fall down." I patted a chair and then gestured to her hair. "Nice wig."

"I trot it out sometimes when I don't want to be recognized."

"Unlike wearing a full-length mink coat."

"Look around. With that cape, you're probably raising more attention than I am."

She was right. So many fur coats were hanging over the backs of chairs that I didn't have enough fingers to count them all. There might be bread lines on Market Street these days, but you wouldn't know it from this crowd.

"You still trying to track down my brother?"

"Yes. Seems like you have a similar idea. This morning, you wouldn't have spit on him if he were on fire. What gives?"

"You spooked me," she confessed.

The chill of the morning had vanished. For now. She paused to light a cigarette, which I began to realize was her way of stalling and giving her time to think about what to say. Al shocked me by gently removing her lighter from her hand and lighting it for her. She smiled at him, and damn if he didn't nearly melt from the wattage.

CHAPTER EIGHT

"I need to know what sort of scheme Helen and Phil have conjured up." She glanced at Al and raised an eyebrow.

"He knows."

"The only thing those two care about is money." She paused to take a drag but had the courtesy to blow the smoke away from Al's face. She seemed less concerned about mine. "Okay, the only thing she cares about is money. Phil isn't completely mercenary. He cares about money, opium, and his side piece. I need to make sure that it's not my money they're contemplating getting their greedy mitts on."

"After I left the yacht club, I went to the morgue at *The Examiner* and read Dickie's columns for the last fifteen years."

"Learn anything new?" Her voice was coy, but the accompanying smile was brittle.

"Not much," I admitted. Then I remembered about the bank. "Commerce Bank. Started by your mother's family or your father's?"

"My mother's. My father's financial genius can best be described as everything he touches turns to dross. Grandfather's turning over in his grave as we speak. Even if Daddy printed greenbacks in the basement of the bank, he'd still lose money. I moved my money, by the way. Thanks for the tip. I had lunch with Dickie today. He vouched for you. If I didn't know any better, I'd say he was sweet on you."

"If I were a rib-eye steak."

At that point, the waiter came up with a bottle of something that was allegedly whiskey.

"Miss Washington?" He held up the bottle for her inspection. There weren't any dead bugs floating in it, so I suppose it was genuine enough.

"Three glasses, please, with ice."

"I'd like a Coca-Cola if you don't mind," I said in a firm voice.

"Make that two," Al chimed in.

"Teetotalers?" Catherine Washington mocked.

"No," said Al. "I have a whiskey now and then. But I teach. Facing a bunch of ten-year-old kids at eight in the morning while wrestling with a hangover is my idea of hell."

"But it's a Friday night." She paused for five beats. "And it's summer."

"So it is," he crooned back and gave her a smile I'd never seen before.

Something was happening here, something that didn't include me.

"What happened between Lucille Stanford and your brother?" I asked in a loud voice.

That broke the spell.

"What do you think? He kept doping. She got smart and dumped him. Daddy was livid, but Phil never liked her. He just liked her—"

Catherine Washington stopped speaking. Her attention was riveted on a man and a woman walking through the bar toward a badly written sign that said Employees Only. The hum of the crowd stopped as everyone watched them mosey their way past the tables. Philip wore a white linen suit that must have cost my year's salary. The confidence I'd seen in that smile in the photograph was more than realized in the way he walked. Sleek and sure, he reminded me of a panther I'd seen at the zoo, and yet, next to the woman by his side, he looked clumsy and positively homely.

As dark as he was light, her skin didn't repel light so much as absorb it. Even though it was freezing outside, she wore no coat. And she so owned any space around her that I could imagine her telling the cold to go away in a bored voice and it slinking out the door, obeying her command. She didn't walk so much as glide through the room. Her black dress shimmered with masses of sequins. Her hair—shorter than even Catherine Washington's—had been clipped very close to her head, as close as a swimmer's cap, and it gleamed in the light from the chandeliers. She smiled and nodded to patrons she knew, stopping now and then to put a hand on their shoulders. Her fingernails were as red as her lipstick. She wore no jewelry, and instead of making her look only halfway dressed, she made everyone around her look fourth-rate while flashing their cheap dime-store glass. In a word? She was mesmerizing.

Before she went through the door at the back of the room, she kissed Phil Washington on the cheek and shut the door behind her. He sat down at a table right at the front of the stage with a big "Reserved" sign on it and a single chair. He hadn't been seated more than a second before he snapped

CHAPTER EIGHT

his fingers. Twice. One of the waiters brought him a drink. He didn't bother to thank the man.

Dickie's antipathy had led him to exaggerate Philip Washington's physical decline. He might be clutching an opium pipe night and day, but he didn't look it, and most definitely not like he'd been working down at the docks.

"Bring your chairs together so he can't see me," Catherine Washington said in a low but insistent voice.

Al and I scooched our chairs together.

The waiter brought our glasses filled with ice and two bottles of Coke. Al thanked him and filled Catherine Washington's glass with whiskey, then poured Coke into my glass, and finally splashed a couple of fingers of hooch into his glass and filled it to the top with Coke. He raised his glass in a toast. He and Catherine Washington clinked glasses and began to sip their drinks while watching each other, not even realizing that I hadn't joined in the toast. I sat there, stunned. Where had the math teacher gone, and when did this sophisticate take his place?

Sometimes, there's just no reason for words. I sat there sipping my drink, the hum of the crowd and the snick of Catherine Washington's lighter the only sounds for quite some time. Al and Catherine traded looks back and forth, and when I say looks, I mean looks. I had no horse in that race. Suddenly, a spotlight snapped on. The sound of clapping brought all three of us back to reality. The stage was bare except for a microphone and a dwarf sitting on a stool facing the keyboard of the piano.

The kid who'd let us in sidled up to the mike and said, "Ladies and gentlemen, the fabulous Miss Velma Jackson." He had trouble making the "J" around his busted lip.

She'd changed into a red dress that left nothing to the imagination. It hugged curves that hadn't been invented yet. In contrast to her previous outfit, this dress had no embellishments. Her body was all the glitter she needed. Her breasts managed to stay mostly behind the deep V of the plunging neckline, but it was a bit of a fight. With her long waist and equally long legs, she looked Amazonian next to the accompanist. She nodded at the dwarf, who played a few bars of intro, and she opened her mouth to sing.

No one made a sound for a long time. All talking stopped. People stopped drinking. The singing was so powerful that Catherine Washington even stopped smoking. The playlist wasn't special, just a bunch of commonplace tunes and plenty of Gershwin: "Fascinating Rhythm," "Oh, Lady Be Good," "Funny Face," "Embraceable You," and "I Got Rhythm," rounded out with the typical standards like "Who's Sorry Now," "Empty Bed Blues," "Let's Do It, Let's Fall in Love" "I'll See You in My Dreams," "It Had To Be You," and "Ain't Misbehavin.'"

There was nothing commonplace about her singing. Songs that other singers sang fast, she sang slow. Songs other singers took their sweet time with, she ramped up the beat. She owned every single note out of her mouth. She sang like no one else had ever sung this song, like it was the first time these notes had ever been heard. When the set was over, we jumped to our feet, screaming for more. She did one encore. She finished with the most marvelous rendition of "My Man" that I'd ever heard and suspected I'd ever hear.

All the other songs she sang to the crowd.

This song?

She looked at Phil Washington the whole time.

It was all for him.

We were just furniture.

There wasn't a second set. We sat at our table, nursing our drinks, waiting for Washington and his girlfriend to come out of that door in the back of the bar so we could tail them home and find out his address. They never showed. We sat there until the barkeep began putting the chairs on the tables and running a mop over the floor. We got the hint and left. Catherine Washington had parked her car near enough to the speak that we could see the entrance to the Ship. The three of us sat there for another hour, waiting for them to show. Catherine and Al sat in the front seat, passing the whiskey bottle back and forth.

The night was cold, your typical freezing summer night in San Francisco. I began to yawn around my shivers and figured this was a bust, realizing too

CHAPTER EIGHT

late that we'd never catch a cab this late in this part of town.

"Let's go. Miss Washington, can you drive us—" I was about to say "to Market Street" when I noticed the lights in the apartment above the speak.

"Al? Check the mailbox for the apartment upstairs and see if the name rings a bell."

"Catherine, may I have your lighter for a minute?" asked Al.

Huh. We were now on a first-name basis. Or at least he was.

She handed it over without a word, and he trotted across the street, ran the light from the flame over the side of the building, stopped, bent over, and then ran back to the car.

"The name Washington rings a bell for me. How about you?"

That answered that.

"I'll take you two home," said Catherine Washington as she turned on the ignition and put the car in gear.

I wanted to ask if she'd known her brother and his girlfriend were living above the speak and that we'd been sitting there flirting with frostbite for nothing. But I didn't. We needed a ride.

"We live out in the Aves. It will take you forever. Just drop us off on Market near the Palace Hotel. We can get a cab there."

She dismissed my protests with a be-gloved hand.

"I drive like a bat out of hell. It will only take five minutes."

It took fifteen, but I wasn't complaining. My feet hurt.

Chapter Nine

We got home after three a.m. I got up around noon. No sign of Al. Ma taught catechism over at St. Ignatius on Saturdays, so we could lounge around for as long as we liked before getting dressed. She'd left a pot of cold oatmeal on the stove for our breakfast. By the time I made some fresh coffee and downed two cups in quick succession that jump-started my will to live, I warmed up the oatmeal. Al stumbled into the kitchen around one, still wearing his pajamas.

He groaned out one word. "Coffee."

I poured him a cup and plopped a bowl of oatmeal in front of him. He ignored the oatmeal and grabbed the coffee.

Once he'd finished his second cup, he said, "This Catherine Washington. What do you know about her?"

He'd purposefully made his face a blank to draw attention away from the fact his interest was anything but "blank."

"Al." I put a hand over his. "She's out of our league." I didn't say "your league" to make the letdown a little easier. "She's from big money. A debutante even. That tells you all you need to know. She lives at the St. Francis Yacht Club on a sailboat that's at least forty feet long. I like her, but I've learned over the past year that this doesn't mean a damn thing."

He sat there sipping his coffee, taking this in.

"What's the name of her sailboat?"

My smart brother wasn't being very smart.

"The *Aurora*. And don't go down there hoping to just 'run into her.' That yacht club is swank city. They'll throw you out on your keister," I warned. I

CHAPTER NINE

did like her. A lot. But Al was booking a room in the Heartbreak Hotel if he thought he was going to make any headway with her.

He scowled into his coffee cup, and I thought he was going to challenge me, but he let it go.

"What's next?"

I had to shake myself. Next? Oh, the case.

"I'm going back to the Ship and talk to Phil Washington. He should be awake by now."

"You need muscle?"

I can't say he was particularly enthusiastic. He clutched his coffee cup like it was the last life preserver on the *Titanic*.

"No, I can handle this."

The stepmother had lied to me enough that I didn't necessarily want to spill Phil's address to her just yet. Her desperation about finding him and the way she slapped three hundred clams down on my desk like she was throwing pennies told me the story was bigger than she was telling me.

I was thinking about taking a bath and scrubbing the smell of smoke out of my hair when the front doorbell rang. Al began staring at the tabletop, a not-so-subtle hint that I should answer it. The doorbell rang again, one long insistent whine. I retied the belt of my robe, tight, and said to Al, "You owe me."

Peering through the peephole, I saw two men standing there. I turned around and said in a low voice, hoping it reached the kitchen, "Al, get dressed right now. Don't argue."

I opened the door. "Detectives Murphy and O'Malley. What can I do for you?"

If the Italians own the fire department, the Irish own the police force. Vince O'Malley and Liam Murphy attended my parish. More often than not, O'Malley's wife would appear at Sunday mass with a shiner the size of a dinner plate. On his days off, he could be found drinking his salary in several Irish-owned bars around town. His wife took in laundry to feed their children.

Irishmen tend to marry late. Fifteen years ago, O'Malley had been a looker.

In his mid-forties now, he had a drinker's gut that hung over his belt and red cheeks lined with tiny broken veins. With his black hair and brown eyes the color of fine whiskey, you didn't notice his small, mean mouth. His hands were the size of trashcan lids, and he was the type of man who hurled a fist first and didn't give a damn about the questions after. The type of man who thought he had a God-given right to slap his wife around because he felt like it. Nick hated him and wouldn't work jobs if O'Malley were involved. "I might kill him, Mags." Nick wasn't joking.

Lots of Irishmen marry late, but there is always a handful who don't marry at all. Murph was of that ilk. A quiet man and half a head shorter than his partner, he was the other type of Irish: redheaded and freckled with a pale complexion that never tanned. He still lived with his mother. You'd see him at mass every day, working the rosary beads. The confessional saw his knees at least once a week, as if he were repenting O'Malley's sins for him. Best friends, they'd lived next to each other all their lives. They'd joined the police force at eighteen, moved up the ranks together, and had been partners for years. Nick said that Murph was the only one who could keep O'Malley in line.

"Detective Murphy, what can I do for you?" I ignored O'Malley.

Al appeared in the hallway, still tucking his shirttails into his pants.

"Hey, Murph. O'Malley. What's up?" he asked.

Al rested a hand on my shoulder.

"May we come in?" asked Murphy at the same time O'Malley barked, "Maggie, where were you at eleven o'clock last night?"

Before Al could open his mouth, I said, "No, you may not. I'm not dressed, as both of you can see. And O'Malley? It's none of your business where I was last night."

Al's hand tightened in warning.

O'Malley decided to get snotty.

"Can you tell us why Harold Washington had a receipt for three hundred dollars in his pocket? Signed by you."

"No, I can't." That was honest. How did Washington get that receipt, I wondered? "And how do you know he had a receipt from me in his pocket?"

CHAPTER NINE

Murph and O'Malley exchanged looks.

"Washington was gunned down sitting in his car last night on Mason at point-blank range by someone in the backseat. Right about eleven. Where were you?" snarled O'Malley.

Shocked, but not, I'd thought something like this might happen, but I hadn't been worried about Washington Senior. I thought it much more likely that the younger Washington would chase a bullet to his gut.

"I wasn't on Mason Street. I'll give you that for free."

"Was Nick working for him?" asked Murphy.

"No, but why don't you ask him? The answer will still be no."

"We just came from his place. We didn't get anything out of that damn lush," sneered O'Malley. "We took him down to the station to sober up. A couple of days in the drunk tank should get him talking."

I looked at Murphy. He gave a tiny shrug.

"He took a swing at us, Maggie. We had no choice but to arrest him."

Like hell they didn't.

"Murph, tell your partner to get off our porch and wait on the curb. I'll tell you what I can, but I will not stand here and listen to him disrespecting Nick."

"Maggie," Al said under his breath in a warning tone.

I ignored him.

"Do you have a warrant, Detective O'Malley?" He glared at me, with that mean mouth of his getting tighter and tighter. "I'll take that as a no. Al, they don't have a right to come in here unless they have a warrant. I might have been gracious and invited them in for a cup of coffee had Detective O'Malley treated me and Nick with some modicum of respect, but he didn't. I'm going to get dressed. When I come back, that man," I said to Murphy as I pointed a finger at O'Malley, "better be at the curb."

As I turned around, I whispered in Al's ear, "Keep your mouth shut. This could implicate your Catherine."

O'Malley yelled at me, "You've learned some nasty tricks from that boss of yours!"

I bit back a very unladylike response.

49

The obvious suspect in the Washington murder would be Helen Washington. *Cherchez la femme.* So why were O'Malley and Murph leaning on me? They should be up at the Washington house grilling his widow. I had a hard time seeing the cultured Mrs. Washington shooting her husband in the back, but then I remembered that one button that shouldn't have been undone. Mrs. Washington wasn't quite who she seemed. She must have an airtight alibi.

I dressed quickly, gearing up for the inevitable confrontation with O'Malley. I put another pot of coffee on the stove. Halfway down the hallway, I realized that I couldn't even call Harvey Cohen, Nick's lawyer. It was the Jewish Sabbath, and he wouldn't be taking any phone calls. I'd have to figure out how to get Nick out of jail myself.

When I reached the front door, Al and Murph were talking about catching the next Seals game. Their bats had been hot lately, hot enough to be in the running for the Pacific Coast League championship. O'Malley was sitting on our front step. Good, but not good enough. He couldn't beat me into submission. He'd have to take my orders and like it. I pointed to the curb and then looked at Murph as if to say, I said the curb, and I meant the curb.

Murph said in response, "Al, why don't you go talk with O'Malley out on the street? He's got an extra ticket to that Seals game we were talking about. Maybe he'll sell it to you if you sweet-talk him."

This was probably the status quo for these two. O'Malley pushing too hard, followed by Murph mopping up and trying to save face all around.

Al looked at me. I gave him the tiniest of nods. Al went out the door and down the steps saying, "Hey, O'Malley, I hear you've got an extra ticket to sell." O'Malley followed Al down the steps, but not before looking back at me with a glower that was supposed to intimidate me.

It didn't.

"Come on in, Murph. Do you want a cup of coffee? I just put on a fresh pot."

Once we were seated at the kitchen table with our coffee, I said, "Washington walked into a bullet last night?"

"Several bullets more like it. Shot in the back. Poor bastard never knew

CHAPTER NINE

what hit him. He was a member of the Pacific Union Club and had been there from around six until he left at around eleven. He tipped the doorman, so we know when he left the building, and we assume that whoever killed him was waiting for him. We've been keeping our lips zipped, but it will be in the afternoon editions. He was sitting in his car when they plugged him. Wallet's gone, but we identified him from the registration in the glove compartment."

"Why aren't you going with a straight-out robbery if the wallet had been lifted?"

"Why shoot him six times? Why shoot him at all? Robbery will get you five years in 'Q.' Murder committed during a robbery is a straight-up ticket to the noose. If I were going to murder someone, I'd plug him good and lift the wallet so us stupid cops would think it was a straight-out robbery. It could just be that, but we can't rule out murder just yet."

"Who found him?"

"Around five a.m., a cook on his way to work at the Fairmont saw Washington slumped over the wheel. What about that receipt?"

"I swear on a stack of bibles, Murph. I have no idea why it was in his pocket. I've never met the man."

"Who did you write it for then? The son? I hear he's a waster."

I shook my head.

"Maggie…" he began.

"You know I can't tell you. But what I can tell you is that neither of Washington's children, Catherine or Philip, could be suspects. Al and I will vouch for their alibis."

"Where were you?"

I shook my head again. "Ask the mayor and the chief of police. They'll vouch for Philip Washington and his girlfriend."

"What in the name of Mary were you doing at the Ship?"

His disapproval was so strong it blew the hair off my forehead. He might as well have added: "A good Catholic girl like you."

"Why we were there is none of your business. I've just helped you cross off three people on your list of suspects. That's all you need to know."

"O'Malley has Phil Washington's girlfriend pegged as the prime suspect."

"He would." I rolled my eyes. "Kill the father so that the son inherits? Except Pop and Junior weren't on speaking terms. Not to mention that murdering your boyfriend's father isn't exactly the way to worm your way into his heart. O'Malley's an idiot. Before he tries to railroad her, both the mayor and the police chief like torch singers if you know what I mean, and I think that you do. If he pursues this, he'll be busted back to patrol faster than you can say speakeasy. You'll both be busted."

He nodded and then finished his coffee in one long gulp. He stood up.

"What was he shot with, Murph?"

"Browning .32. They meant business. Emptied all six shots into him. Poor bastard. Tell your mother I said hello."

Chapter Ten

I could no more march down to the police station and demand they release Nick than I could fly. They'd laugh at me and let him languish with the other drunks until I could get Harvey on the phone to spring him. I didn't have the money or the power; those were the facts. But I had smarts and a telephone, and I knew someone who did.

I called the Mark Hopkins Hotel and had them put me through to the Vance's suite. Mrs. Vance had become something of a religious fanatic. Old age does that. By the time my grandmother died, she was attending mass three times a day and only let go of her rosary when she fell asleep. Mrs. Vance hadn't abandoned the high Episcopalian church of her youth—she had a ringside seat every Sunday at Grace Cathedral—but her days were devoted to listening to strident Baptist radio preachers whose sermons were filled with the sweets of heaven and the horrors of hell. Mrs. Vance knew which gates she was going to walk through, but a little extra insurance never hurt.

"Hello?" said a voice, old, loud, and sharp.

"Mrs. Vance? It's Margaret Laurent. May I speak to Dickie?" I said in a very loud voice, trying to make myself heard over the radio blaring some religious program.

"Young woman, I'm not deaf!" she yelled in that defiant tone of those with major hearing loss. "Richard! Telephone!" she shrieked above the radio preacher yelling at her that we were all going to hell.

In his best columnist's voice, all deep, slow vowels, Dickie came on the line and said, "Hello. May I ask who is calling?"

This was followed by a sharp sound as the phone was slammed down from her end.

"It's Maggie, Dickie."

"If this is about Harold Washington's murder, I want every single bit of delectable gossip you've gathered. I'm all ears."

I wasn't surprised he knew already. He had a bunch of beat cops on his payroll as well. But first things first.

"I need a favor."

He waited for me to say exactly what favor I needed.

"Harold Washington had my receipt made out to his wife in his pocket after they found his body."

I could hear him sucking in his cheeks in anticipation, but all he said was, "Hmmm. Very interesting."

"Very. Unfortunately, Murphy and O'Malley interviewed Nick about it at his apartment this morning. Nick was still, um, ill from last night. O'Malley got nasty with him, as O'Malley does. Nick threw a punch, and Murphy says he had no choice but to call the paddy wagon and let Nick cool his heels in the drunk tank for a couple of days."

"Where Nicholas is sitting as we speak? Yes?"

You couldn't put much past Dickie.

"Yes."

"Did you call Mr. Cohen?"

"The Jewish Sabbath."

As a secretary, I'd have no pull with a judge, even if I had the money for bail. Which I didn't.

"Oh, dear. I'll call the chief after I get off the phone with you. Have you considered that two days without a drink might do him a world of good?"

"Maybe, but it will give O'Malley the opportunity to bring in a wrecking crew and work Nick over some more. As you know, Nick's not too popular with the buttons." I left it at that. "Tell me what it will cost to get him out, will you?"

"Don't be silly, my dear." I imagined him waving that pudgy hand. "Nicholas and I aren't as vulgar as to charge each other. I will get my pound

CHAPTER TEN

of flesh one way or another."

"Thanks, Dickie. You're so sweet."

"I live to serve. Now. Washington."

"Don't know much other than the gunman emptied six bullets into him, a Browning .32. Shot in his car, which was parked on Mason. The gunman must have been in the backseat waiting for him to leave his club. Emptied all six into him."

"That's rather gruesome," noted Dickie in a thoughtful voice.

"Yeah. You knew him. Did he seem like the kind of guy to merit being ambushed like that?"

"Decidedly not, although these days…" His voice trailed off.

I thought of those men slumped over on the sidewalk from exhaustion or hunger. But on second thought, none of them would have access to a gun. If they did, they'd have sold it to buy a meal or three.

"From what I can gather, there doesn't seem to be any chatter from the Fairmont Hotel, either seeing anyone leaving the scene or hearing any shots. Murph didn't say, but it seems they've got nothing other than a man full of bullet holes and a receipt from our office in his pocket."

"The hotel might not have heard or seen anything. Having said that, I can't imagine that they would relish the inevitable publicity that a prominent social and financial leader was gunned down literally steps from their entrance."

"Wouldn't the doorman hear the shots?"

"Not necessarily. Which tells me that Washington's killer has a brain. If I were contemplating murdering someone coming out of the Pacific Union Club, I'd wait to shoot my victim until a cable car rumbled by. When a cable car reaches the top of the hill, they always ring that blasted bell like mad the entire length of Mason between California and Sacramento, which would mask the sound of my gunshots."

"Why do they do that?"

"Purely to annoy everyone. I assume the Fairmont has double-glazed its windows along the cable car route. At the prices they charge for a room, they cannot have their patrons serenaded by endless clanging as their heads hit the pillow. It's pointless complaining to the authorities. Anyway, life's little irritations. How do you figure into this?"

"Murphy and O'Malley went to Nick's place this morning to find out why Washington had a receipt made out to Helen Washington in his pocket with our name on it. Nick played dumb. O'Malley didn't like that."

"Who wouldn't admit to anything purely based on principle? I do admire Nicholas, but sometimes his sense of honor is a little misplaced."

I let that go by.

"Right. Based on the guilty flush on Murphy's face, I assume that they beat Nick senseless because he wouldn't squawk, and they had him hauled off in a paddy wagon to sit in a cell for a couple of days. They know that Harvey isn't available on Saturdays, and on Sunday, nothing happens around here."

"My dear, I'm confused. Why did they make that dreadful drive out to the Avenues to question you?"

"My name's on the receipt."

"Dear, dear."

"My name is on all the receipts, Dickie. I handle the banking. They're grasping at straws. The daughter and son and his twist have alibis. Everyone who has a reason to plug Washington was at the Ship last night, except for the widow, and I assume she has an airtight alibi because they didn't even bring up her name."

He paused and then said, "You didn't hear it from me, but Washington had dinner with his lawyer, Hardesty, at the Pacific Union Club last night. My sources tell me Harold was none too happy with his missus. The word 'divorce' might have been used. And how do you know the others were at the Ship?"

"Caught the floor show last night to see if I could track down the son. You weren't wrong about the girlfriend's singing. She's aces."

"I do hope you took Albert with you." His disapproval crackled over the phone line.

"Sure did. Swanky, with a second helping of la-di-dah, covers it. I ran into Catherine Washington. She's worried about her money and wanted to tackle her brother about any financial shenanigans that he and the stepmother

CHAPTER TEN

may have concocted. Junior walked in with the girlfriend." I left out the part where I'd discovered that Phil Washington was living above the speak and not in the Fillmore. Just like Dickie probably held out something on me.

"He looked fine. The two of them must have gone somewhere for a cure."

"Debatable how long it will last." He sniffed his skepticism.

"It takes him out of the running for his father's killing," I pointed out. "His girlfriend was singing 'Ain't Misbehavin' ' when Washington was shot. Both the mayor and the police chief were in the audience."

"That will make the police's job that much harder. Well, it is not my concern. Now, let me make a couple of calls. Do you think Nicholas has sobered up by now?"

I didn't answer.

"How about you have a cab waiting at the entrance to the police station in, say, an hour, so you can take him home when they release him. When you call DeSoto for the cab, ask for Herman. He'll put it on my account."

"Thanks, Dickie."

I called DeSoto. I managed not to start crying until after I hung up.

Oh, Nick.

***

Just as I reached the police station, a DeSoto cab pulled up, and the cabbie got out. From his undoubtedly numerous legions of lackeys, I can see why Dickie chose this guy to help me. With shoulders the width of Market Street, the man walked on the balls of his feet like a boxer.

"Herman?"

"That's right, Miss. Herman Peters." He tipped his hat, one that had seen much better days. We shook hands.

"Peters?" That seemed a strangely American name for someone with obviously Slavic features. The high cheekbones, slightly slanted eyes, and pointed chin were a dead giveaway. He wasn't very tall, but his broad shoulders and heavy build made me wonder if Dickie also used him for muscle when he needed it—but why would Dickie need muscle? Hauling crates filled with Champagne?

"It used to be Popov, but they changed it when my parents came through Ellis Island. Say, Miss Laurent, I know an Al Laurent. You kinda look like him. You related?"

"My brother."

He whistled and shook his head. "That guy decked me last year. That little drink of water had me seeing stars for two minutes. Lost me the championship." This wasn't said with malice but admiration. "Tell him I said hey, will ya?"

"I will." I grinned.

"Looks like they're springing Mr. Moore."

He pointed to a couple of beefy uniforms with biceps the size of hams walking out the front door of the station with Nick between them. They frog-marched him down the steps. Dickie must have told the chief I'd be waiting. Nick was cuffed, and as they came closer, I saw why.

He must have fought them until they threw him into the paddy wagon. His black eyes had black eyes.

One of the cops growled at me, "This yours?"

I nodded and opened the back door to the cab. They uncuffed him, shoved him inside the back, turned around, and didn't say another word. I gave Herman Nick's address. When we got to his apartment, the two of us hauled Nick up the stairs. Murphy and O'Malley hadn't even bothered to close his apartment door once they'd arrested him.

"Can you hold him for a second?" I asked the cabbie.

I smoothed out the covers to Nick's bed, grabbed his dishtowel, and opened his fridge. A small block of ice sat in a large bowl. The food I'd left there earlier hadn't been touched. An ice pick lay on the counter, but I didn't feel like wrestling with it right now. The room stank of sweat, rum, and despair. I soaked the dishtowel in the icy water and didn't bother wringing it out.

"Please put him on the bed, Herman, will you?"

By this time, Nick was either sober enough or humiliated enough to stand up on his own. He shrugged off the cabbie and walked to the bed and sat down. I handed Nick the dishtowel. Water ran everywhere, soaking his

CHAPTER TEN

shirt, but it would be heaven on his busted-up face.

"Thanks, Mags," he murmured around two fat lips.

"I'll call you later to see if you need anything," I said, which got a weak nod. I walked out of the room, the cabbie on my heels. He had the manners to close the door to Nick's apartment behind him.

When we got to the curb, I said, "Thanks, Herman. I appreciate your help."

"No problem. I do what Mr. Vance says. You need to go anywheres else, Miss Laurent? Off the clock."

Should I go home? No, I needed to go back to the office to see if Ryan had called back with dirt on the Widow Washington. My house shared a party line with some of the nosiest neighbors on God's earth. Any information on her would be all over the parish within ten minutes of that phone call.

"Would you mind taking me to the corner of Sutter and Montgomery?"

"My pleasure," he said and opened the back door for me with a touching gallantry. The ride was filled with anecdotes of the fights he'd won, the fights he'd lost, his plans to get married next spring to the sweetest girl west of the Rockies, the names he'd picked out for the five children they were planning on having, and how he was giving up boxing because it tore her up something fierce to see him get smacked about in the ring, all in the five minutes it took to drive to the office.

"Herman, will you thank Mr. Vance for me?"

"You bet, Miss, and tell your brother that Herman Peters says hi. Say, is Mr. Moore going to be all right?"

"Sure," I lied. "I'll let him know you asked about him."

When I reached the office door, I saw an envelope shoved in the doorframe. I threw it on my desk. Probably another advertisement for a new Cadillac. Car dealerships were sprouting up on Van Ness like mushrooms on a rainy day. I wasn't buying a car anytime soon. It was going to be cable cars, streetcars, and the odd cab for me from here on out, especially since it wasn't likely I'd have a job next month.

I called the answering service for messages. Nothing from Ryan in Boston, nothing from Abramson in New York. I slammed down the receiver in frustration. As I moved to sweep the envelope into the trashcan, I noticed it had my name on it. Not Nick's. And it wasn't typed, it was handwritten. I opened the envelope and pulled out a single sheet of paper.

There's going to be a press conference this afternoon on the Harold Washington murder in the Rotunda of City Hall at five.

No name, no signature. Could this be from the police? Highly unlikely. Then I realized it was probably from one of Dickie's minions.

I looked at my watch. If I were lucky and I caught a cab two minutes ago, I'd just make it.

Chapter Eleven

My luck was good, and I made it to City Hall before the press conference had started. All the dailies had the requisite reporter and photographer in attendance. I knew all the reporters at least by sight, and no one even glanced my way. Who left me the note? I positioned myself halfway behind a pillar.

The mayor, vice-mayor, district attorney, and the chief of police stood on the steps of the Rotunda, talking among themselves. All four men had broken out their finest ties. The better the tie, the bigger the show. The mayor and the D.A. didn't look too bothered. The vice-mayor and the chief of police couldn't stop mopping the sweat off their foreheads.

Crimes like the Washington murder usually cause police chiefs to lose their jobs if the case isn't solved quickly. His obvious nervousness told me that their bats were swinging strikes. It didn't look good for any of them that one of the financial and social leaders in the community had been gunned down right outside his club, but the police chief was especially vulnerable. The residents of Nob Hill had the rep of being immune from such tawdry displays of violence. The police department liked to keep the rough stuff in Chinatown or the Fillmore, and they didn't want it on the front page.

I hadn't seen any headlines about Harold Washington's death at the newsstand when I'd run for the cab, so the newspaper brass must have been holding off until after this press conference. Then they'd flood the late editions with all the dirt on Washington's unexpected demise. That told me that City Hall had been scrambling to find a suspect by the time of this press conference. The sweat on the vice-mayor's brow said they hadn't found a patsy yet.

Nick held that violence was always about money, and if it wasn't about money, it was about power. Harold Washington dealt in money *and* power. The number of people who wanted him dead was legion. In the nine months since the stock market crash, lots of people had lost their homes. If I lost my job, it would be hard work to keep the bank from foreclosing on our house, even with Al's salary as a teacher. I considered us fortunate because we were three paychecks away from packing up. Most people live from paycheck to paycheck. The banks weren't sympathetic. People who'd been solidly middle class now lived out of their cars if they were lucky enough to own one. Only among the monied classes did bankers still enjoy some respect. These days, I bet half the city would be gunning for Washington, especially if his bank was getting mean with the foreclosures. If he could stave off bankruptcy, his bank stood to make a fortune.

The mayor spoke first. A phalanx of cops surrounded him, their eyes alert and continuously scanning the crowd. Murphy and O'Malley stood a couple of feet behind him. O'Malley caught my eye and tried to stare me down. I stared right back at him. He looked away first.

Smiling Tim Stephens had been mayor for years. Something of a showboat, Stephens never went anywhere without a photographer four steps behind him. The type of man who'd invested a fortune in snazzy hats and had grown a bushy mustache to hide the fact he'd gone bald, Stephens had fingers in a lot of financial pies and owned two banks himself. He was running for governor and wouldn't appreciate this scandal with the election only three months away. He'd made his original fortune in shipping, which made me wonder if he had any ties to ABC Shipping.

I needn't have wasted the cab fare. They had nothing.

"We will catch the person who committed this despicable deed..." He droned on and on.

The vice-mayor, Roger Carroll, didn't have anything to say. His job was to clap or smile or look serious or whatever Smiling Tim needed him to do.

Shortly after Eileen had been arrested, I commented to Nick once that Smiling Tim's staff weren't exactly incompetent but were always woefully

CHAPTER ELEVEN

inarticulate and always eclipsed by Stephens at these types of events.

"You think that's an accident?"

"Cooper's pretty ambitious," I pointed out. Theodore Cooper, the D.A. at the time, was milking the papers for every headline he could.

"Hah! That guy's a fool. If he thinks he can outshine Smiling Tim Stephens, he's in for a nasty surprise. Stephens envisions a one-man ticker-tape parade to the governor's chair and has no intention of letting Cooper siphon off any votes."

It wasn't the case when Cooper and Nick were at loggerheads with each other; it was when they weren't that was noteworthy. They'd had a mutual loathing society of two going on for years. Nick had a grudging respect for Tim Stephens because although Stephens is always searching for the camera's angle, at least he's intelligent. He might be ruthless, but he wasn't stupid. Cooper was ruthless but dumb about it. The former D.A.'s desperation for the limelight had been so obvious you could spread it on your morning toast.

As usual, Nick had the beat right. Smiling Tim had made a rare mistake with Cooper. Now, Stephens surrounds himself with bean counters who follow the money. Anyone who tries to hog even a smidgen of the spotlight away from Smiling Tim is spoiling to get canned. And Cooper got canned. He plays a lot of golf nowadays.

This made Cooper's successor, Matthew Doyle, interesting, to say the least. Young and seemingly not too ambitious, he was a looker with a smile that packed some punch. To date, he hadn't made pronouncements or promises that he couldn't keep. Unlike his predecessor. That didn't make him saintly; it just made him smart. Nick didn't have a take on him yet, but anyone would be better than Cooper.

Doyle gave his spiel, but I didn't get any further insight into what made Doyle tick other than grudging admiration for the fine line he walked. He made sure not to embarrass or outshine the mayor, the only person who mattered here—forget Washington—and, like the mayor, gave the impression that he had an ace up his sleeve.

After Doyle wrapped up, the police chief, Bobby O'Sullivan, walked up to the dais. You have to wonder about a guy who still calls himself by his childhood nickname. Rumor was that Smiling Tim couldn't stand him, but Bobby had the support of the rank and file because he handed out promotions like candy, and it would be hard to dislodge him without a fuss. There were rumors that O'Sullivan was eyeing the mayor's seat when Stephens ran for governor. Nick always called him "Booby O'Sullivan," and O'Sullivan's handling of this high-profile case might give Smiling Tim enough ammunition to finally oust him. Based on his speech, full of ums and maybes, Smiling Tim would be figuratively rubbing his hands in glee as Bobby had nothing more to spill to the journalists than vague hints about seditious elements in the community. He didn't come right out and say it was a communist or an immigrant who gunned down Washington, but he sure implied it.

In the end, it all boiled down to they didn't have a clue as to who'd plugged Washington other than the weapon was a Browning .32. The murderer had emptied the chamber into him. Whoever wanted to kill him made damn sure he'd die. Given the lateness of the hour, the streets were deserted, and no one from the Fairmont Hotel heard anything. That was the official story.

When they opened it up for questions, hands shot up, voices shouted, and the photographers positioned themselves for the click. Suddenly I got a whiff of lime and someone's breath tickled the back of my neck.

"Miss Laurent," a low voice said in my ear. "I'm Charlie Stein. I left you the note at Moore's office." The bend of his voice said he hailed from New York. "Don't turn around. A cop is coming straight for you. I'll be waiting for you right here when you come out." He paused. "If you come out."

The smell of lime disappeared, and ten seconds later, a familiar voice said, "Maggie, the D.A. wants to see you."

I glanced over to my left, where O'Malley was standing. This wasn't good. Why send a thug like O'Malley to escort me to the D.A.'s office? It wasn't like I was going to make a run for it.

"Hey, O'Malley, long time, no see. I have dinner plans."

"I don't think so." He cupped my elbow and began to move me toward the D.A.'s office. He held it tight, pinching it in such a way that caused my arm

CHAPTER ELEVEN

to go numb.

"Let go of me right now. You have five seconds before I start screaming that you're hurting me. There are twenty reporters in this room and five photographers. Want to make the front page of the late edition with pictures of me with tears streaming down my cheeks?"

He let go but not before hissing in my ear, "Bitch."

I marched ahead of him. It wasn't smart to bait him like that, but I couldn't let him intimidate me. That would be the ballgame with a bully like him. I'd rather have my hand smashed with a ball-peen hammer than give him that satisfaction.

When we reached the D.A.'s office, O'Malley opened the door and jerked a thumb in my direction. He said to the blonde behind a desk, "Doyle wants to talk to her."

"It's Mr. Doyle to you, Detective." Said by anyone else, it would have come across as a rebuke, but this woman's response was flirty and coy, trying to make the most of a badly done bleach job and a fleshy mouth accented with bright red lipstick, She must be Doyle's secretary. Her nameplate said STELLA KING. I doubted that was her given name. And how she typed with fingernails an inch long, I'll never know.

O'Malley ignored her. After ordering me to sit on a bench against the wall, he shut the door.

Initially frosty—the majority of people who see the D.A. probably deserve the ice treatment—she thawed out around the ten-minute mark. After some encouraging small talk (had I seen *Hell's Angels* yet, and what did I think of Jean Harlow?), it got all girly and chatty. Should she stay platinum? Where did I get my hair bobbed? How did I feel about shorter skirts? Was I married? Where did I live? Oh, I had a brother? Was he single? That sort of stuff.

When Doyle finally appeared, I'd just finished my second cup of coffee. The secretary had been nice enough to let me use the phone to call Ma to tell her I was going to be late and ask her to put up a plate for me. I hoped my conversation with Doyle would be short because it was meatloaf night, and I'm a fool for meatloaf, but I couldn't deny I was also curious about what Charlie Stein wanted to talk to me about.

"Miss Laurent, I don't believe we've met. I'm Matthew Doyle." He held out his hand for me to shake. It was the type of handshake with enough power to intimidate but not alienate. I bet he practiced it on his houseboy when he served up Doyle's pre-dinner martinis.

"Come in." He was playing this jovial like we were old pals. "Thank you, Stella. It's late. Go home. I'll show Miss Laurent out."

"Thank you, Mr. Doyle," she simpered and covered her typewriter with an elaborate move that showed off her figure to great advantage. She liked the shorter skirts and liked them tight as well. Apparently, Doyle wasn't married or if he was, there was no harm in auditioning for the role of Mrs. Doyle Number Two.

I followed him into his office. I'm tall, but this guy was a good head taller than I was and had that slight swagger I associate with East Coast money and privilege. He wore his expensive suit well. I pegged him as closer to forty than thirty-five. He must have some well-juiced backers to be this young in a job that usually required lots of legwork in the political trenches.

In contrast to the utilitarian outer office where his secretary sat, his inner office was mighty impressive. After successfully shipping Eileen off to San Quentin, Cooper, the previous D.A., had outfitted this office with mahogany bookshelves and a matching desk the length of an ocean liner. Shortly thereafter—no doubt at Smiling Tim's request—the newspapers began floating rumors of Cooper using city funds to pay for all this wood. Citing health concerns, Cooper didn't run for reelection.

Doyle's diplomas were hung in a prominent place behind his desk so that when you faced him, you were supposed to cower at the magnificence of his academic smarts. He completed his undergraduate degree in political science, graduating with honors from the University of California, Berkeley, and then topped that off by graduating *summa cum laude* from Harvard Law School. Until Doyle proved himself, I had no intention of being intimidated by all that paper. The jury was still out on this guy.

He flourished a well-manicured hand. "Have a seat, Miss Laurent. Cigarette?"

"No, thank you. I don't smoke." I sat down. "Mr. Doyle, as I told Detectives

CHAPTER ELEVEN

Murphy and O'Malley, I have no idea how that receipt got into Washington's pocket. I've never met the man, dead or alive. Why O'Malley got all snotty with me is a mystery. I can't reveal who my client is, but let's stop being coy. We both know who hired me."

Helen Washington's name was on the receipt. Unless they couldn't read my handwriting, they'd known all along who I was working for.

"Perhaps. Moore wasn't very helpful."

"What wasn't helpful, Mr. Doyle, was him getting the daylights beat out of him."

"I doubt that happened. Have you seen Mr. Moore? Perhaps your concerns regarding Mr. Moore are unfounded."

I gave him a look. "I just came from his apartment. If that's your definition of unfounded, God help you. Of course, some of the boys could have had a go at him once he was thrown into the cooler, but Detective O'Malley's reputation precedes him. He's going to swing at the wrong person one day, Mr. Doyle. He's a powder keg about to blow. At some point, neither you nor Murphy is going to be able to cover for him."

He leaned back in his chair and then yawned, not bothering to cover his mouth.

"I understand from Detective Murphy that Moore threw the first punch."

I didn't want to get Murph in trouble; he was a decent guy. But this conversation left me wondering if O'Malley whaled on Nick in his apartment before the paddy wagon arrived and then got in a few more punches at the station. Why not just slap Nick with a fine and send him home in a cab? They must have thrown him in jail because O'Malley had worked him over but good, and if Nick cooled his heels in the can for a few days, a lot of the swelling would have gone down by the time they sprung him.

"Two against one. Very sporting of them. Have you interviewed Mr. Moore since he was arrested?"

"Can't say I have." He didn't sound concerned.

"If they worked him over again at the station, I'll have Mr. Cohen file a formal complaint."

He didn't respond, which told me that he was well aware that O'Malley had beaten Nick to a pulp for the sheer pleasure of it. If that were the way Doyle planned to play it, using muscle like that, then the jury had reached its verdict. It was time to unload what big guns I had.

"As I told Detective Murphy, it's possible that my brother and I attended a social event last night where we might have seen both the mayor and the police chief with their wives. Philip Washington may have been sitting about fifty feet from me at the exact time someone murdered his father. It's also possible that Catherine Washington and I shared a table at said social event. I suggest you corroborate my story with Mayor Stephens and Chief O'Sullivan."

He yawned again.

"Well, I would, except all of us dined at the mayor's house that night."

"Really?" I raised an eyebrow. "Mrs. O'Sullivan has brown hair, is five feet tall, with small brown eyes, and wears too much rouge. She wore a black dress and a three-stranded pearl necklace that I wouldn't turn down if someone put it around my neck. A black sable fur coat was draped over her shoulders that probably cost as much as your car. Mrs. Stephens is a large woman with blue eyes and red hair, whose bosom is the first thing you see no matter what she's wearing. Last night she wore a green dress that I saw in the window of I. Magnin's last week. Cost Mayor Stephens a bunch of simoleons, let me tell you."

He sat back in his chair and regarded me with wariness and surprise. I didn't flinch under his gaze. While still studying me, he dislodged a cigarette from an engraved silver cigarette case and had it lit and in his mouth in five seconds.

After a couple of drags, he said, "You're not a pushover, are you?"

"I wouldn't be Nick Moore's secretary if I were. I don't have all that paper, Mr. Doyle." I pointed to his diplomas. "I only finished high school. But God gave me lots of smarts, and I know my rights. Who do you think the press is going to believe if City Hall starts leaning on me? I'll sing loud and clear, Mr. Doyle. It will be my word and my brother's word, who's a schoolteacher, by the way, against the mayor, who wouldn't appreciate that kind of publicity, seeing as he's now gunning for governor."

CHAPTER ELEVEN

He laughed. "You don't need a degree, Miss Laurent. You've got it all figured out, don't you?"

"I do all right. Mr. Doyle. If I hear of something I think is worthwhile, I'll let you know. I don't know who killed Washington, but anyone with a mortgage at his bank might be worth looking at."

"That's only ten thousand people," he pointed out.

"Take heart, Mr. Doyle. It's not the mayor, the chief of police, Phil Washington, his girlfriend, Catherine Washington, my brother, or me who killed Harold Washington. For the record, I have no idea why that receipt was in his pocket."

"Was the wife having him tailed? The word on the street is that he's rather frisky around women."

Now it was my turn to laugh. "Is that what they're calling it these days? From what I've heard, he's quite the ladies' man. Ask Mrs. Washington. She'd know. Word is he was two-timing his wife with her while his wife was dying in a sanitarium. She was a lunger. I assume you've interviewed her."

"Now, why would I tell you that?" He wasn't quite what I would call smug, but close enough.

"Because it might make me a little more amenable to contacting you with any information."

He shook his head. "I'll take my chances on your good nature."

"If that's the way you're going to play this, Mr. Doyle. As I said, I'm not book smart, but I'm people smart. O'Sullivan didn't exactly inspire confidence at the press conference. He's got nothing. That was obvious, and that means you've got nothing. The newspapers like Nick. A photograph of him with his nose broken and black eyes down to his knees won't go over well." I stood up and walked across the room, half expecting him to stop me. I reached the door without him saying a word. I turned around. "I've heard that Washington had dinner with his lawyer at the Pacific Union Club last night before he was killed. Maybe Murphy and O'Malley should be grilling his lawyer instead of me and my brother."

I left the office before I could see the look on his face.

Chapter Twelve

When I returned to the Rotunda, the reporter who'd alerted me about the press conference was lounging against a marble pillar, smoking a cigarette. With the show now over, all the other newshounds had fled to file their stories with no story to tell. I saw him before he saw me. Whippet-thin, but not skinny, he reminded me of a younger Nick. Although his chin wasn't as pointy, he held himself with the same casual physical grace and was just short of what I'd call handsome, with large brown eyes and a strong nose. His mouth, wrapped around a cigarette, was wide and sensual, rather like Philip Washington's mouth but not as cruel. His suit—tailored—was a cut above the usual. The wool lay well against his body, and the suit jacket made him look slim but not gaunt. This guy must have some family money because no journalist I knew could afford a suit that fine. Based on his face, I pegged him at no more than thirty, but his temples were graying already. He'd be fully gray by forty.

"Mr. Stein?"

He looked up from his cigarette and threw it into a nearby spittoon.

"Call me Charlie. Cup of coffee?"

More coffee would burn a hole in my stomach.

"I wouldn't mind a sandwich. I'm starving."

We walked in silence to a nearby greasy spoon known as a hangout for the reporters covering City Hall. I ordered a tuna sandwich, which wouldn't set back Stein that much. He ordered a cup of tea, which faintly smelled of bourbon.

"Doyle went easy on you," he noted. "I'd planned to wait another hour at

CHAPTER TWELVE

least. Why?"

I shrugged. "Not much to tell. And before you ask, no, I have no idea who shot Washington. I know most of the reporters by sight, and you don't look familiar. You're not from around here, are you?"

"Nah. Worked for Hearst in New York. They reassigned me to Frisco a couple of months ago to cover the waterfront. Things are heating up here. The International Longshoremen's Association is starting to organize in town. Given the size of this port, when things blow, they're going to blow sky-high."

"When aren't they hot?" With so many men out of work, the ports were taking advantage of the glut of labor, and tempers were beginning to flare. "So why are you interested in the murder of a banker?"

"ABC Shipping mean anything to you?"

"No," I lied.

"I didn't think so," he mocked.

He wasn't buying what I was selling.

"I'm more interested in Washington Junior. Heard a rumor that his father threw him out on his ear for the twentieth time. Financial irregularities are what I believe they call them. Plus, there's something sleazy about him. Just a gut feeling. Did you know he owns that speak? I saw you there last night at a table with Catherine Washington. The guy with you. Is that your brother? You two look alike."

Catherine Washington must have known her brother owned the speak and lived upstairs, so why keep it a secret?

"Yes, he's my brother. Of course, I knew." I tried to sound bored.

"Sure you did," he said, followed by a knowing smirk.

"Mr. Stein, I'm confused. How do you—"

"It's Charlie. I asked the kid with the busted lip about you, and he said you were Moore's secretary. Word on the street? You're working the Washington job because Moore's on the bender of the century."

I was sick of people taking potshots at Nick. I stood up.

"Thanks for the sandwich."

"Sit down, sister. I don't care how drunk Moore is these days. I hear he's the best detective in the city, and I hope that whatever's riding him stops riding him soon. I need a scoop, and I need it bad. The other guys aren't giving me the time of day. You not spending the night in the clink tells me you've got savvy enough to handle someone like Doyle. How about you and I team up? There are places you can't go because you're a da– a woman, and there are places I can't go because I'm a man. I won't spill anything until you tell me to, but if you decide to spill your guts at some point, I won't complain."

I sat down and began playing with the salt and pepper shakers while I considered his offer. There were places I couldn't go. There was Al, but I'd had to strong-arm him to take me to that speak. This guy probably spent half of his waking hours in one.

"I'll give it some thought," I said. "That's as good as it's going to get."

"How about I give you something for free, and then you give me something back?" He wriggled his eyebrows and gave me a wide grin. As grins go, it was pretty nice. "Isn't that how it works?"

"Possibly."

"I already gave you the info on Washington and the speak, and don't give me any bunkum that you knew, because you didn't. Consider this as a bonus. How about Doyle being Stephens' nephew on his wife's side?"

That explained a lot. Smiling Tim was currently the front-runner for governor, and his hand-picked successor will keep the mayor's seat warm until his nephew runs for mayor a few years down the road.

"Your turn," he said and worked that grin some more.

"Philip Washington is well known as a junkie. I've had two people in two days tell me he's poison and to watch my back around him. My bonus info: Washington Senior had planned to divorce his current wife, who's been married at least twice before. None of her husbands have outlived her to date. Harold Washington's number three. Given her marital history, I wouldn't have placed any bets on him reaching his next birthday."

He whistled, and the green in his eyes deepened in color, like a cat about to pounce on a mouse. "You think she's good for it?"

I shook my head. "Nah. Stephens and O'Sullivan would have been grinning

CHAPTER TWELVE

from ear to ear and offered her up to be lynched if they had her to rights. She must have a solid alibi, or they'd have paraded her in front of you guys. Stephens needs this case solved and fast. He's gearing up for the election and doesn't have any serious rivals, but he's been hitting the hooch and showing up drunk in public. He needs a fall guy to take the spotlight off of him. O'Sullivan's perfect for the fall. His reputation isn't the greatest as it is, and if the police don't charge someone soon, Stephens will oust him. Like he's wanted to for the last two years."

"While that cop was marching you to the D.A.'s office, I asked about the wife, and O'Sullivan said that she was having dinner at the home of William Langdon and didn't leave until after midnight. O'Sullivan sounded disappointed."

"I bet. Langdon was the D.A. here in San Francisco several years back and now sits on the California Supreme Court. If Langdon said she was there, she was there. Word of advice. Steer clear of Detective O'Malley if you can."

"The cop with the scowl and two-hundred-and-fifty pounds of muscle behind him who tried to strong-arm you to Doyle's office?"

"Yep. Him. His partner, Murphy, is jake, but O'Malley hates newshounds and will use any excuse to break your nose. Or your neck. I don't think he's too choosy."

"Thanks. I appreciate the warning. Miss Maggie Laurent, we got a deal?"

"Maybe."

"I'll take it." He wrote his phone number on a napkin and handed it to me. "I'm not at my desk much, but I've got an answering service that I check fairly frequently. Call anytime."

"Do you know an Ezra Abramson? Pinkerton. Works out of New York."

"Ezzie? He's the best. Why?"

"Oh, no reason, Mr. Stein. I'll call you. Don't call me." I folded the napkin with his number on it into a tight square and stuck it in the pocket of my coat. I wasn't sure I'd need it, but I might.

Chapter Thirteen

Sunday is the day the Laurent family devotes itself to God. This Sunday's prayers were all pleas to God to help Nick because if anyone needed God's intervention, it was him.

You dress up in your Sunday best—which is my only best—and you pray and take communion. No deviations are allowed. Questions about the Father, Son, and the Holy Ghost are frowned upon or ignored. The little world of the Avenues where I was born was composed of large Catholic families who lived in houses on the small side, no matter how many kids came along. Where I used to think that the biggest sin might be taking money out of the collection box instead of putting it in. Where it was likely that you'd marry your childhood sweetheart.

Nick's world of cheating husbands, stock swindles, bank robberies, and the occasional murder had widened my world beyond the confines of Arguello Boulevard and Park Presidio Drive. I liked that every day was different. That someone who would have been shunned in my parents' world might be a bank robber with a heart of gold. Or a thug who'd plug you with a 22 without a second thought. I began to see people with a much clearer eye. Like a communion veil had been pulled back over my head. Once you see, you can't un-see. Like the fact that O'Malley beat his wife, Father O'Flaherty's breath often smelled like whiskey, and Deirdre Boyle was having an affair with Jackie Reagin's husband. It's like if you don't talk about Bree's black eyes, your husband isn't going to whale on you after a drink too many. It's an apple cart filled with nice juicy apples. And whether their centers were rotten was increasingly a question.

CHAPTER THIRTEEN

For me, nothing upset that nice little apple cart like Eileen Taylor. Seventy-year-old Father O'Flaherty wouldn't have a clue on how to make sense of someone like her. He'd say, "Oh, my child, God works in mysterious ways," his answer to pretty much all questions beyond his understanding. It must be nice to have things so simple. But the world isn't that simple. Sure, I knew you couldn't answer those questions with a bunch of meaningless platitudes, but I was now searching for a way for things to fit again, even if the answers weren't what I wanted to hear. Maybe there weren't answers. The Church had answers for everything, even if it all boiled down to having faith. I've found that wasn't enough. I had faith, but I still wanted answers.

We socialized in the church hall after mass like we always did. O'Malley was there. We avoided each other. Bree began sneaking muffins and cookies into her coat pockets like she did every Sunday. All of us looked the other way like we always did. Sometimes, Ma made extra batches of cookies, telling Bree that she'd accidentally doubled the recipe, so would she take the extras before they went stale? Another lie. Did Ma confess these lies? As I said, the world isn't simple.

Ma would have had a fit if I'd gone into the office that day, so I stayed in my room and scanned the Sunday editions for news on Harold Washington. His attorneys, Hardesty, Hardesty, Chambers, and Danvers, had issued a statement eulogizing Washington as one of the guiding financial lights in the city of San Francisco. That his bank was on the verge of bankruptcy wasn't mentioned. Once I'd skimmed through all the articles that said virtually nothing other than Harold Washington had been murdered, I lay there cataloging what I knew so far, what I didn't, and what I should find out.

Washington Senior had been gunned down on Mason Street in the shadow of the Pacific Union Club. Earlier that night, he'd made loud noises to his lawyer about divorcing his wife over his steak and kidney pie.

Philip Washington owned a speakeasy, operating out of what looked like a moribund shipping company. Even to my relatively naïve eyes, this place was obviously *la crème de la crème*. The mayor and police chief, being part of the regular clientele, told me it was the toniest one in the city and juiced up to the eyeballs. Phil Washington wouldn't need to bribe Stephens to keep the cops away from the speak. Stephens' presence signaled to the monied types that it was a safe bet against any raids.

At first glance, Helen Washington had seemed on the up and up, but as I've found out, appearances can be deceiving. Although her money was good—even without Catherine Washington's calling nerts on the brother working down at the wharf—her story about wanting to find her stepson was fishy enough to call Boston and get her history. And then there was her husband's untimely demise. Until I talked to Ryan or Abramson, I had no answers, only suspicions.

Catherine Washington? The last bit of the puzzle. Why did she lie to me about her brother? If they were on the outs, why would all that muscle let her in the door without a holler? I noticed that she didn't pay for that bottle of booze with its fancy label. Based on the speed with which Al was guzzling down his drink, I bet it tasted neat and not like someone's socks boiled in alcohol. So, where did the high-class hooch come from? Could ABC Shipping be a conduit for whiskey running? Canada had done its own flirting with Prohibition but hadn't outlawed exporting booze. Go figure. I guess the Canadian government was looking for loopholes to tax the liquor companies. ABC Shipping could export it, but no one could buy it legally. Unless you sold it under the table to speakeasies like Washington's. What a sweet deal. Washington could use his ships to ferry the booze down from Canada, outfit his speak with decent liquor, and cut out all middlemen. Was he selling his cache of smuggled booze to other speaks? And maybe the rumor that he was short on cash was nothing more than a smokescreen to hide the fact he was swimming in dough.

First things first: I needed to find out if the rumors about the divorce were true. A quick thumb through the telephone directory for Hardesty, Hardesty, Chambers, and Danvers told me their office was in the Flood Building, one of the most prestigious addresses in the city. Hat-and-gloves territory for sure. Hopefully, my shoes would be ready by tomorrow morning.

Chapter Fourteen

The shoemaker took pity on me and gave me a nice discount. The Irish in me said I should decline the offer, while the French side of me reminded me I now had lunch money for the week. Pragmatism usually won out over pride where food was concerned.

With my gloves, hat, and newly polished shoes, I looked swell enough to brave the hallowed offices of Hardesty's, as they were known on the street. Nick and I didn't bump elbows with these hoity-toity lawyers too often. Unless there was a dispute regarding a will that the law firm didn't want to sully their hands dealing with, we rarely interacted with the higher-end attorneys who were all about mergers, trusts, stocks, and bonds. Not Moore Detective Agency territory.

Hardesty's monopolized the entire top floor. The elevator opened onto a pair of massive oak doors, at least twelve feet tall, with enough beveled glass to outfit a small cathedral. Did one knock? I looked for a doorbell. Nothing. I walked in. The doors opened onto an enormous room filled with a bunch of women my age, typing away. Probably most of their business these days dealt with bankruptcy filings. The sound of thirty typists pounding away filled the air. The back wall was composed of wall-to-wall doors of frosted glass, with the names of the lawyers etched on the glass. The size of their names indicated their status in the firm, with the principals in big letters and the other lawyers in a font so small I had to squint to read their names. I hadn't a hope in hell of talking with any of the principals, but maybe one of the lesser attorneys would give me five minutes. I'd planned out my strategy, saying I'd been hired by Mrs. Washington to find her stepson—they could check with her if they wanted—and then hope like hell I'd get a few crumbs to work on.

An older woman, pushing a hard sixty, marched toward me, a real Mrs. Grundy type, with her severe black suit and a bun so tight it must give her headaches. She eyed my bob and then the length of my skirt with disdain. There was no way I'd get past her.

"Yes?" she said in a voice that clearly said "No."

Scrambling for an excuse to be there, I stammered, "I'm wondering if there are any openings. I'm an excellent typist."

"No, there aren't any openings." She turned and began to walk away from me.

"Excuse me," I called after her. "I'm really awfully good. May I show you how accurate and fast I am?"

"No, you may not. I told you once there aren't any openings. Now leave before I have you thrown out."

She didn't have to be this vicious. When she reached her desk, she turned around and pointed at the door, then lifted the receiver of her phone to make good her threat about security.

What makes people so angry? Her. O'Malley. I made for the ladies' room to splash some water on my face. As I was patting it dry with my handkerchief, the door opened. I half expected that witch to appear, making sure I was going to leave the building.

It wasn't.

"Don't let Miss Carruthers get you down. She's just like that," said a petite blonde in a dark blue suit with a skirt so long, she had to be part of Hardesty's typing pool. She filed past me to open a window and then pulled a cigarette out of her bra and fished a lighter from behind a vase. She lit up and on her first exhale, sighed with relief. "Miss Carruthers would fire me if she caught me smoking. We really don't have any open positions. I'm sorry. Are you okay?"

"Yeah, I'm fine. Boy, is she mean. I guess you get a lot of people looking for work these days."

She nodded and waved a hand in the direction of the office. "All of us hate

CHAPTER FOURTEEN

her. Last week, she slapped one of the girls who'd made a typo on a will. But we're super grateful to have a job, and it pays okay."

"What would happen if someone slapped her back?" I asked.

That set off a round of giggles between the two of us.

"My name is Jane Morris. Everyone calls me Janie. If you give me your name and phone number, I can call you if there are any openings."

My first reaction was no way, no how. I'd never work under that Carruthers hag. I'd scrub Market Street with my toothbrush before I'd let that woman slap me around. But realistically, even a couple of days of temporary work might give me some information I'd normally not be privy to. I gave her my home phone number.

"I'm Maggie Laurent." I held out my hand. "Nice to meet you, Janie. I read in the newspaper that you guys were Mr. Washington's lawyers. It must have been horrible around here when you got the news."

"Oh!" Janie squealed with a lot more glee than was appropriate. "You have no idea. Mr. Washington had come in the morning of the day he was killed, stomping his foot, screaming and yelling in front of the staff that he needed to see Mr. Hardesty Senior that second! He wanted to change his will and change it right there and then, and divorce that 'hussy.' Those were his very words! He wanted Mr. Hardesty to fly down to Mexico with him the next day to get one of those quickie divorces. Well! Mr. Hardesty Senior was up at the capital that day for some reason and wouldn't be back until after five. We all knew that Mr. Hardesty would lose his noodle if anyone else even thought about amending that will without his looksee. Washington screamed that one of the flunkies, he used that very word, could do it. But then Miss Carruthers calmed him down and told him that Mr. Hardesty would be back later that day, and she could make an appointment for them to have dinner together at the club. And then! Then! He was murdered! Can you imagine?"

"Sounds like quite a scene!" I exclaimed, trying to match her enthusiasm but falling way short. She didn't seem to mind.

"It was great. You can imagine there aren't a lot of chuckles around here."

"No, I bet they're in short supply. Did you know Mr. Washington?"

That got a snort. "My backside did. You learned pretty quickly to glue yourself to your chair whenever he walked into the room. I hate men who can't keep their hands to themselves, especially since he knew we couldn't complain about it or we'd be fired."

This tallied with what else I'd heard about him. Sounds like the son wasn't the only louse in the family.

"What about his widow? Have you ever met her?"

"Once or twice. She seemed okay. I mean, no one who comes into Hardesty's treats the secretaries with any respect. Mrs. Washington mostly ignored us, but at least she didn't expect us to dance around her getting her tea and biscuits like most of the wives do. That counts for a lot around here."

"Well, I should go before that witch starts patrolling the halls and escorts me out the door. You've been very kind, Janie. Thanks! And if something should come up, let me know!"

Chapter Fifteen

Armed with this information, I decided to offer my condolences to Widow Washington.

I picked up some flowers in North Beach and took a cab across town to Sea Cliff, where the big money lived. The mansions lining the street had a bit of the fairy tale about them this morning. Indistinct in the heavy blanket of fog that hadn't yet burned off, they appeared to float as if on water. As I looked down the block, the fog swirled around lampposts and chimneys, and even my ankles. This road curved around the cliff face and eventually became Ocean Avenue, which fronted the beach. This morning, it felt like this was the edge of the world.

Sea Cliff real estate was judged by its proximity to the ocean. The homes overlooking the Pacific were the biggest and the most expensive. The Washington house was relatively small compared to the mansions across the street. Still, our entire house would probably have fit in the living room twice over.

My bouquet of lilies looked meager and cheap in my hand.

I rang the doorbell. I waited. Counted to fifty and then rang again. A butler opened the door just enough to show his face, which was round and plump with the faintest of mustaches over his upper lip.

"Yes? May I help you?"

I managed to hide my shock. His voice had that mannered, odd combination of clipped speech around long vowels favored by the upper-class limeys I've run across.

"I've come to pay my respects to Mrs. Washington." I held up the flowers.

He didn't even bother to look at them.

"I will tell her."

He made to shut the door, but I wedged my foot between the door and the threshold.

"You don't know my name," I protested, never mind that he made no moves to take my flowers.

"On the contrary, Miss Laurent."

That stopped me. I'd have to play a card I hadn't wanted to play just yet.

"I have news of Mr. Philip Washington."

"I shall relay the news to Madame."

That wouldn't do me any good.

"I'd rather tell her myself. It's confidential."

I would later understand that little smirk he gave me before saying, "As you wish."

He opened the door and, with a manicured hand, bade me to follow him. One black braid hung down his back, so long it skimmed the top of his waist. The silk beanie on his head was even darker than his braid. Although clothed in head-to-toe black silk pajamas, his feet were encased in white socks. The tap-tap-tap of his clogs against the marble floor echoed throughout the foyer. His braid swayed back and forth as he walked. The pomade on his hair smelled of dying gardenias and was so potent that its heavy aroma made me slightly nauseous as I followed in his wake. A short man, only a little over five feet, he seemed as wide as he was tall and gave the impression of rolling on wheels as he walked.

He stopped in front of an ornately carved door twice my height. It looked heavy, like it might take both of us to swing it back on its hinges, but he had no trouble opening it and ushering me in.

"Miss Laurent," he announced, bowed, and left the room.

No sooner did I cross the threshold than the scent of flowers overwhelmed me, and I had to fight off a sneeze. Huge arrangements of lilies, mum, carnations, and glads covered every surface in the room. The Flower Mart down at 5th and Howard must be cleared out. Whatever Washington's monetary woes, he was jake with the elite of San Francisco.

CHAPTER FIFTEEN

I coughed to hide my "Oh" of surprise. Philip Washington, slender in a black wool suit, was leaning against the marble facade of the fireplace, smoking a cigarette. He didn't look particularly bereaved.

Helen Washington sat on a sofa, clutching a snifter of brandy. At an hour shy of noon, I thought it a little early to be hitting the hooch. The cut-glass decanter in front of her stood half-empty, and I'd bet my neck that it had been full that morning. Her black suit, the height of fashion, made me wonder if she had anticipated her husband's demise. Despite the deep black of the wool, that suit kissed her every in and out.

The entire room had been decorated in white silk; the walls, the upholstery, and the marble floor, even the pillows gleamed white. It was like standing in a snowstorm. The only spots of color in the room were their clothes and the deep red of Helen Washington's lips and nails. The combination of the two of them against all that white gave the living room the feeling of being in a movie.

"Miss Laurent, I believe?" Washington held out his hand for me to shake. I had to do an awkward shifting of the flowers from one hand to the other.

"Nice to meet you," I stammered, out of my depth here.

"As you can see, Philip has returned home." Helen's voice was too loud. Like she'd had one too many snorts but was trying to hide it. She waved a hand in his direction, and her drink sloshed over the edge. "Obviously, I won't be needing your services any longer."

"I wanted to convey my condolences." I raised the flowers.

She didn't bother to stand up, just nodded at me, which was more of a jerk than a nod, and ignored my outstretched hand offering her the flowers. Her hand clutched her glass so tightly, I could see the white of her knuckles. Jeepers. Any more wound up, and she'd break the glass.

"Don't I get any flowers?" mocked Washington.

I wanted to throw them at him, but I didn't.

"I'm truly sorry for your loss, Mr. Washington. I was devastated when I lost my father."

My not-so-subtle hint that he didn't look at all devastated was not lost on him. He grinned.

"Touché." He picked up a cigarette case from the mantel and held it out. "Cigarette?"

"No, thank you. I don't smoke."

"Helen?" He crossed the room with his cigarette case with an easy grace, confirming my original impression of him as a jungle cat.

"Please."

Again, her voice was too loud, and her hand shook a little as she brought the cigarette to her mouth for him to light. His hand? Rock steady.

He returned to the fireplace to improve his lounging abilities. Not that he needed any pointers.

"Did you enjoy the floor show the other night, Miss Laurent?"

In the few seconds during which he'd lit their cigarettes, I'd regained my composure, but that question shook me.

I stammered, "It was s-swell. She's quite a singer."

I bet he knows the names of everyone who crosses the threshold of his speak. I should have counted on that.

"Yes, she is." That might have been the only honest sentence he'd uttered in months. "How's Nick doing these days?"

"He's fine. Do you know Nick?"

Flicking his ash into a cut-crystal ashtray, he drawled, "Oh, we've run into one another now and then. One does."

Does one?

"I'm doing his legwork right now. He has a bad case of the flu. It's his chest. He's having a hard time shaking it. Since the war…" I let the phrase trail off.

"Is that what they're calling it these days? How do you know Catherine?"

That's why they let me in the door. They wanted to grill me about his sister.

"I don't."

"Oh? You looked pretty cozy the other night at the speak."

"She shared her table with me and my brother. That's all. I was working on behalf of your stepmother and had asked her some questions that morning about your whereabouts. I heard through the grapevine that you frequented

CHAPTER FIFTEEN

a speak down at the waterfront, and my brother and I went to check it out, hoping you'd be there. Once I found you, I was supposed to persuade you to return home. That's it."

I had no intention of letting him know that I knew he owned the speak and that he lived above it.

"As you can see, the prodigal son has returned," he drawled and then bowed. "Does the grapevine have a name?"

Although he phrased it as a casual question, I detected some bark behind it. He hailed from those echelons of society where the de facto tone of voice was a drawl. Nothing mattered, life was a chore. People like him had only two speeds. Sarcasm or boredom.

Nick says that everyone has a tell, and you should watch for it, that it always surfaces when someone is hiding something. Philip Washington's tell was how the grip on his cigarette changed. When he wasn't fussed, the cigarette made its way in a leisurely mosey up to his mouth. When fussed, his fingers tightened on the butt, and he moved the cigarette so fast it became nothing more than a blur. Philip Washington had his cigarette pinched between his fingers so tightly that it was a miracle he didn't kill the flame.

"How about 'grapevine'?"

"Advantage, Laurent. Do you play tennis, Miss Laurent?"

"Yes. I'm not sailing to England to play at Wimbledon anytime soon, but I do okay. I'm a better golfer."

"How good?"

"Ten under par good."

He stopped lounging against the mantel and stood up straight to leer at me. "Perhaps we should play a round."

He wasn't talking about golf.

"I've got a pretty mean swing, Mr. Washington." Right then, I wanted to brain him with a nine iron. I glanced over at Helen Washington. A minuscule shake of her head warned him to back off.

"Should I be afraid of you, Miss Laurent?" He stated it like it was a harmless question, wrapped up in a toothy grin, but his sharp squint told me he meant business.

"I'm just a secretary, Mr. Washington. I'll go now. I don't want to intrude on your grieving."

He laughed out loud at that.

Dickie Vance wasn't wrong. This guy was poison.

"Philip, ring for Wai-Ling."

There wasn't a "please" in that voice, and the glare she leveled at her stepson was cold enough to send a shiver down my back.

"Helen, your wish is my command." He pulled on the bell rope, but not without smirking at her as he did so. "Nice to meet you, Miss Laurent."

I didn't return the sentiment.

I nodded at Helen Washington and said, "I'm very sorry about your husband."

The manservant must have been lurking in the hallway because I barely got those words out of my mouth before he appeared. He waited for me to exit the room first and then closed the door behind me. As he escorted me down the hallway, I could hear the screech of Helen Washington's voice yelling at her stepson, but I couldn't make out what she was saying. I'd barely crossed the threshold before the front door was slammed behind me.

I still had the bouquet of lilies in my hand.

Chapter Sixteen

Sparring with Philip Washington had made me hungry. I stood on the sidewalk, debating whether to walk over to Geary, where I'd be sure to find a coffee shop nearby, or catch a streetcar and have lunch at home. The blare of a car horn got my attention. Someone was waving at me from across the street. It was Charlie Stein. He pulled around in front of me and opened the passenger door.

"Want a lift?"

"If you're going someplace where I can get a sandwich, I sure do."

Without waiting for his reply, I hopped in.

"How'd it go in there?"

I answered with a question of my own. "How long were you casing the house?"

"Long enough to see you arrive with a bouquet in your hand. That's nice of you."

"Not really," I admitted. "It was the only way I could think of to shoehorn my way into the house."

"They boohooing in there?"

I rolled my eyes. "Hardly. The widow is guzzling brandy like it's going out of style, although wearing a spiffy suit while pounding them back. The son? Acted as if his father had died two hundred years ago, not two days."

"What about the sister?"

"Not there. I'm not even sure if she knows about her father. I assume so, but she lives on a boat down near Crissy Field, so maybe she hasn't heard."

"A boat? That seems a little low-end for that crowd."

"You haven't seen the boat. Keep driving. We'll hit Ocean Avenue in a minute. We can find a place to eat near Playland."

"Playland?"

"You need to get out more. It's an amusement park. Just head in the direction of screaming kids. My dad used to take me there when I was small. Al worked there as a teenager selling tickets to the Big Dipper. He'd let me ride for free."

"The Big Dipper?"

"A roller coaster. I spent one entire summer doing nothing but endless loops around the tracks. Talk about heaven."

"You ever been to Coney Island? Bet it has this place beat."

"No. Never been outside of California. Someday, I'll get to New York."

He pulled up in front of the Cliff House and parked. Even though the windows to his car were rolled up, I could hear the seals out at Seal Rock barking away. The fog clung to the shore, and if it weren't for the endless shush of the waves, you wouldn't know you were five hundred feet from the ocean.

Perched on a cliff overlooking the Pacific Ocean, the Cliff House was like a palace, all white and elegant. I'd snuck into the lobby once, marveling at how posh it was, and breathed in the briny scent of freshly shucked oysters and lemon. My father used to take my mother there for dinner to celebrate their wedding anniversary. She'd put on her smartest hat and whitest gloves while he'd pin a corsage on the lapel of her coat. They'd waltz out the door hand-in-hand. I doubted I could even afford a cup of coffee there, never mind a sandwich, and I was sure that Charlie Stein didn't have that kind of dough either.

"Hey, I can't—"

"Pipe down. You're a source. I haven't used up my budget for the month."

"You're lying. Let's find a hot dog stand. There's bound to be one near Playland. Keep driving. It's not far. And we'll go Dutch. My pocketbook ain't flush, but it can handle a hot dog."

Stein gave me a speculative glance. "I'm beginning to think you're okay."

"Is that what your life is like? Everyone's working a con?"

CHAPTER SIXTEEN

"Until they prove me wrong."

I couldn't argue with that sentiment. Going those few rounds with Eileen Taylor had me dialing up the cynicism first. I didn't give many people the benefit of the doubt these days.

"Let's find that hot dog stand. I'm on the verge of gnawing on my left ankle I'm so hungry."

We drove down Ocean Avenue, picking our way through the fog. It was still a bit pea-soupish. Once parked, we got our dogs and then sat on a bench facing the ocean and chowed down.

"You've got a pretty nice ride there." I pointed to his car parked at the curb.

"Hearst gave me a nice fat bonus for moving out here. Say, when does the sun come out in this town?"

"September and October are the best months. Warm days, cool nights. Nice. All the tourists have fled by then, so the city isn't very crowded."

"I've had my heat on every single day since I arrived."

"July's the worst. You'll get used to it."

We sat there for a while, letting the sea breeze kick past us. The sun was doing its darnedest to peek through the fog. I could have sat there all day, but I needed to talk to Dickie again. I was just about to stand up and ask Charlie for a lift to John's Grill when he coughed to get my attention.

"I talked to Ezzie."

"Look, Stein, this is my case, and I don't—"

"Keep a lid on it. He's a pal of mine. Gave me the scoop on the Merriweather jewel heist. I owe my career to him. You can trust him, and you can trust me. I don't plan on stealing your thunder. Just out of curiosity, why are you doing this? Keeping the agency afloat while Moore floats on a sea of booze."

I hadn't even considered walking out, even when the possibility of not being paid became less of a possibility and more of a fact.

"Because Nick's the best egg there is. Sure, I can type and take shorthand. So can every girl who's graduated high school. His was the thirtieth door I'd knocked on. Either they weren't hiring, or I was too young, or I didn't

89

have any experience. I told him I was a hard worker and could type eighty words a minute. My shorthand was iffy, but it got the job done, and I needed the money to help support my family. He gave me the job on the spot and handed over a hundred smacks as a hiring bonus. That's the kind of guy he is. Sends my mother flowers on the anniversary of my father's death. His office space isn't exactly the Ritz, and I work weekends some times, but short of murder, I'm going to do anything to keep this agency going until he gets back on his feet."

Stein put his hand over mine for a moment. He wasn't grabby or anything like that. Just being nice.

"How long do you think it will take to dry him out?" he asked.

I shook my head and looked out to watch the breakers hit the shore. I didn't want him to see me cry.

"That dame do it to him?"

I nodded. Huh. The gossip about that case had even reached New York.

We sat there for a while. When the sun finally began to inch its way through the fog, I said, "What did Ezzie have to say?"

"Nuts to the society babble that Widow Washington is from Boston. That angle's a bust. She grew up in Hong Kong. Family are English and monied." That explained the accent. "Father moonlighted as a diplomat. The real dough comes from his hoity-toity position in a shipping company."

My eyebrows hit my hairline at that.

"Yep. Rang some bells for me, too. Anyway, the word out of Hong Kong is that her family seems on the up and up. They shipped her off to a boarding school in New York to weasel her way into high society and find a rich husband. She's found at least two of them. Washington's number three. When she's not married, she parks herself in an apartment on Fifth Avenue. Both of her marks were out of Boston because she wasn't stupid enough to nail chumps where she lives. Maybe she'd run out of potential husbands on the East Coast and decided to ply her wares on the West Coast."

That explained how she had no problem rubbing elbows with San Francisco's social elite without raising any red flags. She'd had that type of upbringing.

CHAPTER SIXTEEN

"What if she knew about Harold Washington because both families are in shipping? Word in New York was that Harold's wife has T.B., prognosis grim, and Helen moves to San Francisco to scoop him up before someone else does."

He nodded. "Good guess."

"Are her parents still in Hong Kong?"

"Father's dead, mother went back to the family manse in England."

"Siblings?"

"She's got an older brother. Half-brother. Illegitimate. To give the father his due, he brought up the children together and treated the brother like he was his own son, paid for his education, the whole ball of wax. He was sent off to a boarding school in England when she was shipped off to New York."

"A brother? Dickie's columns didn't mention her brother. Is he still in England?"

"No idea. Ezzie hasn't found hide or hair of him in New York. He's put out some feelers in London. Give him a few days."

"Rats. There's no real dirt on her other than two of her previous husbands bought the farm before the wedding cake went stale."

"Still smells a little fishy, but not super lousy," Stein pointed out. "Both husbands were a lot older than her, had bad tickers before she married them, and both died of heart attacks. She'd been married to one guy for a year, the second guy for two years."

"What if she played the loving wife until it got to be old hat, bumped off the hubbies, scooped up the money—you can bet she'd carved out a sizable bequest before the 'I do's' were uttered—and lived high on the hog until the bank accounts got low? Then she'd look around for another mark. Based on her history, I'd say Washington's number was nearly up. What if she deliberately chose wealthy men who had dickie hearts and then poisoned them so they'd pop off? That's what I'd do. Feed them digitalis with their mashed potatoes. With a bad heart, it wouldn't take much."

He gave me a look. "Maggie!"

"With her looks and a fondness for lots of money? Sure. Easy."

He laughed. "You're too much."

When he laughed, his forehead smoothed out, and the brackets around his mouth disappeared. He was younger than I thought. Twenty-five rather than thirty.

"I haven't heard any dope about Washington's health," I told him. "But he was probably in his mid-sixties, so his profile fits. I'll try to shake down the daughter again. Philip Washington won't give me the time of day anytime soon. They might all be in some con together, but I don't think the venom with which Catherine spoke of her stepmother was acting."

"How did you get into the house? I staked out their house for hours. Aside from a bunch of vans delivering flowers, no one was admitted."

"Surprised me, too. Something is going on for sure. I don't know if it has anything to do with Washington's death, but something's not right. First, Catherine Washington claimed to be *incommunicado* with both father and brother for years. Yet, she was at the club the other night and didn't pay a single smack for her drinks or ours."

"Brother must have known she was there."

"You got it in one. Anyone entering that nightclub is screened by that kid at the door and then by the bruiser in the basement, who looks like he could snap your neck using only his pinkie. Washington asked me how I liked the floor show. He knew Al and I were there. How did you get in? Pretty pricey joint."

"Dickie Vance vouched for me. Both of us work for *The Examiner*. What if the stepmother was afraid that the brother and sister were cutting her out of some deal the three of them had cooked up? She hires Nick, or you, as it turned out. Your interviewing the sister was part of the stepmother's plan. She never wanted you to find him. She wanted to warn them that they'd better not pull any funny stuff. Where'd you get the info on the speak?"

"Dickie, of course. I told Catherine Washington that I'd had lunch with him, so I guess she knew that I'd hit the speak at some point. What if she went down there that night to warn her brother that someone was on his tail? When Al and I show up, it only confirms that the stepmom had upped the ante. I doubt either of them expected their father to walk into a bunch of bullets, but Philip Washington couldn't even be bothered to shed a crocodile

CHAPTER SIXTEEN

tear or two."

"But why let you into the house?"

"Because they're all terrified that they're double and triple crossing each other. I'm sure that's why Washington tried to grill me about why Al and I were at the club and what, if anything, Catherine had said about him. It took forever for the manservant to answer the door. I think they were debating whether to let me in or not. If they think that Catherine is double-crossing them, then it makes sense that Washington would try to squeeze out of me whatever information he could. At some point, stepmother and stepson must have mended their fences. That might mean they're muscling out the sister."

"Think she's in on it?"

I shook my head. "I don't know. Oh, by the way, Washington stomped into his attorney's office the morning he was killed, screaming that he wanted to divorce his wife like yesterday. He called her 'that hussy.' A direct quote, by the way. In front of the typing pool, no less."

His whistle was long and not particularly low.

"How you'd get that info?"

"Girl talk. I went to Washington's attorney's office and asked for a job, hoping to get a foot in the door. No such luck. The head secretary threw me out on my ear, but one of the girls from the typing pool followed me into the ladies' room to help me dry my tears. She spilled that Washington was furious over something his wife had done and wanted out. The receipt I wrote to her for our services was found in his pocket after he was shot. What if something happened that made him question her devotion?" I said this with a large helping of snide. "He goes rifling through her purse and finds the receipt. Confronts her. She probably lies, he challenges her, and eventually, she spills about trying to find Junior, only confirming his suspicions that those two were having an affair—"

"Seriously? Come on," he scoffed.

"She's easy on the eyes, right? Junior doesn't strike me as the type to be too choosy. He might have made the first move. I could see him sticking a metaphorical shiv in his father's back, given they were constantly on the outs," I noted.

"Yep. If she's bumping off husbands left and right, an affair with her stepson would seem like small potatoes. Tsk, tsk, tsk. Seems like things are heating up. But the stepmother, the son, and the daughter all have excellent alibis. Who plugged him and why? Are you going to drop this now that Mrs. Widow has given you the heave-ho?"

"Like hell I am! I don't like being played, Charlie Stein, and that woman played me like a violin. Something is going on in that family, and whether she used me to shake down her stepdaughter or her stepson, it doesn't matter. She paid me for a job. and I'm going to find out what it is."

"There's my girl," he said with a smile and punched me on my shoulder.

I stood up. "I'm not your girl. Let's talk to Dickie about getting Nick some help before he kills himself."

Chapter Seventeen

Even before I talked to Ma about my plan, I needed to talk to Dickie. Besides, Ma would say yes because she's got a soft spot for Nick. Dickie said he'd help, but I didn't know how far I could push him. I'd pushed it pretty far already.

"Drive down Geary until you hit Mason, and then make a right," I ordered.

"Feel like cutting me in on the action?" groused Charlie.

"Oh, sorry. I plan to have Nick stay at my house with my mother. She used to help my dad out in his office, so she's got some nursing chops. I'm betting Dickie knows a doc that can help out. Al will be there. Nick can stay in my bedroom. I'll bunk at his apartment downtown. It's much closer to the office, and it will make hunting down whatever dope I can find on the Washingtons much easier if I don't have to factor in taking cabs or streetcars to my house out in the Aves."

What I didn't mention was that I needed to wrap this thing up with the Washingtons and fast. What with the cab fares, back rent, and back salary, the Washington moolah was nearly gone, and there weren't any new jobs pounding on our door. I bet O'Malley was squawking about Nick's current love affair with Jim Beam to anyone who'd give half an ear, discouraging any future clients. I needed to get Nick sober and fast. He'd always pounded them back more than he should have, but you could say the same thing about lots of people in this town. To my knowledge, he'd never gone on a bender like this before. But then, he'd never met a woman like Eileen Taylor before.

"I know nothing about getting someone sober, do you?"

Charlie's mouth thinned to a grim line, and he didn't say anything for a few blocks.

"Yeah," he said in a bitter tone that didn't invite more questions.

We drove another few blocks before Charlie said, "My old man dried out. Again and again and again. Sometimes it takes. A lot of the time, it doesn't. It never did with him. If they're lucky, the docs shoot them full of dope, so they don't go into the DTs."

Nick needed to sober up for a lot of reasons. First, I liked my job and wanted to keep it. Second, with Nick's various underworld connections, he might have information on Philip Washington that I'd never have access to, information not even Dickie Vance was privy to. But the most important reason was that I absolutely couldn't bear to see him slowly kill himself with hooch over a woman who'd killed at least two men, and those were only the ones we knew about. There was no doubt in my mind that Eileen Taylor's past was littered with suckers willing to take the fall and a bunch of bullets for the lingering kisses and false promises in those blue eyes. Based on the hatred I saw in her eyes before the rope snapped her neck, she would have plugged Nick, too, without a backward glance if given half a chance. Nick had a reputation for being fast and loose with the rules, but even in his rough-and-tumble world, you don't turn a blind eye to cold-blooded murder.

"I don't think he'll go into the DTs. I mean, gosh, I hope not."

"You know, he might get violent. Why don't you ship him off to some clinic to dry him out?"

That idea was all wet. It would ruin Nick's reputation in this town, and it'd taken enough hits as it was.

"Nick spars a lot with City Hall and usually wins. If he gets a reputation as a rummy, City Hall will walk all over him. This is a hard-drinking town, and no one is going to blink at someone tying one on now and then. But this is different, and people know it's different. No dice to shipping him out to some clinic. My brother looks like a drink of water, but he's fast with the fists."

Charlie rolled his eyes.

"He's won the amateur boxing title in San Francisco three years in a row.

CHAPTER SEVENTEEN

Have a little faith, Mr. Stein."

There was that whistle again.

"You Laurents are something."

"You better believe it. Turn left on O'Farrell. The restaurant is on the right. Dickie has said in the past he'd help Nick. I need some scratch to pay the doctor, and we don't have it."

I might need to hire an additional someone to help Al out if Nick went off the track. The cabbie Herman came to mind. He might like the extra jack.

We pulled up to the front of John's Grill and parked. Dickie would be plowing through his first dessert. I always timed my visits so he'd be smoking his post-lunch cigar, but today, there was nothing for it. Charlie opened the door of the restaurant for me. Nice. I like a man with manners. The waiter I'd seen a couple of days earlier was back manning the podium, just as old, his shoes just as polished, and his apron just as long and white. Lunch was still in full swing, chatter filling the room. Against the dark wood paneling of the room, the cloth napkins, perched like little tents at each seat, made the tablecloths seem even whiter. I'd never pushed Dickie for anything more than the occasional pot of tea and had never eaten here. The prices were out of my league.

"I shall tell Mr. Vance you're here, Miss Laurent. Please wait here."

Charlie said in a low voice, "Jeez, you rate mighty high with Dickie. How do you know him?"

"He and Nick go way back. I think they met in the army. Dickie's grandfather on his mother's side was a general or something like that. Big military hoo-hah. Think he's related to Robert E. Lee. Anyway, Dickie did his four years, met Nick along the way, demobilized here, and became the West Coast version of Walter Winchell."

Charlie scratched the back of his neck. "Hard to see Dickie in a uniform. Last time I looked, bright blue socks weren't standard issue."

I stifled a giggle as the waiter returned and, with a stately "Mademoiselle," bade us follow him. Dickie stood up when he saw us and leaned toward me. Today, his shirt was a headache-inducing lime green, and his bow tie shocking pink. Should Dickie ever try to disappear into a crowd, he was doomed to failure. I've only seen that color combination on hummingbirds, which works in nature, but not so much on a man over six feet tall and roughly three feet wide.

We air-kissed. Either he'd finished his dessert, or the waiter had removed his plate so as not to be rude.

"Charles, my good man." He shook Charlie's hand. "And with the delightful Margaret Laurent. To what do I owe this surprise?" In an undertone to the waiter hovering near the table, he said, "A glass of my specially blended lemonade for the gentleman and a black tea for the lady." Then, without preamble, he sat down, tilted his head like a bird, and asked, "Do you have dirt on the Washingtons I can use?"

I wondered how much to tell him. If he spilled all my info, it might hamper me from getting the scoop on what was going on with that family.

"When Harold Washington was getting plugged on Nob Hill, Helen Washington was having dinner with the Langdons. Like I told you yesterday, Catherine Washington was holding down a table at her brother's speakeasy, and her brother walked in with his gorgeous side piece just as his father's face was hitting the steering wheel. All have airtight alibis. Whoever plugged Washington, it wasn't those four. Or me for that matter."

Our drinks arrived: my tea, steeped very dark the way I liked it. The lemonade in Charlie's mug looked and smelled like Champagne.

"And you, Charles? How are you involved in all this?" Dickie's voice wasn't exactly stern but didn't contain his usual lilting bonhomie. As he spoke, he pointed at Charlie with a menacing finger.

"Saw her at the speak with her brother. They were warming the chairs with the Washington dame. I quizzed the bouncer, and he told me that they'd gotten in on Moore's hook."

"That tells me how, but not why."

"Need a scoop," he replied and grinned. "I'm betting that if I follow her around, I'll get to announce to the world who killed Washington."

"Take care, Charles," he warned. "If anything happens to Margaret, I shall hold you responsible."

Charlie's grin fell, and he ducked his head to swallow a large mouthful of

CHAPTER SEVENTEEN

Champagne.

Dickie sighed. "I'm very disappointed. I've been waiting for the news that Philip Washington had been arrested for his father's murder. I was so sure he'd done it that I'd already written a column on how young Washington was an example of greed triumphing over familial affection. Of course, I'd have gladly shot my father, but I was never given the chance."

"Dickie!" I chastised.

"Well, maybe not actually kill him, but I certainly thought about it. Horrid man. I don't know what Mother was thinking in marrying that cad. But I can't complain now, can I? Anyway, I'm still not sure young Philip isn't guilty. He might not have pulled the trigger, but given the company he keeps, he could snap his fingers, and ten people would do his bidding." Then he said sotto voce to Charlie, "A most deplorable young man. Watch yourself around him." In a more normal tone, he railed, "Curses and blast! Now I'll have to write another column for tomorrow, and I was planning to catch a picture show this afternoon. Thank you for that little tidbit, my dear. My date with the Marx Brothers will have to wait, but that's not your fault. I haven't exonerated young Washington, because, really, that young man is capable of murdering ten fathers, but there is another suspect to consider. Have you contacted Dillard Reade?"

Charlie and I looked at each other. We both shook our heads.

"Brother to the late and very-much-lamented Aurora Reade. Before he died, Reade Senior bypassed his son, Dillard, and handed over the reins of the bank to Washington, effectively demoting Dillard to a jumped-up file clerk."

Dickie pronounced clerk as "clark." You can take the boy out of the East Coast aristocracy but not the East Coast aristocracy out of the boy.

"Is he local?" I asked.

"Oh, yes. He's at that table over there. His sister's death destroyed him. His brother-in-law's mismanagement of the bank has enraged him. Hence, his sad addiction to, shall we say, lemonade."

Dickie gestured with his eyebrows toward a guy at a window table with only a lone coffee cup in front of him. His hand was shaking so badly that the "lemonade" slopped over the side as he brought the cup to his mouth.

The ghost of a good-looking man gone to complete seed, Reade had the physical characteristics of hard-core alkies who drink their meals: thin arms and legs, a bloated belly that hung over the table edge, and those deep red cheeks pocked with spider webs of veins. The elbows of his suit were shiny with wear, and his despair hung around him like faded perfume.

Charlie snorted. "That guy couldn't hold a gun steady for more than half a second."

"True," Dickie agreed. "But he has enough of a trust fund to hire a gunsel. Now, what may I do for you?"

"I need the services of a doctor."

Dickie brought a napkin up to his mouth and gave his lips a dab before speaking: "One who is versed in, say, the vicissitudes of excessive alcohol consumption?"

Nothing got past Dickie.

"Yes. I'm going to take Nick to my house and have Ma watch over him until he dries out. I want a doctor there… You know, just in case."

What neither of us was saying was that this doc might have to pump Nick full of dope to keep him from getting violent or going into the DTs.

"Sounds like a very good plan. I know just the fellow: Dr. Simon Chase. His middle name is discretion. I shall give him a ring and ask him to pay your lovely mother a visit at, say, four p.m.? You will have Nicholas there by that time?"

"Yes, I will," I said with confidence. Hell or high water, I was going to get Nick out of that horrible apartment that reeked of despair, booze, and sweat, even if I had to clonk him on the head to do it. "Can you add the doctor's services to my account?"

"The account that will forever have a zero balance? I shall."

"Thank you, Dickie. You're an angel. I… I…was thinking of hiring Herman for a few days. Just to make sure that Al has some backup at night."

"Excellent idea. Mr. Peters will be thrilled. I shall call him."

I wondered how much work Herman did for Dickie. As in, Herman relaying back to Dickie, who took cabs to those houses they shouldn't be taking cabs to. In the dead of night.

"And you will keep me abreast of events regarding the Washingtons?" he said in a low voice in case the remaining diners were within earshot.

"I'll do my best. I promise." And if I crossed my fingers while saying it, he didn't have to know. He'd get it all in the end, but how much I'd tell him along the way, I wasn't sure.

"That's a good girl." He turned toward Charlie. "I charge you, sir, to keep an eye on this treasure of a woman. I'd marry her tomorrow if I were the marrying kind."

"Not if I get there first," said Charlie and wriggled his eyebrows.

"Stop it, both of you," I said as a blush hit my hairline. Dickie was laying it on thick today, but reading between the lines; he was serious about Charlie protecting me from harm. Or warning him that he shouldn't try any funny stuff. Probably both.

I stood up, "Charlie, we need to move a leg if we're going to get Nick to my house by four. Thanks a million, Dickie."

"You're very welcome, my dear." But this wasn't said in his usual effusive air. He was looking at Charlie and not with affection.

Chapter Eighteen

We drove to the office first to pick up the spare key to Nick's apartment. Next, I called Ma, told her my plan, and got Al on board. As we drove to Nick's place, Charlie asked me what I'd have done if my mother or brother had said no dice.

"They wouldn't."

"But what if they did?" he insisted.

"Were you raised by wolves? This is what people do for each other. Nick's a great guy with a tremendous amount of integrity in a town where most everything's for sale. He isn't, and he took the hit for it. If my family can help him weather that hit, we're going to help him."

Once we turned onto Post, I pointed to a green-painted apartment building.

"That's it."

We parked on the street in front of Nick's place. Herman was waiting for us on the stoop, his cab parked a few car lengths away.

"Mr. Vance sent me, Miss Laurent." He doffed his hat.

Dickie, my guardian angel.

"Charlie Stein, this is Herman Peters." I thought for a second, debating on how to describe exactly what Herman did for Dickie. "Herman helps Mr. Vance now and then." That seemed good enough, as he collected dirt for Dickie's column now and then. "Mr. Stein works for the same newspaper as Mr. Vance."

"You work with Mr. Vance? You're jake with me," said Herman.

They shook hands and did that weird sizing-up thing that men do to each

CHAPTER EIGHTEEN

other. I suppose they both passed muster because by the time their hands were back at their sides, they were trading grins back and forth.

"So's Mr. Vance said you might need some help with Mr. Moore."

"That's right, Herman. Mr. Moore is taking a little vacation at my house. We live out on Ninth Avenue."

"Mr. Vance filled me in," he said in a confident voice. I got the impression that not much rattled Herman Peters.

"Let's go," I said with a lot of bravado, wishing I had half Herman's confidence.

I had the slimmest of hopes that we'd knock on Nick's front door and he'd answer it, freshly shaved and in his best suit. No such luck. After pounding on his door for a good three minutes, I turned the key in the lock.

The apartment smelled of vomit, bourbon, and sweat. Nick wasn't even in bed. He'd passed out in the bathroom, his body curled around the toilet bowl. Fortunately, he was dressed, sort of, in a stained T-shirt and his shorts. Charlie and I shared a glance, but it was Herman who voiced what we were both thinking.

"Someone worked him over real good. Is he alive, Miss Laurent?"

I swallowed my tears and knelt to feel for his pulse. It wasn't the strongest pulse I'd ever felt, but he had one. He stank. Like he hadn't bathed in a bunch of weeks. I brushed back the hair from his forehead, careful not to touch his face. His face was one big bruise, courtesy of O'Malley's fists, and rough with stubble. Seeing him with that scruff on his face? Oh, Nick. I'd never seen him without the closest of shaves. He even had a sink installed in the office so he could spiff up in the afternoon.

I had another one of those swallowing-down-tears moments.

"Nick, it's Mags."

I counted to ten, waiting for a response. Silence.

"Nick, it's Maggie," I said in a louder voice. "I'm taking you to Ma's. Okay?"

No response.

"He needs a bath," said Charlie.

Even as I covered my mouth to escape from the smell of Nick, the bathroom, and the room behind me, I bit back a snide, "Oh, my, your reporter skills sure are something."

Instead, I said, "Not now. It's for the best that he's out like a light because he'd probably fight me if he were conscious." His bathrobe was hanging up on the back of the bathroom door. "Once we get him into his robe, we can haul him down the stairs and into Herman's cab. Charlie, I hate to ask, but will you ride with him in case he comes to and panics? I'll follow you in your car."

As we began to maneuver Nick's arms into the robe, Charlie asked, "Can you drive?"

"Of course I can drive," I said. It was proving a lot harder to get a robe on a passed-out person than I'd ever imagined.

"Of course you can," he mused.

"Okay, that's that. If you two can help to stand him upright, I'll tie the belt."

The fog hadn't come in yet, so it wouldn't be too cold out, but Nick wouldn't want his neighbors to know the color of his shorts. With a snug pull on the belt, he was as decent as we could make him.

"If the two of you—"

"Never you mind, Miss Laurent. I can handle him." Herman promptly hoisted Nick over his shoulder and began to make his way out of the bathroom, as if Nick weighed no more than a kitten.

"Is he a piano mover or something?" asked Charlie in a low voice.

"Boxer." I added, "Al has KO'd him three times. Will you help Herman with the front door while I grab Nick some clean clothes?"

I rifled through Nick's drawers, grabbing underwear, socks, a pair of shoes, two pairs of trousers, two shirts, a pullover sweater I'd never seen him wear, a tie, and his best hat. I plonked the hat on my head and rolled the rest of it up in a towel. I reached Herman's cab just as Charlie was settling himself in the back seat, with Nick slouched against the opposite door, still unconscious.

"Herman, I live at—"

"I knows where you live, Miss."

Dickie comes through again.

"Thank you, Herman. My mother is expecting you. Charlie?" I held out

CHAPTER EIGHTEEN

my hand, palm turned up, and he dropped his car key into my palm.

"You look cute in Nick's hat."

I rolled my eyes. "I'll try not to dent your fender, but I can't guarantee it."

If Herman and I broke a few thousand traffic laws that afternoon, I'm not telling. Once we arrived at my house, Herman hauled Nick out of the back seat and, like before, threw Nick over his shoulder and headed up the steps. My mother had opened the front door just as Herman had pulled into the driveway. She stepped back when Herman passed over the threshold and said, "Mr. Peters, I presume. Please take him down the hall and place him on the bed in the bedroom at the end and to the right."

She didn't beef or grumble about me dumping Nick on her. Her first words to me were: "What happened to his face?"

I didn't mince words. "O'Malley claims he resisted arrest, and Murph sort of backs him up. When this is over, I plan to file a formal complaint."

"That might make things difficult for Bree. Is he conscious?"

I shook my head.

"Good. I can give him a sponge bath and maybe a shave. Those bruises. My goodness, Maggie, he stinks!"

"You should smell his apartment. Ma, you've met Herman. This is Charlie Stein. He's helping me out with the Washington case. He's a reporter for *The Examiner*."

"Nice to meet you, Charlie. Keep an eye on this one." She pointed to me. "A bit of a pistol."

He gave me a glance that he probably thought was mischievous. "Not telling me anything I don't know, Mrs. Laurent."

"Excuse me!" I glared at my mother first and then Charlie. "I'm standing right here."

Fortunately for both of them, the doctor arrived. He was a slim older man, with a fussy pince-nez perched on his nose, and even though he was wearing a hat, it didn't hide that he was bald as a bowling ball. Ma stepped forward and held out her hand. "You must be Dr. Chase. I'm Katherine Laurent."

Funny, I never thought of her as a "Katherine." She's always been Kitty to our family.

His expression changed from what looked like a perpetual half-frown into a smile.

"How nice to meet you. I'm Dr. Chase. Mr. Vance gave me a rough idea of what's going on. Would you care to fill me in?"

Over the last few weeks, I'd kept Ma briefed on Nick's rounds with the hooch. While she updated the doc on Nick's current condition, Charlie and I went into the house and down the hallway to my bedroom. Al and Herman were getting Nick settled in my bed.

"You're a brick, Al. Thanks. Albert Laurent, meet Charlie Stein. He's a reporter for *The Examiner*. He's helping with the Washington case. He was at the speak the other night. Saw us with the sister."

Charlie stuck his hand out, and they shook. But I noticed there wasn't that immediate ease between them that had characterized Charlie's interactions with Herman.

I placed Nick's hat on my dresser and the rolled-up towel containing his clothes on the floor. I grabbed my suitcase and threw in a dress, my best suit, several pairs of shoes, stockings, and gloves. I pushed the rest of my clothes to the side of the closet, unrolled the towel containing Nick's things, and hung up what I could. I piled his underwear and socks where my suitcase had rested on the top shelf of my closet.

I said to Herman over my shoulder, "Herman, I don't—"

He interrupted me. "I'm thinking I'll stay about five days if that's okay with your ma," said Herman. "Mr. Moore should be out of the worst of it by then. All he'll need after that is about six squares a day."

I turned around. "Herman, you don't have to—"

He held up a hand. "Mr. Vance says to take care of Mr. Moore, and that's what I'm going to do, Miss. Plus, Al's gonna teach me some of his boxing moves. Maybe I K.O. him next time."

"In your dreams, pal," said Al in some good-natured ribbing. "Herman and I are going to take it in six-hour shifts and hot-sheet it. We'll clear it with the doctor, but with Ma's help, I think that will cover all the bases."

Herman feinted a one-two punch. "Big talk, tall guy."

While those two continued to verbally spar with one another, I angled my

CHAPTER EIGHTEEN

back so Charlie couldn't see me scooping up some underwear. I added two pairs of dungarees, a heavy sweater, and a couple of everyday blouses. I laid my best hat on top. Washington's funeral was tomorrow, and I had every intention of attending.

Once I'd snapped the locks of my suitcase shut, I turned to Al. "We should probably wipe him down before the doc examines him."

Al nodded and left the room in search of a basin of soapy water and a washcloth.

"Herman, I'm going to be bunking in Mr. Moore's apartment for now. If you need anything, call me. He's got a phone. I'll write his number—"

"No need, Miss. I got it up here." He knocked three times on his forehead with his knuckles.

Never cross Dickie, I said to myself.

"Charlie, let's—"

"Miss, Mr. Moore is trying to say something. Sounds like your name."

I leaned over Nick, holding my nose as he tried to speak. His breath was rank enough to blast off my eyebrows. "Nick?"

"M. M. D. Doc. A B. Ssss. Sh. Sh," he managed to mumble before he passed out again.

I gave him a weak shake of his shoulder. Waited. Nothing.

I stood up to face Charlie. "Did you hear him?"

"Sounded like gibberish to me."

"No, he was trying to tell me something."

At that point, the doctor came into my room, followed by Al with a washbasin and my mother with a towel.

"Charlie, let me grab a bottle of bleach. Can you give me a lift to Nick's place? I'll only be in the way here."

"Sure thing."

I kissed Al and Ma goodbye, thanked Herman again, and shook hands with the doc before we headed off, with the bottle of bleach and a sponge in my lap.

I didn't realize that Charlie intended to help me clean Nick's place, but he took off his tie and rolled up his sleeves. I washed all of Nick's bedding in the bathtub, even the blankets, and hung it all out on the line at the back of the apartment building. It was doubtful they'd be dry by nighttime. The fog was hanging off the mouth of the Bay, threatening to roll in any second. I'd sleep on the mattress in my coat.

After a couple of hours, we were done. All traces of alcoholic bender had been scrubbed away.

"Hungry?" he asked.

"Always," I admitted.

"Let's get a bite to eat. Recommendations?"

"The Pig 'n Whistle is my favorite. Their chicken pot pie is to die for. Let's walk. It's close. I need some fresh air."

Once we were seated and had ordered, Charlie asked, "Any clue on what he was trying to say?"

"The 'm' was clearly my name. Then I heard a mushy 'dee' and maybe an 'oh.' The 'a' was clear, as was the 'b,' but then it was nothing but a bunch of esses."

Charlie lit up another cigarette, his face slack with thought, while I sat there twiddling my fork through my fingers, trying to piece it together. Nick's voice had a strange East Coast curve to it. He grew up in Philadelphia and Baltimore, one city being resolutely Northern Protestant and the other being Southern Baptist. He told me his brain had given up on reconciling the two.

I let the fork fall to the counter and snapped my fingers. Twice. "ABC Shipping. Bet the 'd' was for 'dock.' We got hung up on all those esses. The first one was a cee, not the first ess."

"That's it. How come you're so smart?" he cooed and stubbed out his cigarette as the waitress plunked our plates in front of us.

He must really want that scoop. I gave him a stern look.

"I eat my vegetables. Are you going to the funeral?"

"Wouldn't miss it for the world. Want a lift?"

I nodded as my mouth was wrapped around a hunk of pastry.

"Funeral's at ten. I'll pick you up at nine. The crypt will be packed."

Chapter Nineteen

The swankiest of the swank live on Nob Hill, but their social standing didn't matter one jot in 1906. Whatever the earthquake didn't destroy, the subsequent fire finished the job but good. Twenty-four hours after the earthquake, the fires finally reached the top of Nob Hill. The mansions of the Big Four—Hopkins, Stanford, Huntington, and Crocker—were reduced to ash. Although the Fairmont Hotel survived the fire, her windows cracked from the heat. The hotel was one of the few buildings left standing. The rich rebuilt, but they are still subjected to the ringing bells and clanging of the cable cars as they pull their way up Powell Street *en route* to Taylor or Hyde Streets. And if the operators ring their bells with extra vigor while operating through Nob Hill, well, what of it?

It had taken over twenty years to drum up enough dough to start rebuilding Grace Cathedral, and they were still only halfway through construction. Services were being held in the Founders' Crypt where they'd set up an altar and pews. Gigantic candles had been lit to hide the absence of windows. It hadn't worked. The space remained gloomy and dark. All the candles did was provide enough light so that we didn't trip over the legs of the pews. The word "crypt" made me think of rows of sepulchers, and Founders' Crypt suggested that this was where the big donors had been interred. I guess they moved the bodies out and the pews in. Even though Charlie and I arrived nearly an hour before the service began, we had to stand along the wall. There wasn't a seat left.

I tapped Charlie's shoulder and then pointed to an empty spot along the wall near the top of the nave. I wanted a better look at the front rows where the family was seated and an even better view of the rest of the attendees.

At the bench closest to me sat Catherine Washington, her face nearly eclipsed by a pair of large black sunglasses. She sat alone at the last space at the far end of the bench near the wall. The entire bench was empty except for her. Across the aisle sat Philip Washington on the edge of the bench closest to the center aisle. Next to him sat Helen Washington, sporting a veil so thick it was impossible to see her face. Surprisingly, Mrs. Washington's manservant sat next to her, with various family members filling the rows behind them. The rest of the congregation had been crammed into the pews according to their social status in the hierarchy of San Francisco's elite. Dickie would be having a field day cataloging all the attendees. There would be several photographers waiting at the exit, catching the somber faces as fast as they could click their shutters. This funeral would be the social event of the season.

Not surprisingly, Dickie and his mother sat two rows behind Catherine Washington. He'd eschewed his usual garish attire for a white shirt and a deep gray tie that matched his suit. We made eye contact. He didn't smile, but there was a glint of both amusement and approval in his gaze. I recognized various society types seated next to him, their real selves looking much smaller than in their photographs in the newspaper. Also much older.

On the opposite side of the aisle, two rows behind the son and the widow, sat the top brass of San Francisco's government: the mayor, police chief, and D.A., accompanied by their wives wearing their best hats. Judges, lawyers, and bankers filled in the rest of the audience. I scanned the crowd. No Dillard Reade. Odd. I kept my eyes on the entrance, waiting for Dillard to appear. I wasn't the only one. Catherine Washington kept looking over her shoulder, obviously searching for someone. Based on my knowledge of her family, I assumed she was waiting for her uncle.

Dillard Reade still hadn't shown up by the time the service began. The High Episcopalian isn't that much different from the Catholic service, except it's in English as opposed to Latin. I knew most of the religious cues and noticed that Charlie watched me closely to mimic my responses. I'd have to confess that I attended a non-Catholic service, even for a funeral liturgy.

CHAPTER NINETEEN

Willfully breaking this rule was worth a few rosaries. I needed to see the players in action. Plus, I thought this rule was stupid.

At the final "amen," I saw Catherine nip out a side door in a near run.

I murmured to Charlie, "Stay here. Watch the Washingtons."

I followed Catherine out the door. The fast click of her heels on the stone steps told me that, having done her familial duty, she was desperate to flee the nave. I caught up with her just as she was exiting onto the lawn surrounding the construction site. She stumbled, and I caught her arm before she went down.

"Are you okay?" I asked.

She looked up in confusion, shaking her head like she didn't know who I was and why I was following her. Then she knew me.

"Miss Laurent?"

"Today and every day. And it's Maggie. Are you okay?" I repeated, taking her by the elbow and leading her over to a bench so we could sit down.

She didn't respond but reached into her purse to pull out a package of cigarettes. Her hands were shaking so badly that she had trouble getting the lighter to work.

"Here. Let me," I said and took the lighter from her hand.

Using my body as a shield from the wind, I flicked it once. The flame caught. I lit her cigarette and then handed back her lighter. Made of solid silver with her initials etched on its flat side, it was surprisingly heavy. If I threw it at someone's head, it'd give me enough time to run away. I should pretend to smoke to justify having a lighter like that in case I needed to brain someone.

"For someone who doesn't smoke, you're pretty handy with a lighter."

"I used to light my dad's pipe for him," I said.

We sat there for a couple of minutes in silence, her smoking, me thinking about my next move.

"It's so silly," she said.

I turned towards her. Her tears, heretofore hidden by the sunglasses, had now made their way down to her chin. The pallor of her cheeks, her black suit, and the deep red of her lips made her look a little unearthly, like a benign vampire.

"He was about as good a father as he was a husband, but still…" Her voice trailed off.

"He was your father."

She nodded, and the hand started to shake again as she brought the cigarette up to her lips.

"I saw your uncle at John's Grill yesterday. I gather he wasn't on good terms with your father."

She rolled her eyes and took a drag of her cigarette before saying, "That's one way of putting it. He was supposed to be here. We'd made plans to meet, but he hasn't shown." She paused. "I'm worried about him. He took my mother's death so hard. He'd always been a hard drinker, but my mother kept him from tipping over into being a drunk. When she died…well." There was another pause. "How'd he look?"

"Not so good," I admitted. "Where does he live? Shall we ask the police to check on him?"

"I'm going to his place right now and see if he's all right. There's supposed to be a cocktail party at the house afterward. I don't plan on attending. Helen's calling it a reception, but it's just an excuse to break out the booze and hobnob with her society friends."

"Do you want some company? What if I drove?" I put this out there, not expecting her to agree to either suggestion.

Her shoulders slumped. Although she didn't make a sound, the tears began to flow again. "Would you mind? I'm so… I don't know what I am, but I probably shouldn't drive."

"I don't mind at all. Let's go. Where are you parked?"

As long as a city block, her car, a late-model canary-yellow convertible that purred along California Street so easily, it felt like the car was driving itself. With the merest flick of my hand on the steering wheel, the car would hug the corner with a wee ho-hum. I'd never driven a car like this. I sensed the impatience of the engine, begging for long stretches of California coastline with the top down, the driver oblivious to everything but the thrill of the wheel in her hands, the rush of wind past her face, and the briny scent of the

CHAPTER NINETEEN

ocean as the breakers hit the shore. Al would have crawled to Los Angeles and back on his knees to drive this baby for only five minutes. We didn't talk except for Catherine's brief instructions to turn right or left. By the time we arrived, she'd pulled herself together. She'd reapplied her lipstick and re-anchored her hat against the wind.

Dillard Reade lived in a fake Tudor-esque mansion out in Pacific Heights on the hilly end of Vallejo Street with a panoramic view of the Bay. All the half-timbers, bricks, and mullioned windows looked out of place in a sea of large Victorians and ornate Italianate mansions. Given that the 1906 earthquake was a mere twenty-something years ago, it took some nerve to build a brick house. But then brick doesn't burn as readily as wood. Choose your poison.

During the summer, the water usually has a gray cast to it, reflecting the dull, overcast sky. Today, the water was cut with whitecaps, and I could just see the far end of Alcatraz, the military prison, squatting right in the middle of the shipping lane. The leaves of the trees shimmied in response to the wind roaring up the hill. I shoved my hatpin further into my hair to make sure my hat stayed put. It was my best one, and I had no intention of losing it to one of San Francisco's errant gusts of wind.

"Pull into the driveway. There's Uncle Dill's car, so he must be home. He wanted to go to the graveside. Dad's being buried at the cemetery on Laurel Hill. We can give him a ride. No sense in taking two cars."

"Some house," I said.

"I grew up here. Before the earthquake, we lived in a Victorian monstrosity with about forty turrets. When they rebuilt, my mother insisted on going full Tudor. She was an unrepentant Anglophile. Once my grandfather ceded the bank to him, my father insisted we move to Sea Cliff. 'To be with our kind,' he liked to say. Broke my mother's heart. One of my father's many sins. My uncle bought it from him in a stock swap deal. Real estate will always bounce back. It's less certain that the bank will survive. Let's go."

We got out of the car, our hands on our hats. We stopped short at the same time. The front door was swinging on its hinges.

"Miss Washington, we should—"

I couldn't even finish saying, "Call the police," when she strode ahead and began shouting for her uncle.

"Uncle Dill, where are you? Uncle Dill! Uncle Dill!"

With every footfall, her voice became increasingly frantic.

We found him in the library, lying in a pool of blood with a bullet wound in his head. A gun lay next to his right hand. He was very dead.

Chapter Twenty

The moment we saw the body, I dragged Catherine out of the library. She clawed at me for a minute, screaming at me to let her go as she tried to free herself from my grip. It was obvious her uncle was dead, but in her hysteria, she didn't want to believe it. After a few seconds, all the fight left her, and she became limp and docile. I led her into the living room and sat her down on one of the sofas. She curled into one corner and pressed her hands to her face, sobbing with that awful, bone-deep sorrow that never really leaves you. I phoned the police, made sure the front door was still open, and held her while she cried into the fabric of my suit.

All of Reade's faded, wasted beauty had been destroyed by the bullet. I feared it would be the type of image I'd never forget. It was bound to appear in my dreams, like a snapshot. Whoever did this should rot in hell.

When her sobbing had ebbed to the occasional whimper, I said, "We can't do anything for him. He's dead."

I pushed away the image of the remainder of his shattered skull.

After a couple of minutes, she whispered, "He was the only family I had left."

Now was not the time to remind her she still had a brother.

We sat like that, side by side, holding hands and waiting for the police to arrive. I heard the wail of sirens tearing up the hill but didn't move. O'Malley and Murphy walked in, followed by D.A. Doyle. Murph was the only one who made eye contact with me.

"He's—?"

"In the library. Second door on the right."

The others didn't even glance our way as a beat cop led them down the entrance hall to the library. The big grandfather clock in the corner of the room chimed the half-hour before they approached us, still seated in the living room. At the sound of their footsteps, Catherine pressed her face into my shoulder. I tightened an arm around her shoulder.

"It's okay," I whispered. "I'll handle this."

Doyle had the flushed cheeks of someone who'd been drinking, but the demeanor of being able to hold his liquor. The buttons must have dragged him away from the funeral reception. O'Malley and Murphy stood against the wall of the living room, notebook, and pencils in hand.

Initially, Doyle asked Catherine to leave so they could question me alone. And I'd thought the former D.A. was a pretentious bastard. Doyle pulled his "I'm the D.A., cower before me" act. He and Nick will be at loggerheads for sure.

"This is an official investigation," he said in his pompous best and tightened the knot on his tie. "And as D.A. of this county—"

He didn't even get to finish before Catherine wrenched herself away from my shoulder and started screaming at them that this was her house, and if they thought they could order her around like she was some maid, they had another thing coming.

"And I am a Washington, Mr. Doyle. I'm staying right here. I asked Miss Laurent to drive me here. If you don't want me to drag the mayor away from the reception and his fifth highball, then I suggest you shut up." Her voice, as raw as a common fishwife's, so startled Doyle that he immediately assured her that she could stay while they questioned me. She burrowed her face into my shoulder again.

"Maggie, what a pleasure to meet you again." He didn't sound particularly pleased. I ignored O'Malley's snort of derision. Doyle raised an eyebrow at Murph, who then gave O'Malley a little kick on the ankle to remind him to behave. Doyle began again. "Can you please tell me what happened?"

"I attended the service for Mr. Washington. Seating was tight, so I ended up standing along the wall near Miss Washington at the front of the nave. At the end of the service, Miss Washington fled out the side door. I was

CHAPTER TWENTY

worried about her, so I followed her."

"You were worried about her." This was said deadpan, with a generous side-helping of snide, like I was a human rock, totally bereft of empathy.

"Yes. My father died about ten years ago. I knew what she was going through."

He flushed with embarrassment. I went on.

"I followed her out of the crypt, and we sat outside together while she collected herself. Miss Washington expressed her concern because her uncle, Mr. Reade, hadn't shown up at the funeral."

Doyle turned toward Catherine. "Were you expecting him?"

She nodded and sat up straight to answer his question. She didn't let go of my hand though, clutching it so tightly that my hand would be numb for a couple of hours once we left the house.

"I phoned him from the yacht club last night. We'd arranged to meet at eight-thirty a.m. I was to save him a seat if I arrived first and vice versa. Miss Laurent was kind enough to sit with me after the service and drive me here. I was pretty upset. As you can imagine, Mr. Doyle."

No mistaking her contempt for him in that last sentence.

"We arrived," I looked down at my watch, "roughly an hour ago. Miss Washington told me to park in the driveway behind Mr. Reade's car. I did. As we exited the car, we saw that the front door was swinging on its hinges in the wind."

Doyle interrupted. "Is that correct, Miss Washington?"

She nodded.

"Miss Washington ran up the steps ahead of me, calling out her uncle's name. We arrived at the library at the same time and found him." I avoided the words "his body." "It was obvious he was dead, so—"

"How many dead bodies have you seen, Miss Laurent?" O'Malley sneered from behind me.

I turned my head to glare at him and counted to five, trying to tamp down my temper. O'Malley was trying to get my Irish up, and I had no intention of giving him any satisfaction. I wanted to lay him low, but Catherine began to tremble against me, her hand tightening even more.

I turned my attention back to Doyle. "You've seen Mr. Reade." I left it at that. "I brought Miss Washington into the living room, sat her down, and then called the police. Before you ask, we did not touch the body or anything in the library. We left the room the second we saw the body. We sat here in the living room, waiting for the police to arrive. Other than my calling the police, we have not moved from this sofa."

Doyle sat on that for a few seconds.

"Miss Washington," he said in a voice filled with all the respect that had been lacking in his exchange with me. "Would you say your uncle was suicidal?"

She blinked several times as if such a question were absurd.

"No, I wouldn't. He hated my father and had plans to take over the bank before my father ran it into the ground. Uncle Dill wanted to attend my father's funeral to gloat."

"Miss Washington, it's well known that he took your mother's death very hard, and I'm—"

"Mr. Doyle, I'm not sure Mr. Reade committed suicide." I interrupted. Reade, as a suicide, would make his life a lot easier, but I wasn't convinced.

I swear I heard Doyle's teeth grind.

"The gun fell from his hand onto the floor after he shot himself, Maggie. It's as plain as the nose on your face. What other possible scenario is there?"

Behind that manufactured panache was an ambitious man who'd relish squashing little nobodies like me. He was as vicious as O'Malley. He just hid it better with that cocky "prestigious law school" grin.

"Your face, not mine. I had lunch at John's Grill yesterday, Mr. Doyle. I noticed Mr. Reade sitting at a table fairly near me. Have you ever eaten there?"

He rolled his eyes. "Of course I have. I grew up in this town."

I had, too, but besides my meet-ups with Dickie, I had yet to unfurl one of their napkins on my lap.

"Then you know that the dining room is fairly small. There was no mistaking him."

"You know him? Isn't he a little out of your league?"

CHAPTER TWENTY

I'd called it. Vicious.

"No, but Dickie Vance does."

That shook him a little. He blinked a couple of times, and his jaw firmed up. He wasn't going to like what he was going to hear.

"As I sat finishing my tea with Mr. Vance…" I nearly said "we," but I didn't want or particularly need to drag Charlie into this. "…I saw Mr. Reade drinking his 'lemonade.'" I emphasized the word lemonade so that he knew that I knew it was hard-core booze in that coffee cup. "His hand was shaking so badly he could barely lift the cup to his lips."

"So? The man had the reputation of being, well, fond of 'lemonade,'" he snapped. "My apologies, Miss Washington. A lot of people drink 'lemonade,' Maggie. I've been known to have a cup or two myself now and then."

At Doyle's smug smile, complimenting himself on his heavy-handed wit, I waited for him to reach around and pat himself on the back.

"Yes, lots of people do, but I don't. And it's 'Miss Laurent' if you don't mind."

Even if it turned out that Reade had killed himself, I was making Doyle look foolish for jumping to conclusions. Challenging him in front of Murph and O'Malley might not be a wise move, as his response proved.

"You're just a secretary, Miss Laurent. Leave the police work to your betters."

The gloves were off.

"I'll do that, Mr. Doyle. But just for the record, Mr. Reade was left-handed." Murph, O'Malley, and then Doyle's face went blank with surprise. "If I were going to commit suicide, I wouldn't do it with my weakest hand. But then I'm just a secretary."

At that point, Catherine held up her left hand. "Everyone in the family is left-handed. Maggie's right."

"The person who shot him didn't know that." I turned to Catherine. "I'm sorry."

After a few seconds of silence, she shoved her sunglasses into her hair and lay back against the back of the sofa with her eyes closed. "It's all right."

At this point, Murph peeled himself off the wall to cross the room. He whispered something in Doyle's ear.

"Does your uncle own a gun?"

She sat up straight and opened her eyes, which were dark and mean.

"Yes. It's usually kept in the safe."

"Could you identify it?"

She began shaking again.

"I'm not an expert on firearms, Mr. Doyle. I couldn't tell his gun from your gun. I'm not going back into that room, so don't bother asking me again."

"What about the combination of the safe?"

She stood up and pulled me upright.

"I don't know the combination of the safe, but you have my permission to bust it open. I don't think my uncle committed suicide. Before you put out the word that he did, you'll need to prove it. I have the best lawyers in town. You publish his death as a suicide, and I'll personally sue you and move heaven and earth to get you fired. Not even your uncle will be able to save you. Am I clear?"

She might have been shaking like a leaf, but you'd never know it from the tone of her voice. With her free hand, she shoved her sunglasses back over her eyes.

Doyle didn't react until she shouted, "Am I clear? Do you understand me?"

He nodded stiffly, even as his face glowed with anger.

"I can't add a single thing to Miss Laurent's narrative," she said in her normal voice. "If you need to contact me any further, I live on the *Aurora* down at the St. Francis Yacht Club. Have them take my uncle to the McAvoy O'Hara funeral parlor. Miss Laurent and I are going to leave now. Come on, Maggie."

The Washingtons were San Francisco elite, and if Catherine Washington said we were leaving, we were leaving.

Privilege has its pluses.

"Where might I find you, Miss Laurent? Moore's place? Just in case I need to clear up a few things, you understand." Doyle feigned sweetness and light now that Catherine Washington was buttering my bread.

CHAPTER TWENTY

Had they seen us take Nick there? How did he know I was bunking at Nick's? In addition to casing our house, they must be listening on the party line. Another reason to keep all my conversations with Al vague. They must have seen me leaving my house with a suitcase in hand.

"I'm staying at the Normandy right now." I named a popular women's hotel in the city. To make my lie extra credible, I added, "Room 124."

I had no intention of staying there. Although cheap, they had a strict curfew, and I had plans for tonight that didn't involve staying in my room and tatting doilies.

The enmity in his eyes told me he'd have me down at his office at 7:00 a.m. sharp to continue his harangue. He'd probably send O'Malley to fetch me, who wouldn't have the nerve to rough me up but would be as unpleasant as he could be without breaking the law. I hadn't meant to make an enemy out of Doyle, but he dealt those cards.

I didn't say anything else. I followed Catherine out the door. Once we reached the entrance hall, I turned in the direction of the library and made the sign of the cross. "Rest in peace, amen," I whispered and crossed the threshold to the front porch.

Chapter Twenty-One

Once we were down the front steps, she said in a low voice, "I'll drive. I need to do something with my hands, or I'll go nuts with the cigarettes, and my throat is already raw."

I handed her the car key.

"That Doyle is a real piece of work," she muttered. "My parents used to socialize with his parents. Stuck up snobs who think they shit rosary beads."

"Lace-curtain Irish are the worst," I agreed.

She drove like she'd been driving since birth. Red lights were nothing more than caution signs. Yellow lights meant flooring the pedal and sailing through an intersection. Privilege even extends to traffic lights.

"Thanks for giving Doyle the rundown on what happened," she said. "I'm usually pretty good at keeping my cool. Do you want me to drop you off at the Normandy?"

"No." I laughed. "I flat-out lied to Doyle. They'll have me down at the station tomorrow morning before the sun is even halfway above the horizon. I'd planned to stay at Nick's place, but once they realize I'm not at the Normandy, they'll head straight to Nick's."

"You can't go home?"

"Nah, we've got company. That's why I'm staying at Nick's," I lied.

The less Catherine knew, the better. I could stay with one of my friends, but I didn't want them involved in two murder investigations, even peripherally.

"Stay with me. It's not the Ritz, but I've got an extra bunk in the boat and lots of blankets. Frankly, I could use the company."

CHAPTER TWENTY-ONE

That would solve a lot of my immediate problems.

"You sure?" My hands gripped my seat as she drove through another stop sign.

"I'm sure. You were a godsend today. I don't know what I would have done without you."

She took her hand off the wheel to pat me on the shoulder.

After a brief stop at Nick's for me to pick up my toothbrush and pajamas, we drove to her dock. After stowing my stuff in the cabin of her boat, we ate a late lunch at the yacht club. The dining room had all the elegance of John's Grill, but none of its charm. Too stuffy by half. Although I was wearing my best suit, it didn't feel formal enough for this place. Not bothering to wait for the waiter to seat us, Catherine strode across the dining room to a prime table with a view of Fort Point, the old Civil War post. The fog hadn't come in yet. The outline of the fort was so clear, I felt like I could put out my hand and touch it.

"A double martini, no more than a teardrop of vermouth, and two olives, Carl," she said, not even bothering to look at the waiter who'd followed us across the dining room; all her attention was on the water. "And the steak. Rare. Maggie, what do you want?"

"Oh, the steak, but, um, medium-rare." I glanced at the menu but didn't recognize half the items listed. What were oysters Rockefeller? I loved oysters, but I didn't want to eat them with anything weird on them.

"Anything to drink, miss?"

"A root beer?" I didn't mean for it to come out like a question.

"Very good," he said, even as he sniffed his disapproval as he walked away.

"Don't worry about the cost," Catherine said. "I have an account here."

I bet she did.

We sat there for a few minutes in silence, her sunglasses hiding her thoughts.

"I hear they're going to build a bridge from the Presidio to Marin. It's going to take at least three years," I said in a pathetic attempt at small talk.

"That's nice," she replied without an ounce of enthusiasm. "What does your brother do?"

"He teaches high school math and going to night school to become a lawyer."

"Does he have a girlfriend?"

I stifled the impulse to lie.

"No, he's picky. He doesn't cotton to women who are all fluttery and helpless. The ones who bat their eyes. He's living with me and Ma to save money so he can go to law school full-time. He's a swell guy, one in a million, and I will rip out the heart of any woman who hurts him."

She didn't back down after that warning. She laughed. It was hard not to admire her for it.

"He thinks he's protecting you, right? The older brother shtick. But it's really the reverse, isn't it?"

I conceded with a smile.

"I've never batted my eyes at a man in my life." She paused. "And I'm not helpless."

"To quote Doyle, you're a bit out of our league."

"I don't particularly like my league, Maggie."

All conversation stopped at that point as our food arrived. I kept waiting for her to rescind her invitation to spend the night, but she didn't.

For dessert, we both had a slice of lemon meringue pie, followed by a cup of coffee for me and another double martini for her. As she sipped her drink, she watched the fog begin its slow roll over the Marin headlands before it tumbled into the Bay.

She waved a hand in the direction of the water. "The tide's coming in. Do you sail? Oh, I already asked you that. You golf. My uncle was good enough to have gone professional. He should have gotten out of the banking business, away from my father. I'm my uncle's sole heir. I get the house and his shares in the bank. When my mother died, my father got her shares. Unless my father has changed his will and left everything to that gold digger, Phil and I should receive equal shares."

"Which means you've got more financial muscle than he does," I pointed out.

She didn't answer right away, pressing the metal of her cigarette lighter

CHAPTER TWENTY-ONE

against her lips for a couple of minutes. "If I have another cigarette, I'm going to be sick." She dropped the lighter on the table. "Maggie, I've done everything I can short of moving to Outer Mongolia to leave that world, and now it's sucking me back in."

"Do you want to fight your brother for control of the bank?"

"I don't know. He'll fight dirty, but there are too many instances of his greedy paws in the till for them to trust him. But he's a man, so they might side with him. I'd have to buy him out."

"If I were to place bets, I'd put my markers on you winning that fight."

"Thanks for the vote of confidence." She turned in the direction of the water. "Look at that fog. Coming in so fast, it's like a puppy tripping over its own feet. Do you know that at this time of year, you can set your watch by it? If Phil gets the bank, I give him six months before he runs it into the ground."

"And the house?"

"Fuck it," she muttered to herself and lowered her head to hunt through her purse. The cigarettes appeared, and a waiter was there at her side with a light even before she had shaken one out of the pack. It was that kind of place. After the first drag, she said, "I smell my mother's perfume every time I walk in the door. I know it's not real, but I can still smell it." She finished her drink in one long gulp.

I understood that. Some days, when the wind blows just right, I imagine I smell the thick aroma of my father's pipe when it's only the wind whipping down the chimney. Still, I fool myself every time it happens.

"It's a big house for one person." My voice was noncommittal.

"True. What do I need with a house that big?"

"My mother still smells my father's pipe smoke. They'll take her out feet first. Sometimes memories need a lot of space."

Her face jerked toward me. "How did you become so wise?"

"I eat my vegetables."

"I eat mine, too, for all the good it's done me. I'm exhausted and sad, and all I want to do right now is to curl up with a book and try to escape from this goddamn awful day." She stubbed out her cigarette in the ashtray; even that small movement seemed to take everything out of her. Leaning back in her chair, her shoulders slumped against the chair back, she faced me and said, "Maggie, you have no idea how tired I am. Let's go."

On our way out of the dining room, I stopped at the *maître d's* podium. He gave me the once-over and then sneered. I sneered right back at him.

"Catherine, I need to check in with Al. I'll meet you on the boat. May I borrow the phone here?"

"Sure. See you in a tick." There was a little wobble to her gait, the gin finally hitting her. The *maître d'* handed me the phone with as much trepidation as if I had a full-blown case of head lice.

"Thank you," I said in my most saccharine voice.

"Al, it's Mags. How's our friend doing?"

I'm not book smart—more savvy than anything else—but Al is both savvy and book smart. He picked up right away from my voice that our guest needed to remain as anonymous as possible.

"Asleep. Woke up about three hours ago. Still… You know, but okay. Ate some chicken soup. Probably the first real meal in days. Not talking much other than to say thank you now and then." The tension I'd been carrying across my shoulders for the last three days eased a little. "Are you calling from you-know-who's place?"

"No, staying at the Normandy. I'll tell you about it tomorrow."

There was a pause. Thank heavens Al realized that this party line might not be safe. He had no idea how unsafe it was.

"Maggie, is everything all right?"

"Why wouldn't it be?" I said with fake innocence. "Tell Ma I'm fine. I need to go. I'll come home tomorrow to check in, I promise."

I hung up. Several copies of afternoon editions of the various newspapers in town were stacked on a credenza for the members. Only *The Examiner* had a story about Reade's murder; the typeface was huge: SOCIETY SON SHOT DURING FUNERAL, by Charles Stein. The title was deliberately misleading, implying that Reade had been gunned down at the funeral, but then again, this was a Hearst publication, so par for the course.

Below the headline was a lurid photograph of Reade splayed out on the

CHAPTER TWENTY-ONE

floor, dead. The black-and-white photograph took some of the edge off the gruesomeness of the scene. The first few paragraphs confirmed that the coroner thought that Reade had been killed close to ten that morning while all potential suspects were at Washington's funeral service. How convenient. And no mention of suicide. Catherine's threats had worked.

There were several other headlines. D.A. Doyle was planning to hold a news conference the next morning to outline his plans to catch the "murderous thugs roaming our streets," as if these were random murders by lunatics with guns who'd just happened to target members of the Reade and Washington families. The entire front page was devoted to filler stories about Washington's bank and Reade's failure to wrest away control of the bank after Reade Senior had died, bracketed by old society photos of Washington posing with wife number one and wife number two.

I put the newspaper back on the credenza. Catherine didn't need to see a photograph of her uncle with his brains splattered all over the carpet. *The Examiner* excelled at printing lurid photographs of tragedies. I'd heard that their photographers were paid better than the other newshounds so they could bribe the cops to let them photograph crime scenes.

Even though it was several hours away from sundown, we changed into our pajamas on the boat.

"Take the bunk on the right. Mine smells like smokes." Catherine gestured at the stacks of books piled everywhere. "Help yourself. Biographies, histories, potboilers, you name it."

We climbed into our bunks, settled down with a couple of books, and spent the next few hours talking and reading. I told her about the Taylor case. I left out the part about Eileen being hanged.

She told me about her childhood and how, despite being twins, she and her brother had never gotten along. Eventually, he was sent away to boarding school because her mother couldn't stand their arguing, plus they were terrified he'd start selling the family silver.

"He's smart, I'll give him that. But while at school, he used his charm as a way of fooling people into trusting him. Eventually, he was kicked out for stealing other boys' money and watches. Sometimes, it's hard for me to believe he's my brother."

That made two of us.

Once it got dark, we retreated to our books, lulled into silence by the waning light and lapping of the waves against the hull of the boat. The soft thump of something hitting the floor brought my head up from my book. Catherine's history of the Roman Empire had thudded onto the floor. She was asleep, her hand wrapped around her half-finished highball. I picked up her book, removed the glass, and tucked the covers over her shoulders.

The stakes were increasing. I put my book aside and turned out the light. I played my usual mental game, wondering what to do next.

We had Helen Washington, the not-so-grief-stricken widow with a mysterious past and, no doubt, a nice payout from Washington's will. Then there was Philip-the-Lousy, now flush with bank shares and a possible inheritance from Pop. And Catherine-the-Reluctant-Heiress, also flush with bank shares and her uncle's estate, never mind what she might inherit from her father. All three had a motive to off Washington and Reade, and all three had airtight alibis for both events. There had to be a fourth player, the one who knocked off Washington and the person who killed Reade. Doyle wouldn't like it, but these two murders were obviously connected.

Follow the money, darling. I wish I had a dollar for every time Nick had whispered that in my ear. Reade had been the perfect patsy. Reputation as an alcoholic, a well-known antipathy to his brother-in-law, bitter about Washington's takeover of the bank and his sister's death, Reade as a suicide played well. Washington's death could have been labeled as unsolved, put down to a no-name thief or a communist. They were always good for it. Even I might have bought it. But with Reade's death looking like a murder, City Hall couldn't convincingly claim that Washington's murder was a random act of violence.

I lay there playing mental chess with myself, trying out various scenarios and always coming up short. Who was that extra player? And how did ABC Shipping fit in? At a certain point, I gave up, listening to the plaintive moaning of the foghorns until I fell asleep to their sad siren song.

I woke up to the sound of the door smashing against the side of the cabin.

CHAPTER TWENTY-ONE

I barely got in one blink of surprise before a ball of fire blasted into the cabin.

"Catherine!" I screamed. "Wake up!"

I grabbed my pillow and started smashing out the flames before they ignited the floor. No sooner had I put out the fire when smoke began to surge into the cabin.

"Catherine! Get up!" I screamed at the top of my lungs. I covered my mouth with my pajama top to protect myself from the smoke. I turned toward her, expecting her to sit up.

She wasn't moving.

I poked my head outside of the cabin and saw orbs of flame dotting the wooden deck. I didn't have time to put them all out. I had to get Catherine out of the cabin. I shook her, trying to wake her. She still didn't move. This was more than the martinis and highballs. She'd been doped. I didn't wait to find a pulse. I hauled her up by her armpits and dragged her to the ladder to the deck. The smoke, thick as molasses, filled the cabin. I'm strong, but I couldn't quite make it to the top of the steps. The flames on the deck were growing larger. Any second now, the entire boat would be engulfed.

I slapped her across the face as hard as I could. "Wake up!" I hit the other cheek. "Catherine! Wake up!"

That roused her a little. She moaned and stiffened just enough so that she wasn't a total dead weight. I got her up the stairs and onto the deck. The gangplank was in flames. I couldn't throw her into the water. She'd drown. I began screaming for help, trying to find an air pocket free from the smoke.

The heat was tremendous, the flames licking around our legs. An ember landed on a sleeve of her pajama top and ignited the material. I propped her up against the mast and held her up with one arm to batter the ember out before it spread. She'd have one hell of a bruise in the morning.

I dragged her toward the side of the boat to throw her overboard onto the dock when, suddenly, the boat slammed against something. Several people had pulled the boat to the edge of the dock while others were throwing buckets of water on the deck, trying to douse the flames.

"Give her to me!" someone shouted.

I hauled her over to the side, pushed her over, and several people caught her before she fell to the dock.

"Jump," shouted a familiar voice.

It was Charlie.

I jumped.

As the fire gained in intensity, boat owners stopped trying to save Catherine's boat to save their own. Cars driving down Marina Boulevard. stopped mid-traffic and jumped the curb to drive across the fields to help man bucket brigades. While waiting for the ambulance, I sat on the dock, shivering in my pajamas and holding Catherine upright in my arms. Someone put a coffee cup up to my lips, and I drank in tiny sips. It was so hot it burned my throat, or the smoke had scorched it raw. I didn't know which, but it tasted like ambrosia.

The fireboats arrived before the ambulance, drenching all of us in seawater. Within a couple of minutes, they'd put the fire out. Once in the ambulance, the crew wrapped us in blankets before racing off to Letterman Hospital in the Presidio. Although a military hospital, it was the closest. The staff could see the fire from the hospital, and the nurses marveled that we had survived. I had only superficial burns on my hands and still had my eyebrows and eyelashes.

Doctors and nurses huddled over Catherine in the bed next to me. They pumped her stomach, assuming she'd just overdosed on booze. Although she'd drunk quite a bit while at lunch, it couldn't have been the alcohol that made her so groggy. They gave me a shot of something designed to put me under. The last thing I heard before dropping off was Catherine asking me how I was doing. I had just enough energy to say, "I'm fine," before everything went black.

Chapter Twenty-Two

When I woke up the next morning, Ma was sitting on the edge of my bed with her eyes closed, one hand on my ankle and the other holding a rosary.

"Ma," I croaked. "How's Nick?"

She opened her eyes. "Had a bit of a rough night, but Al and Herman handled him. That Herman. What a nice young man. The doctor gave Nick a shot to calm him down. He's fine now. The doctors here told me that you escaped with only minor burns. How are your hands?"

I flexed them a couple of times. Sore, but manageable. "I'm fine." I held them up for her inspection, although they looked twice as big as normal because of the bandages. "They look worse than they feel. How's Catherine?"

"Who's Catherine?"

"The woman in the bed next to me. Catherine Washington."

Catherine was propped up, sipping what looked like weak tea.

"Catherine, this is my mother, Kitty Laurent. Are you okay?" I asked her.

She nodded. "Nice to meet you, Mrs. Laurent. Seems like someone nearly broke my jaw last night, and that same someone gave me a bruise on my arm that goes from my shoulder to my elbow. Thanks. You saved my life." She began to cough. When she'd finished, she said, "They're going to keep me here for a day or so. My boat?"

I shook my head. "A goner, I'm afraid."

"What about the other boats?" She sat forward, concerned.

"They're all fine. Those closest to you managed to sail out. Being berthed on the end helped."

She sat back in bed. "Thank God. What happened?"

I had a good idea.

"I'm still piecing it together. I'll tell you about it later." I glanced at my mother for the briefest second as if to say, not in front of my mother. She nodded. "Ma, how did you know I was here?"

"Charlie called me."

At that moment, Charlie walked up with a bouquet of roses in his hand.

"How are you doing?" he asked, his forehead puckered with worry.

"Great. More or less. Only superficial burns." I held up my hands.

He handed the roses to my mother. "Your hands. Ouch."

"They're fine. I love roses. Thanks." I turned to my mother. "Can we go home, Ma? I'm starving."

"When Maggie's starving, all's right in the world," said my mother. She squeezed my ankle and then slipped her rosary into her coat pocket. "They gave me some salve for your hands. How about we head home for breakfast with lots of pancakes and bacon and a day of doing nothing?"

There was no point in protesting. I didn't even try. I said goodbye to Catherine and told her I'd visit her tomorrow. Ma had brought me some clothes and a pair of shoes. With my hands bandaged up to the size of catchers' mitts, I couldn't manage the buttons on my blouse. She had to help me get dressed. I tried not to care that my best suit and shoes—the ones I'd just paid to have resoled—had gone up in flames.

As Charlie drove us back to 9th Avenue, he told me what had happened after I'd left the church pursuing Catherine. He kept waiting for me to return, and when I didn't, he'd attached himself onto Dickie's coattails and finagled an invitation to the gravesite and the post-funeral gig at the Sea Cliff house.

"Dickie wasn't very happy about me being there. I don't think he likes me. Anyway, I hadn't been there for more than two minutes when the phone rang. Their Chinese butler moseyed up to Doyle and whispered something in his ear. Doyle downed his drink in one go and nearly ran out of the room. I followed him to the Reade joint. Based on all the buttons lolling about, I figured something big had happened. I saw you and Catherine leave in her

CHAPTER TWENTY-TWO

car. Torn between following you or getting the scoop—"

"You stayed for the scoop."

He grinned. "My editor loves me right now. Front page of the afternoon edition."

"Congrats. What were you doing down at the docks last night?" I whispered.

"I decided to see where Washington berthed her boat. I saw a light on in the cabin and thought, well, what if brother Philip shows up? I was sitting with my back to a tree, smoking, and I guess I fell asleep. All of a sudden—"

I made the slashing motion across my throat to get him to shut his mouth. I glanced at my mother, who was sitting in the backseat.

"Let's talk about it after breakfast. I'm so hungry I'm about to start chewing on your upholstery."

"Yes, let's hear all of it." Ma's lips were pursed in that "You are in big trouble, Miss Margaret Mary Laurent" expression.

I spent the rest of the drive mentally concocting a story my mother would swallow without too much trouble. If I told Charlie the truth about what had happened in front of Ma, she'd lock me in the house for the next two years.

While my mother made breakfast, we sat in Al's room. Herman had just gone down for a nap, and it was only me, Al, Charlie, and Nick, who was asleep. I told them that I thought that Reade had been murdered, but it was set up like a suicide. We kept our voices low.

"Are you kidding me? Doyle claimed that he was the one who put the word out that they were considering Reade's death a murder."

"Your outrage on my behalf is touching, Charlie. He's a liar. Was all ready to go with the suicide angle until I pointed out that Reade was left-handed, and the gun had been staged so that it looked like it had fallen from his right hand. Whoever killed him didn't know Reade was left-handed."

"How did you know that?" asked Al, genuinely puzzled.

"Charlie and I saw Reade at John's Grill two days ago." Could it only have been two days ago? "It was obvious he was left-handed. Catherine is also left-handed. It usually runs in families."

"You're so smart." Charlie leaned over to flick me on the shoulder.

"Not really. Doyle has a big head to match his big law degree. He jumped on the suicide idea right off the bat because it let him off the hook for both murders. He'd have appeared in one of his expensive suits and announced that the police had determined that Washington's death was due to a robbery gone wrong. Now, he has no choice but to pull out all the stops as these two murders are linked. He hates my guts right now."

I cocked an ear in the direction of the kitchen and heard the bang of some pots and pans, but no call to come to the table. I lowered my voice even more.

"The cops must be listening on the party line. Doyle knows that Nick's here and that I had intended to sleep at Nick's. I told him I'd booked a room at the Normandy. I needed a place to stay, and Catherine offered me a bunk on her boat for the night."

"Why didn't you go to the Normandy?" said Al.

"I lied to throw Doyle off. He was as snotty as all get out during that interview at Reade's house. I didn't want to give him the opportunity to haul me down to the station at the crack of dawn for another going-over. At some point, he'll get me down there, but if I can delay it by a day or two, I'll have Harvey Cohen, Nick's lawyer, pull out his legal guns. Also, Catherine needed the company. She was pretty shaken up by seeing her uncle like that." She wasn't the only one. I didn't much feel like being by myself either. "Anyway, someone Mickey-finned Catherine's whiskey. She'd downed plenty of booze at the yacht club while we ate a late lunch, but she fell asleep before she could finish the highball she'd poured for herself when we got into bed."

If she'd finished that drink, it probably would have killed her.

"I assume she lit up her bedclothes with her cigarette," said Charlie.

That was the story I'd spin to my mother. Ma was an anti-smoking vigilante, convinced that my father's love of his pipe had contributed to his death. I wouldn't say explicitly that the fire was caused by Catherine's cigarette. I'd only hint at it.

"No, although I wouldn't be surprised if that was the narrative the killer

CHAPTER TWENTY-TWO

was hanging his hat on. You'd only have to stand next to her for five minutes to realize she's a chain smoker. It was a simple plan. Dope her booze. Ball up a bunch of newspapers and light them on fire. He kicked open the cabin door first and then hurled a couple of those fireballs into the cabin. She had a bazillion books in the hull. Whoever doped her booze must have seen all those books. It's a sure bet that the boat would have gone up like a matchstick with all that paper. But to make sure she wouldn't make it out of that cabin alive, they planted similar balls of lit newspaper all over the deck as well. Pretty diabolical. That's why the boat went up so fast. I managed to put out the fire in the cabin, but there was no way to contain all those fireballs on the deck. Catherine would have been murder number three."

My mother appeared at the door with a spatula in her hand.

"Breakfast is on the table. And while we eat, Maggie, why don't you tell me what happened last night."

Al and Charlie left the room before me. I bent over Nick to pull the covers over his shoulders. He said very quietly, "Thanks, precious. Watch your back, Maggie. ABC Shipping. The docks, not the speak."

I gave him the tiniest of nods. I was on it.

Chapter Twenty-Three

Two stacks of pancakes, six slices of bacon, a bowl of oatmeal, and twenty-four white lies later, I nagged my mother into letting Herman drive me to Philip Washington's apartment down near Pier 29. Whatever the issues between the siblings, he should know his sister was in the hospital. She'd probably refuse to see him, but he should know. Ma refused to let me go until I took off the bandages and showed her my hands. Not even a blister. I managed to keep my smile bright and perky. Didn't even wince when I flexed them for her inspection, though it hurt like the dickens.

"They're tender in spots and a little red, but they're okay. Feels like a sunburn," I assured her.

I even got her to agree to let me stay at Nick's that night under the condition that I had to call her later with a health update.

"I hear even a hint of exhaustion, and you'll have to come home. And no arguments, missy." As if she needed to say that. No one ever argued with Ma.

"Sure, Ma. But I feel tip-top."

Which was true. So hopped-up on the events of last night, I had to restrain myself from running to Herman's cab. Charlie had already left to attend Doyle's press conference, but we'd arranged to have dinner that night at the Pig 'n Whistle. As Herman drove me to the waterfront, I'd relayed the events of last night, with specific instructions for Herman to repeat every single detail to Dickie Vance. I wasn't in over my head. Yet. But I trusted Dickie, and I didn't want my naivete to land me in a stupid jam. Whoever set

CHAPTER TWENTY-THREE

Catherine's boat on fire meant business. Ugly business. Limited to smarts and pluck, my skill set had served me well until now, but was it enough? At some point soon, I'd insist that Al teach me some boxing moves. Like tomorrow if my hands could handle it.

Once we arrived at the speak, I asked Herman to wait for me.

The storefront for ABC Shipping still looked like the front door hadn't been opened in a month of Sundays. Old newspapers still littered the entryway, with the shades drawn tight over the windows. Nothing ventured, nothing gained. I looked around. The docks were teaming with men unloading the ships, but on this side of the Embarcadero, not a single person was in sight. I tried the windows along the storefront and broke four nails for my efforts.

Rats.

I climbed the stairs to the flat above the speak, holding on to the railing with a firm hand because the wind kept throwing me off balance. Except for Pier 29, the other docks were filled with ships of all sizes, topped by flags from different nationalities proclaiming their allegiance. The force of the wind caused the flags to snap against their lines with a fast rat-tat-tat like a tap dancer. The shirts of the men working the ships billowed in the breeze.

Once I reached the top of the staircase, I knocked first. No answer. Knocked again. Counted to one hundred, but still nothing. I turned the handle, and it opened without so much as a whisper.

"Mr. Washington?" I called out.

No answer. I tiptoed down the hallway and eased my head around the corner of the large archway leading into the living room. The acrid smell of ammonia had me reeling back on my heels. I covered my nose and mouth with a hand. Magazines, newspapers, and random debris lay on every surface. Clothes had been draped over all the furniture like shrouds. Velma's finery, so brilliant in the glow of the speakeasy's chandeliers, looked cheap and tawdry in the morning light. Women's shoes had been indiscriminately toed off and lay scattered here and there. The shades were drawn, and the room, bathed in a sepia light, resembled a photograph. There wasn't a sound. I put one tentative foot forward and then another, and walked in. Plates grimy with food, dirty glasses with the remnants of half-finished drinks, and coffee cups covered every surface.

Since I was here…

I tiptoed through their apartment. It wasn't anything special, but it was bigger than Nick's, with an honest-to-God dining room and a couple of bedrooms in the back. No one in the kitchen. The first bedroom was in a similar case of chaos as the other rooms: an unmade bed bracketed by two end tables piled high with more coffee cups and glass tumblers, a chair piled with more clothes, and a full-length white fur coat had been tossed into a corner. No Washington. The second bedroom seemed to be the actual office of ABC Shipping as opposed to that nearly barren room on the first floor leading to the entrance of the speak. A huge desk dominated the room. In one corner sat an overflowing wastepaper basket, surrounded by several large boxes half-filled with paper. Someone was emptying a file cabinet. Seemed like someone was leaving town.

I flipped through a few of the files. There were ships' manifestos of goods being loaded in Hong Kong, more goods taken on in Marseilles, a stop in Vancouver, then all of the cargo was unloaded in San Francisco, and it started all over again. It had been going on for a couple of years. The manifestos claimed that all loads contained tea. They made the loop twice a month. It seemed above board, except why would you pick up tea in Vancouver and Marseilles? Not exactly the climate for cultivating tea.

I walked back to the living room and put my hand on the doorknob when I saw her.

But for a long brown arm trailing over the side of the couch, I would have missed her. Her full-length red silk kimono blended into a red velvet sofa that had been pushed against one wall. Velma lay on her side, still, the front of her facing the back of the sofa. That arm dangling over the side didn't make sense until I realized she'd been trying to reach for a long pipe lying on the floor but had fallen asleep before she could reach it. Or she'd died. I ran over to the sofa and knelt to press two fingers to her wrist. Doped up to the nines, her pulse beat too slowly for comfort, but it was strong and steady.

CHAPTER TWENTY-THREE

"Velma? Are you okay?" I said far too loudly.

I turned her over on her other side so that we were face-to-face. She didn't fight me. One eye was swollen shut, the other nearly just as bad, and her lip was split. She wouldn't be singing the blues any time soon. If someone had belted me around like that, I might have reached for an opium pipe, too. Junior must have socked her and then backhanded her in the bargain. I already disliked Philip Washington. Now, I hated him.

She came to and lisped, "Who are you?" Between the dope and the busted lip, it was almost impossible to understand her. Her speaking voice was the same as her singing voice: a melody. An American Circe.

"It's Maggie Laurent. I saw you at the speak the other night. I'm looking for Philip."

She didn't open her eyes when she spoke. "No here. At the bitch's house. Gettin' scratch for the trip."

Trip?

"What trip, Velma?" I tried to make my voice casual.

"France. Gay Paree." She began humming a tune I didn't recognize, lost in a drug-fueled dream.

"When are you leaving, Velma? When?"

She stopped singing and brought her hands together as if in prayer, shoving them under her cheek. I waited for a couple of minutes until I realized she'd fallen asleep again. I tried to push the pipe under the sofa with my foot in case she woke up and reached for it again, risking overdose. But something heavy was in the way. I ducked my head to see what was under the sofa and immediately scooted back.

A gun.

I didn't know what to do. This might not be related to the previous murders, but it might. Velma couldn't have murdered Harold Washington because she had an airtight alibi courtesy of me. But what if they hired someone to kill the Washington patriarch with this very gun and set the presumptive heiress's boat on fire as well? That fourth person. We weren't that far away from the dock where Catherine's boat was docked.

Think, Maggie, think. Anyone, even a child, could have balled up a bunch of newspapers and lit them on fire. But the foot that booted the cabin door open was that of a man. I was sure of it. It would take a strong kick to bust the locks, and if Velma were hitting the pipe every night, I doubt she'd last even one round with a kitten. But I bet Phil Washington could do it. Did he have an alibi for last night? Based on the night we attended her show at the speak, she didn't take the mike until around 10:00. That would leave Washington plenty of time to reach the dock, wad up a few newspapers, kick open the cabin door, light the boat on fire, and then return to the apartment to don his suit and escort Velma downstairs to the stage.

He had the opportunity. Did he have a motive? Phil wouldn't be Catherine's heir, given her antipathy toward him, but I bet he'd be the recipient of her shares in the bank should anything happen to her. I doubted the Board of Directors would let the shares out of their control, thus hamstringing her from donating her shares to an orphanage or something. I'd promised her I'd see her today, but that was before I discovered Phil packing up to leave town. And I still had no answer as to why Catherine was at the speak if she and her brother were estranged. She claimed it was because she was worried about her brother trying to pull some financial shenanigans, but surely a lawyer could deal with that? All those questions would have to wait.

I now had a date with District Attorney Doyle.

I decided to leave the gun where it was, but I'd tell Doyle about it. New techniques for matching the rifling of bullets to the gun had been around for a few years. If this was the piece used to kill Washington Senior, then Junior had some explaining to do.

Velma began to sing the mournful refrain of "I Can't Give You Anything but Love." Her beautiful face, mauled by that bad egg's fists, made me sick to my stomach. I went back into the kitchen and grabbed a dishtowel. They'd plugged up the sink for a block of ice. There might have been dishes on every surface in the living room, but an ice pick lay on the bare counter. They certainly had their priorities. Based on the number of unwashed dishes throughout the apartment, washing up wasn't important compared to pouring a scotch on the rocks. I soaked the towel in the icy water that

CHAPTER TWENTY-THREE

had collected around the block of ice. I didn't wring it out too much, but folded it into a square and returned to the living room.

"Velma, I'm going to put this on your face. It's nice and cool, and it will take down some of the swelling."

No response.

I gently placed it over her face. She jerked a bit, but she was too out of it to say anything. That I'd done the same thing for Nick hadn't escaped my notice.

I bathed her face one more time and then left.

Herman was standing next to his cab, reading a newspaper.

"Herman, could you take me to the D.A.'s office?"

"Sure thing, Miss Laurent." He held the door open for me. "Say, your ma is an awfully nice lady. That must be why you and Al are so nice."

I was discovering just how not-nice a lot of people were. It's not that I'm naïve or anything. Plenty of unsavory stuff comes in over the transom when you work for a gumshoe, but that scene upstairs left a nasty taste in my mouth.

"Thanks, Herman. May I borrow your newspaper?"

"You can have it. I'm done."

We took off. I flipped through the pages until I found the arrivals and departures for the ships. *La Chanteuse* was arriving tonight with the tide at around six tonight at Pier 29. Right across the road from the speak. It was scheduled to depart two days later for Marseilles.

I had two days to figure this all out before Philip Washington, and his little canary skipped town.

Chapter Twenty-Four

Herman drove me to the D.A.'s office and then headed back to Ma's. Doyle's secretary wasn't nearly as chatty as last time. In fact, I'd say she was downright hostile.

"Is Mr. Doyle available?"

"I'll see, Miss Laurent," she snapped and moved her chair back a foot like I had mustard stains on my blouse. With a deliberately elaborate move, she pressed a button and spoke into the phone. "Miss Laurent is here to see you. May I send her in?" After a couple of seconds, she sneered, "He's busy right now. Do you want to wait?"

"Yep." I sat down. And waited. And waited. At the thirty-minute mark, a part of me wanted to get up and give that snotty little secretary's desk a kick on my way out the door. What did it matter to me if Philip Washington skipped town? Not my beef. I'd done my job and had been paid. The Washingtons could march straight to hell. My Irish was up, and that's never a good thing.

Then the practical French side said: You need to tell them about the gun and that Junior's skipping town. Velma might not be a murderer, but someone thought she was important enough to beat her something fierce. As a warning not to shoot her mouth off to the D.A.?

Fortunately, the French half usually wins my internal debates because when I give in to my Irish temper, all hell breaks loose every single time.

Fifteen minutes later, he came out of his office and pretended to be surprised to see me still sitting there. Maybe he was surprised. He escorted me to a seat in his inner sanctum. He'd ditched yesterday's black suit

CHAPTER TWENTY-FOUR

dedicated to funerals and weddings. Today, he wore a subtle navy pinstripe that complemented the color of his eyes. Buttoning up his suit jacket was another power move I bet he learned in his first year of law school. Shows the other person who's boss.

"Have a seat, Miss Laurent."

I sat.

"I hear you had quite a time last night."

"You could say that. But I'm fine. Thanks for asking."

Not that he'd asked.

"I'd greatly appreciate it if you'd sit down with Detective Murphy and verify some facts. He needs to interview Miss Washington sometime soon."

"Sure," I agreed. "But I have no idea what you're going to get out of her. Someone drugged her booze. I had to haul her out of the boat. She couldn't even stand up."

His hand stilled, the flame from his lighter hovering over the ubiquitous cigarette.

"Are you telling me this fire wasn't an accident? That someone set the fire?"

I refrained from rolling my eyes, but if someone said to me, "Someone drugged her booze," I'd take that as being deliberate.

"Yes, the fire was deliberately set. And if I ever hanker to start drinking, this little experience has made me a teetotaler for life. Whoever set that fire didn't count on me being on board. I'd assign her a police detail if I were you."

He sat back to study me while finally lighting his cigarette, narrowing his eyes, either to protect them from the smoke or in obvious dislike. Probably a healthy mixture of both.

"Are you telling me how to do my job, Miss Laurent?" He leaned forward. There was that smile again, nasty and tight.

"Of course not, Mr. Doyle. You seem to be doing a bang-up job." I'd said this with a straight face, but he wasn't buying it based on the glare he was giving me. "I'd be happy to give Murph a rundown of last night's events, but later. I'm here because you have much bigger fish to fry."

"You weren't at Moore's place, nor were you staying at the Normandy. You lied to me. Twice."

"I'll confess it on Sunday. Sure did. You had no right to round me up, and you know it."

He didn't disagree, but he didn't appreciate me spelling it out. The glare got glarier.

"What other fish?"

Now, he was wary, sitting back in his chair and letting the ash on his cigarette grow.

"Philip Washington and his side piece are leaving town. The ship *La Chanteuse* is due in tonight at Pier 29, just across from the speak. It departs for Marseilles in two days. It's part of the Washington family shipping holdings. Washington's real office for the business is in their apartment above the speak. He's packing up. Boxes are everywhere."

I handed him Herman's newspaper and pointed to the arrival and departure times of the ships.

"The two of them are skipping town?" The ash on his cigarette got longer.

"If the boxes weren't enough of a tip-off, his girlfriend confirmed it around a split lip the size of Alcatraz. They're leaving for Europe. I'm not the District Attorney, but it seems to me that either of them skipping town with two murders still unsolved would look bad. And you, on the job only two years."

"The newspapers would have a field day," he murmured to himself. He narrowed his eyes even more. "May I remind you, it's only one murder at this point."

"Pull the other one."

"Split lip?"

I nodded. "She's been beaten up. Badly. I assume Washington did it. But what if they've been paying their supplier with nothing more than promises based on his inheritance, and she was beaten up as a warning to come up with the Benjamins and fast. She was high as a kite when I left her. You might get something out of her. Like where's Washington? She told me he was at the widow's house trying to weasel some dough out of his stepmother for their trip. Might be a lie."

CHAPTER TWENTY-FOUR

"Probably," he drawled. "The day I take the word of a druggie is the day I should be fired. We'll check it out."

I paused. "Have you done any tests to see if the gun in the library was the gun that killed Reade?"

"Of course, we've done tests," he said, working his own roll of the eyes.

"And?" I said through gritted teeth.

"I can't divulge that information, Miss Laurent. Anything else?"

"I can't divulge that information, Mr. Doyle."

We were back at square one.

In response, he leaned back in his chair, fumbled in his desk for a new pack of cigarettes, and then turned away from me to smoke down a few while looking out his window at Van Ness Avenue below. I fished for a nail file in my purse and began to work on my nails. As I filed away, I heard Nick's voice: *It doesn't do to give them even an inch, darling. It only guarantees their initial impression that you're weaker than they are, and they will push you every time.*

I'd rather be Doyle's enemy than his punching bag.

After about twenty minutes, the squeak of his chair as it swiveled around to face me again brought my head up.

"Doyle, I've got smarts and gumption, and I know my rights. Nick taught me well. I didn't come here to get in your good graces. I came here because two people have been killed so far, and it's all tied up with the Washingtons. Deny it. Why is Junior hightailing it out of here? Because he had someone kill his father or because he's afraid he might be next? I was nearly incinerated last night. Now, it's personal. I'm not stopping until I find out what's going on. Do we understand each other?"

We stared at each other for a bit, not blinking. He blinked first, sighed, and stubbed out his cigarette. People were always sighing around me for some odd reason.

"The gun on the floor of the Reade library is not the gun that killed him. The caliber's too small, and the bullet casing doesn't match. And it hadn't been fired in about ten years. It's registered to Reade. The housekeeper says he kept it in the safe. The safe was open and cleared out by the time we arrived. The housekeeper said that he kept a pile of spare cash in the safe; Reade often raided the safe to pay her salary, but she couldn't say how much was in there or the denominations. Just that it was a large stack of greenbacks. Miss Washington might be able to give us some idea of how much was stolen. You two missed the safe," he pointed out.

"Like you missed that he was left-handed. Just to be clear: The safe was empty while you were drilling me and Miss Washington?"

"That's a possibility," he conceded.

"Which, in addition to the left-hand thing, is another check in the 'he was murdered' box."

"Not really." He pointed his cigarette at me to make his point. "That safe might have been empty except for the gun, and he opened it to get his gun because he was so distraught that he didn't bother to shut the door."

"Before he killed himself. With his right hand even though he's left-handed. With a gun that hadn't been fired in years."

"We didn't know that at the time."

"Stop whining, Doyle. You—"

"I'm not whining," he whined.

"Have it your way. You've jumped to a lot of conclusions because Reade's suicide would have let you off the hook. Now you have two murders to solve. I'm guessing whoever shot him threatened him with their gun and ordered him to retrieve his gun out of the safe to make it look like suicide. Or maybe it was a straight-up robbery gone bad."

"Makes sense," he grumbled, not very graciously.

"Does Reade have an alibi for the night of Washington's murder?"

He waited a few seconds before saying, "Yes. He was having dinner with Herbert Fleishhacker. Reade was hoping the Fleishhacker brothers would bankroll a takeover of Commerce Bank and wrest control away from his brother-in-law."

Based on Dickie's information, Commerce Bank was about to go bankrupt, so the deal between Dill Reade and the Fleishhacker brothers would be a bankruptcy sale for pennies on the dollar. That made the suicide angle even more improbable, and the murder of Washington by Reade doubly so. Reade

CHAPTER TWENTY-FOUR

was out to humiliate his brother-in-law and take back control of the bank.

"You got any money in Commerce Bank?"

"Not anymore. If the Fleishhackers are sniffing around the bank, chances are the bank is in serious trouble. They've never lost money on a deal yet. Now, why are you here?"

"There's a gun under the sofa at Washington's apartment. I saw it myself. What if Velma killed Reade? She couldn't have killed Washington because both she and Junior had alibis for that particular shooting party, but what's to say he didn't hire someone else to plug his father? Promised some poor sap cargo containers of dope if only he'd kill his old man. That's the way I see it so far."

I paused to give Doyle a chance to protest, but he stayed silent. Guess the rumors about the company Ole Phil kept had moved beyond society gossip.

"I'll have the police chief send a couple of bulls over to Washington's place and check out your story. Where are you going to be for the next couple of hours?"

"Here, in the basement in the records department."

"Why?" He narrowed his eyes. "What mischief are you up to?"

"I'm curious about a few things."

He pointed a menacing finger at me. "Stay there. Don't move. I'll find you."

Chapter Twenty-Five

Philip's clearing out of the records of ABC Shipping was curious. If this business was on the up and up, then why all the subterfuge? Plus, in all the print I'd read about the Washington family, ABC Shipping only garnered a minor mention, with the real wealth in the banking end. And yet they had a berth at the waterfront with a warehouse at one of the busiest ports in the United States. Although the storefront was just that, a storefront, Washington was conducting business out of the back bedroom of their apartment. It was a real business, but no one wanted to bring attention to it. Why?

The man running the desk at the records office was hunched over a crossword puzzle and ignored me until I mentioned that Doyle had given me permission to root through the files. Doyle had done nothing of the sort, but he didn't know that.

"Waterfront. Shipping. Boats," I said.

"Corridor F. Aisle H," he yelled back. He motioned toward a door and went back to finishing his crossword puzzle with a magnifying glass in his hand.

When I opened the door, it was corridor after corridor of file cabinets. It took me a while to find Corridor F because the signage was so bad and the light so poor. Eventually, I found myself at the records for the waterfront. Two years ago, ABC Shipping sold controlling interest to a firm listed as Hong Kong Exports—a limited liability corporation. I had no idea of what that was, but I filed it away as something to ask Harvey about.

Digging farther back into the file were dunning letters reminding Harold

CHAPTER TWENTY-FIVE

about unpaid dock fees, business fees, et cetera. When Hong Kong Exports took over, all that type of correspondence stopped. Hong Kong Exports paid their bills on time. There were no names associated with this corporation other than Philip's name as their U.S. contact, with the home office based in Hong Kong. They were paying a premium for yearly licenses for the dock and the warehouse. I had a hard time seeing tea bringing in enough money to pay those kinds of fees. And yet all the shipping manifestos made it clear that the entire cargo consisted of tea, at least on the runs I'd thumbed through.

I bet that Philip was operating this on the sly and that Washington Senior had no idea what his son was up to. Somehow, Junior got the financing to set this up, bought the company from his father, and hid it behind this other entity. He owned the speak as a cover for the shipping operation, where he was making his real money. With the mayor and the police chief as trusted clients, you could be sure that no one would start asking questions. Plus, he ran a decent club. The booze was the real stuff, not your bathtub gin. More reason not to question his business practices. The run to Vancouver made sense if they were loading honest-to-God-hooch, but the stop in Marseilles still had me puzzled. I'd heard it was the crime capital of Europe, but what they could be transporting from there had me stumped.

I leaned against the open file drawer, cleared my brain for a few seconds, and read over the business license again. I had proof of a relatively new company whose representative was listed as Philip Washington. The obituary of Harold Washington had only a tiny mention of ABC Shipping as a business he once owned. But if Senior knew that Philip was part of Hong Kong Exports, then why make such a fuss and kick Junior out of the bank? And why would Junior be so stupid as to steal money from the bank, drawing attention to himself? Unless he wasn't fired because he was lifting money. He was fired for some other reason.

Or he wasn't fired at all.

What if the widow's eagerness to find the wayward son had nothing to do with the bank? What if Philip had taken a temporary powder and his stepmother needed to find him? He'd been fired from the bank numerous times; that story would hold water. But her insistence that her husband be kept out of the loop regarding Philip's whereabouts now seemed fishy. All I knew was that she was desperate enough to find Philip that she was willing to hire Nick. And I bet that Helen Washington knew nothing about the apartment over the speak, or that would be the first place she'd look for him.

Doyle found me two hours later, sitting on the floor, trying to make sense of all this.

"Let's go," was all he said. He didn't wait to see if I was following him and began walking at such a pace that I had to half-run to keep up with him.

"Where are we going?" I asked, before sliding into the front seat of his car.

"ABC Shipping. Velma Jackson was murdered."

He was silent through the entire drive with a set to his jaw that warned me not to utter a peep. When we pulled up to ABC Shipping, the street was thick with beat cops, some tapping their batons on their thighs. The wind hadn't abated, and most of them had their free hand on their hats. A space in front of the building had been left open, and Doyle pulled in. The outside door to the speak had been busted off its hinges. Murph and O'Malley were standing beside the broken door, handkerchiefs tied around their mouths.

"The chief here yet?" asked Doyle.

They shook their heads. Doyle closed his eyes like my father used to do when he wanted to swear up a blue streak. In my head, I imagined Doyle saying the Lord's name in vain in about twenty different ways.

"Update," he ordered.

"Washington's squeeze upstairs is dead," said O'Malley. He could have been talking about a bunch of wilted dandelions for all the empathy in his voice. "The speak's been cleared out of all the booze. No one is on site. Nothing left down there but the tables and chairs. Looks like Washington's skipped town. His clothes are all gone."

A shiver raced down my spine to my ankles.

"Doyle, she was alive when I left her, I swear."

"I believe you," he said in a quiet voice. "Murph?"

"We've begun interviewing the businesses around here, but so far, no one

CHAPTER TWENTY-FIVE

saw anything amiss. No moving trucks for the last several days."

"There's a door in the kitchen that probably leads to the speak," I said. "What if Washington moved the boxes down to the speak. How he got them out of there without anyone noticing, I have no idea."

"Let's go," he said to me and began walking toward the stairs to the apartment.

"Sir," Murph said in a low voice. "I don't think Maggie should—"

"She was here earlier this morning, and the dame was still alive, Detective Murphy. I need Maggie to tell me about the scene before someone decided to silence Washington's canary for good. See if anything's missing or has been moved."

"It's okay, Murph." I placed a hand on his arm. "Really."

Doyle had finally realized that he needed to stop this carnage and fast. The newshounds hadn't arrived yet, but it was only a matter of time. Some cop who needed to pay a doctor's bill would have made a quick phone call to both *The Examiner* and *The Call-Bulletin*. I was surprised Charlie hadn't arrived yet.

I followed Doyle up the stairs, reciting Our Father to give me courage. It couldn't be worse than seeing Reade, I told myself.

When we reached the top, he said, "Did you touch anything?"

"A dish towel. I dunked it in cold water in the kitchen sink and placed it over her face a few times to take down the swelling. That's it."

He paused to give me a look I couldn't decipher.

"What?"

"Nothing. Let's go."

We stepped over the threshold and immediately covered our mouths. By this point, the apartment had been baking in the morning sun, and it smelled five times worse than when I entered it several hours ago. The acrid scent of the fireplace having been used recently vied with a sickeningly sweet aroma. Doyle handed me the handkerchief sticking out of his breast pocket. I tied it around my face. It helped, but only a little.

Velma was where I left her. On the sofa. Whoever had killed her had rolled her over onto her back so they could kill her fast. Had the murderer turned her over so that she faced the sofa back, we wouldn't have even noticed the ice pick sticking out of her. Except for the pool of blood dripping over the side of the sofa and staining the floor beneath her. The dish towel still covered her face like a bridal veil.

At the sight of her, Doyle and I both made the sign of the cross. I turned away. This was far worse than Reade. I didn't know this woman, but I'd seen her look at Philip Washington; she was crazy about him. She'd do anything for him. Maybe even murder someone. Even when she was completely doped up, I'd heard the hope in her voice when she said, "Gay Paree."

"Everything the same?"

Doyle's voice brought me around.

I studied the room.

"They moved her. When I left her, she lay on the couch, on her side, but facing the room. Not on her back."

My voice, muffled because I was speaking through the handkerchief, didn't sound like me. All flat and stupid, like someone else was talking. I turned away and began talking to the windowpanes. I didn't want to see her again. Once was enough.

"And someone's been burning paper." I pointed at the fireplace. The embers were still smoking. "The opium pipe on the floor's gone. When I went to shove the opium pipe under the sofa so she couldn't take another hit and overdose, the gun was in the way. That's how I discovered it."

Doyle murmured to someone, "Check for the gun."

A few seconds later, O'Malley said from under his handkerchief, "It's gone, sir."

"Let's check out the kitchen," said Doyle, placing a firm hand on my elbow to lead me to the kitchen. I found I didn't mind. His hand was warm, and I began to shiver, not from the cold, but from something else.

"Looks the same," I confirmed. "Except for the—" I couldn't say it.

"The ice pick. Let's check out the bedrooms."

O'Malley and Murphy followed us as we walked through the first bedroom. Nothing had been moved or changed. But the boxes in the second bedroom were missing, and all the drawers in both file cabinets had been emptied.

CHAPTER TWENTY-FIVE

"He's cleared out," I said in a dull voice. "When I was here earlier, the file cabinet still had some files in it. I guess he burned what he couldn't haul out of here. There were—" I thought hard "—three boxes half-filled with papers. How could they have cleared this out so fast with none of the other businesses noticing?" I had a thought. "What if he burned all of it?"

"Could be. O'Malley, look around the bedroom, will you? See if you can find any clue where Washington might be. Train or bus information, stuff like that."

Pushing the sleeve of his jacket over his hand, Doyle opened the desk drawers; all of them empty. He turned to me, and whatever he was going to say would never be said because Murph walked into the room holding a white fur coat up by its shoulders. The front was stained with blood and bits of something else. Something worse. I swallowed down the sick in my throat.

"She stuffed the lining with a bunch of bills." He opened the coat to show us the torn lining. The green from the bills bled through the thin white silk lining like mold on white bread.

I turned around and ran out of the room, moving so fast my feet barely touched the floor. I ignored O'Malley's loud shout of "Hey!" and made it all the way down the outside steps before I felt a hand on my shoulder. I shook it off. The hand came back and kept me in my place.

"I'm sorry, Maggie, but I need to talk with you about the fire and today," said Doyle, his voice determined.

My shoulders slumped in surrender.

"Can we walk? I need…" I didn't know what I needed, but getting away from that apartment was a good start.

We walked along the Embarcadero in the direction of the Ferry Building. A cop car followed us at a discreet distance, watching over Doyle or watching over me. I don't suppose it mattered.

I didn't say anything for a couple of blocks, letting the wind wash over me. I breathed deeply, trying to clear my lungs of the awful smell of that apartment and the visual of that coat. I'd wash my clothes as soon as I got back to Nick's place. They stank of death.

Once well away from the speak, Doyle said to me out of the side of his mouth, "Look, I'm sorry I wasn't very polite before. I'm under a lot of political heat right now. Washington was a big cheese in this town, and the mayor wants answers."

I guess apologies didn't come easy to Doyle. Every word sounded like he was talking with a mouth full of ground glass.

"I'm on your side, Doyle. Why wouldn't I be? But if you're so sorry, then I want you to apologize to Nick for letting O'Malley tear him apart. You either authorized that beating or looked the other way."

"Moore doesn't have the best reputation with the mayor's office." Some of Doyle's previous belligerence was sneaking back in.

"And the San Francisco Police Department doesn't have the best reputation with the folks who live and work in this city," I shot back.

"Fair enough," he admitted. "I'm sorry that I had to drag you back to that apartment. I didn't have a choice."

The French side of me told me I'd made my point and let it go, even though the Irish part of me was all for holding a grudge into the next century. But people were getting shot and stabbed, and this needed to stop. I swallowed a couple of times and then said, "Apology accepted. Truce?"

"Truce."

We walked on for several yards before I said over the roar of the wind, "How can people live like that? In such squalor."

"They just do."

"Did you ever hear her sing? I swear, Doyle, it was like an angel opened her mouth. She must have shot Reade and then cleared out the safe, stuffing the greenbacks in the lining of her coat. How does someone shoot another person in cold blood like that?"

He shook his head. "I don't have any answers for you. Are you ready to talk?"

I nodded and told him about the fire. Then I told him about trying to find Washington because his sister was in the hospital, and that's how I ended up at the apartment. I don't remember turning around and heading back to the speak, but we must have done. Suddenly, we were standing in front of

CHAPTER TWENTY-FIVE

ABC Shipping again, the beat cops still trying to stop their hats from getting blown away.

"You need to have a look at the business files for ABC Shipping. There's something hinky going on."

"Is that why you were in the records office?"

I nodded. "Some sort of shell company owns it now. Washington sold it a couple of years ago, except it looks like his son is running it. The runs are limited but like clockwork. Which is a lot of tea for one city, with stops in Marseilles and Vancouver. If I were a betting woman, which I'm not, I'd say the stop in Vancouver involves whiskey running. The stop in Marseilles? More booze? Drugs? I don't know." I shrugged. "But it's unclear whether Philip's father knew he was running it. Setting up the speakeasy here," I waved a hand in the direction of the building, "in a shipping office that had been deserted because of the sale would mean that the brass wouldn't look too closely at its business practices, with the mayor and the police chief with their reserved tables."

"I leave you alone for two hours, and look what you come up with," he teased. "What made you look into it?"

"Nick says that it's often what isn't said that's important. Washington's obit had only one oblique reference to ABC Shipping, hinting it was a past holding. What was that ammonia-like odor?" No one had taken a mop to that place in months.

"Cooked opium smells like that. Walk through an opium den. Your nostrils won't thank you."

"I'll pass."

"Did you pick the locks to get in?"

"No. The door to their flat was unlocked. I left it unlocked. Anyone could have walked in and killed her. I don't know how to pick locks. Yet." I fingered the hairpins in my coat pocket.

He frowned at me like I was his kid sister, with a lot of bark but no bite.

"I'm going to have to keep an eye on you."

"You can try."

"Laurent. That's a French name, isn't it?"

"My father was French. Ma is County Cork through and through."

"That explains a lot."

We smiled at each other because this was a language we both understood: that secret verbal semaphore between the Irish.

He asked a few more questions and then said quietly, "Do you want a lift to Moore's place or your mother's house? One of… There's Chief O'Sullivan. About time. Murph's car is up the block. You want a lift somewhere?"

"St. Patrick's, if you don't mind. I want to light a candle for Velma and Reade."

"Can your mother handle another invalid?" That answered that question. Yes, he knew about Nick staying at my house.

"If I ask her to, she will. Why?"

"I talked to the docs over at Letterman. They're planning to release Miss Washington tomorrow morning. Can she stay at your mother's place?"

"So she doesn't get killed, you mean?"

"So she doesn't get killed," he repeated.

Al will do handsprings when I tell him the news.

"Sure. The more, the merrier. Maybe you should assign a couple of cops to—"

"Done. I've already got a couple of buttons casing your house."

I gave his shoulder a light punch. "You've also been listening in on the party line. Why?"

"Your receipt in Harold Washington's pocket." He pointed at me. "You still haven't come clean on that."

I rolled my eyes. "Jesus, Mary, and Joseph, give me patience. I'm telling you flat-out, I have no idea why my receipt was in his pocket. The missus hired me for a job, I did it, and we're done."

He made to speak, and I held up a hand.

"It's not relevant to the murders. If it turns out later that it is, I'll spill. I gather that Washington wasn't too happy with wife number two. What if he found the receipt and it sealed the deal for him?"

"His lawyers are squawking. Seems there's a little dispute over the will. Think Junior's good for it?" He glanced at the apartment.

CHAPTER TWENTY-FIVE

I shuddered at the savagery in the way Velma was killed. I didn't know how many times she was stabbed, but it wasn't just once or even twice. I shook my head.

"He might have wanted her out of the way, but all he had to do was put a pillow over her face. That—" I waved a hand in the direction of the speak "—was vicious. Oh, I could see him backhanding her now and then, but not..." I shuddered and didn't bother to finish my sentence.

He chewed on that for a few seconds.

"How about that lift?" He raised a hand and beckoned Murph over to where we were standing.

"Doyle, one more thing. Keep O'Malley away from me. I don't like him."

Chapter Twenty-Six

We pulled up to the front of St. Patrick's. Murph turned to me and said, "Do you want me to wait for you? If not, I'll go." He grimaced. "I drew the short straw. I need to tell Velma's parents about her. Christ, I hate this part of the job."

His hands were gripping the steering wheel, his knuckles impossibly white.

"Where do they live? The Fillmore?"

"Nah, East Oakland. She has a bunch of priors, so I least I don't have to hunt down her next of kin. Father works the line at the Chevy plant. Mother's a teacher. If I hurry, I might be able to grab him getting off his shift. Want to come with me?" he said with a tense smile.

He meant it as a joke, but I didn't take it that way.

"Yeah, I'll come with you. Let's go."

"You sure?" His hand hovered over the ignition, the key tight in his fingers.

"I'm sure."

"I'll admit I'd be grateful for the company, but the chief will string me up if he hears about this," he warned.

"I won't tell if you don't."

Murphy was a good soul. He'd relay the bad news with some sympathy, but I wanted her parents to know that... I don't know... In a crazy way, to let them know that she was loved, at least by Philip Washington. That people sat still as boards when she sang, barely breathing. That it was like hearing an angel singing. The beat cops, O'Malley, and even, to a certain extent, Doyle, were treating her death as a big headache. Some junkie finally got what was coming to her. It would only be because Velma was tied to the

CHAPTER TWENTY-SIX

Washington family that her murder would get any attention. She inhabited that underworld the brass wanted to keep hidden, where power and money gulp down their free booze in defiance of the laws, but the woman who sang for her supper and mesmerized them night after night wasn't worth anything now that she'd been silenced.

We took the Creek Route Ferry to Oakland. The ride was rough as the boat's prow sawed the waves with a thud. I held onto the rail with both hands, staring out over the water at the approaching shore. Murph was silent the whole time, sucking down one cigarette after another. Despite the chop of the water, we made good time. After docking at the bottom of Broadway, we drove straight to 73rd Avenue.

The automobile plant occupied a city block, and we could hear the clanging of machinery through the concrete walls as the factory churned out cars. Murph showed his badge to the foreman, a small man with a mean mouth and a big beer belly hanging over his belt, and told him we needed to speak to Mr. Jackson about a family matter. The man didn't look surprised. He nodded and led us into a small office off the plant floor.

The foreman returned two minutes later.

"Tom says he doesn't have a daughter anymore. Died ten years ago."

"Sorry, he does. She's—"

"He says no, Detective. If that's what the man says, then I need you to leave. I don't want no trouble here." He pulled out a small sack of tobacco and bit off a chew; his teeth were black. "His wife teaches over at the Fifteenth Street Church. Mebbe talk to her," he mumbled around the wad of tobacco and turned around, letting us find our own way out.

Near the plant, we found a beat cop directing traffic who steered us in the direction of 15th Street. It was about twenty minutes away. The church was built up to the sidewalk, with an oversized dome on top that gave the impression that the walls were struggling to stay upright. Large windows squatted over a pair of tall doors with smaller windows to the left and right. Only one window was of stained glass. I bet that every Sunday, there were pleas for the window fund.

Murphy asked a young man swabbing the steps of the church if Mrs.

Jackson were there.

"Still teaching."

"I need to talk to her."

"School lets out in five minutes." The mop never stopped moving.

"Round back?"

"Yeah, and down the stairs." He kept his mop moving without glancing at us once.

If this had been O'Malley, he would have grabbed the mop and broken it over the kid's head. As it was, Murph ignored the barely concealed hostility. The longer he had to wait to tell this woman her daughter was dead was okay by him.

As we made our way to the back of the church, a parade of children came tumbling down the path leading to what must be the church hall. Their voices were a medley of happy chatter until they saw us. The chatter stopped, and they began to walk by us single file, silent, with their eyes downcast. We let them pass.

The back of the church lot was nothing more than a field of raggedy grass and a makeshift baseball diamond that doubled as a parking lot on Sunday mornings. A staircase at the back of the church led down to what must have been the church hall. Murph led the way down the stairs and made for the door handle. I stilled his hand and knocked. A tall woman opened the door. At the sight of us, her face crumpled for the tiniest fraction of a second and then stilled into an admirable stoicism. That beauty that her daughter wore with such command had its ghost in this woman's face. Although stern, even unforgiving, her expression gave the impression of having lived through many tragedies, and this was one more to be borne, and she would bear it with dignity.

"It's about your daughter, Mrs. Jackson," Murph said.

"I figured as much. Come in."

Velma had also inherited her mother's physical grace. She didn't rush to her desk, but picked up a stray pencil here and there and straightened a chair that some child had pushed out of the way in anticipation of school letting out. Once sitting at the lone desk, ramrod straight, she clasped her hands

CHAPTER TWENTY-SIX

together as if in prayer. We followed her and stood in front of her desk like errant kids who hadn't bothered to do their homework.

"Now," she said. "Tell me."

Murph introduced himself as a San Francisco police detective, giving her the barest of details, only that Velma had been murdered by "persons unknown" and that the police would do their best to apprehend her killer.

A raised eyebrow conveyed her skepticism.

"Were there drugs involved, Detective Murphy?"

The tone of her voice was so blunt that both of us blinked at her in surprise.

"We don't know," Murph admitted.

She turned to me. "Why are you here, Miss…"

"Laurent. Maggie Laurent. I'm a friend of Detective Murphy's. I demanded to come with him to tell you this awful news. I… I heard your daughter sing this week. It was like hearing God singing through her. Every note, so pure. I guess I came along to tell you that. That people stopped everything, even almost not breathing, to hear her sing. She… She was blessed. In a way," I finished lamely, embarrassed. This woman knew her daughter could sing.

Again, she shocked us by smiling at us.

"Yes, it was a miracle when she opened her mouth. She started singing here in our choir when she was four years old." Mrs. Jackson waved a hand in the direction of the church. "Then, at sixteen, someone gave her a glass of whiskey, and we lost her. To drink, to drugs, to whatever man would buy her a fix. In some ways, my prayers have been answered. She is free now."

We're told that death is the ultimate place of peace. Free from life's cares and woes. There was nothing peaceful about Velma's body lying on that couch with her blood pooling on the floor.

"Mrs. Jackson. I am sorry for your daughter's death. Just so you know, we went to your husband's place of work first. He denies her existence," said Murph.

She gave him a minute shake of the head and stood up to lead us to the door.

"We handle grief in different ways, Detective Murphy. His way is not my way, but who am I to judge? We need to bury my daughter and celebrate her final journey to the Lord. Where may we find her body?"

The calm in her voice was belied by the grip she had on the doorknob.

Murph stood there, unable to speak. She would have been taken to the city morgue, and he couldn't utter those words with any dignity or compassion.

"You are a man of faith, Detective Murphy?"

He nodded.

"And you, Miss Laurent?"

I realized then that I'd been fingering the cross around my neck during the entire interview.

"Yes."

"Then I ask both of you to say a prayer for my daughter. Now, where may I find her to bring her home?"

* * *

Murph and I sat in the inside cab on the ferry ride back to San Francisco. He'd handed me his handkerchief, and I cried into it nearly the length of the Bay. We drove back to St. Patrick's Church, where we knelt side-by-side to say our prayers.

Although convinced that Velma had killed Reade, I was willing to hand over Velma's soul, asking God for His divine mercy and to bless her mother and give solace to her father so that they might find some peace. Sometimes, the church's tendency to let everything fall into God's hands—that he would mete out justice and it wasn't our right to question Him—angered me. What right did God have to take my father from me when I was just a child? They didn't need doctors in heaven. When I questioned him about my father's death, Father O'Flaherty muttered the usual stock phrases: Oh, Maggie, we mustn't question God's master plan. Based on her reaction, I'd say that Mrs. Jackson didn't question God's plan to have her daughter's life end with an opium pipe in her hand and an ice pick in her chest. Yes, I had faith, but I also had questions.

The sun filtered through the stained-glass windows, bathing me in a warm

CHAPTER TWENTY-SIX

glow. I began the nine days of the Novena for the dead. Using the buttons on my coat as a makeshift rosary, I prayed for both Reade and Velma, unable to judge either of them. He was someone's son, and she was someone's daughter. I lit candles for both of them.

"Is it always that bad?" I asked Murph as we left the church together.

"No. It's the ones that go like this that kill me. Like they've lost hope and are waiting for someone like me to knock on their door."

Chapter Twenty-Seven

Murph drove me back to Nick's office. I had my hand on the car door handle when he said my name.

"Maggie, I'm going to ask you something."

I sat back and turned to face him.

"Lay off O'Malley."

Of all the things I thought he might say, that wasn't one of them.

"Not likely. Did you see Nick's face? When he stops using the world as his punching bag, I'll—"

"I'm asking you in all charity. Lay off of him."

Charity is a big gun in Catholicism. It shut me up like he knew it would.

"He's got something riding him, and sometimes it gets too much."

That wasn't enough for me.

"Lots of people do. They don't go around beating the daylights out of their wives on Saturday night after hitting the bars all day. Or stand on people's front porches without an ounce of civility, making demands he knows he doesn't have any right to make. He's a bully, Murph. I told Doyle this and I'm going to say it to you as well. Someday, and I think it's going to be soon, he'll go too far. He'll hit the wrong person, and that will be his career. I don't know why you always cover for him."

He had no answer for that, just clutched the steering wheel like it was a lifesaver and stared down Montgomery Street. I waited and was about to get out of his car when he said, "Please. For the love of God, please."

That expression is often tossed around but I knew he meant every single word. That if I loved God...

CHAPTER TWENTY-SEVEN

I wanted to counter, "Will you ask the same of him?" but I knew Murph wouldn't because O'Malley wouldn't respond to a plea like that.

Love of God. I took a deep breath.

"I'll try. Take care, Murph," and slammed the door in my wake.

I locked the office door and sat behind Nick's desk in the dark. Where was I, case-wise? Philip would sail out with the tide in less than two days unless I could prove he'd had his father killed. I doubt that Velma would have gunned down Reade unless it was on Junior's say-so, but with Velma dead, that would be damn hard to prove. Nailing Junior for his father's death by hire was a much more likely option. If they matched the bullet that killed Washington Senior with the bullet that killed Reade, then Doyle would be free to sweat Junior something fierce.

Assuming Velma was good for the Reade murder—the fur coat seemed evidence enough—I was still missing the person who committed Washington's murder. It seemed logical that the person who'd killed Washington had also killed Velma, but damn if I could connect the dots there. The antipathy between father and son provided motive enough for Phil to hire a button man to bump off his father. Plus, he stood to gain financially. But I had a difficult time seeing Philip ice-picking his girlfriend to death; it was far too gruesome. There was total rage behind her murder. I'd pegged Philip as more calculating than anything else. He might leave her on the dock or even turn her over to Doyle to take the heat off himself, but stabbing her repeatedly? It didn't play for me.

Then who killed her? Was it a dope deal gone wrong, and her murder a message to Junior: pay up or else you'll get it, too? And Washington? Was it nothing more than a random robbery gone wrong? My mind began turning somersaults, trying to make sense of it all, and ended up with nothing but a throbbing headache.

I needed to call Ma before I did anything else.

"Ma—"

Before I could continue, she interrupted me. "How are you feeling?"

"Great," I lied. The less she knew about Velma's death, the better. "May I bring Catherine back to the house and have her stay for a few days? The docs are releasing her tomorrow morning."

More omissions followed. Like the part where Doyle thought there might be a hit out on her, or that an arsonist had nearly burnt both of us to a crisp, or that we were now looking at three murders, which would have been upped to five murders if the person who'd set fire to the boat had been successful.

I was between a rock and a hard spot. If I told Ma that Catherine was being targeted for murder, then I was putting the entire household at risk. But if I told my mother all the details about the fire, she'd still insist that Catherine stay, but she'd chain me to the dining room table and never let me out of her sight. I had to trust Doyle that he had a couple of cops watching the house night and day. At the first opportunity, I'd tell Al what was going on. He'd put up a fuss, but I don't think he'd rat me out to Ma. Also, Nick might be down, but it wasn't for the count. Both Nick and Al had mean left hooks.

"Of course. Catherine seems like a nice girl. Al can sleep on the sofa."

"Perfect. I gotta—"

"Are you coming home for dinner?"

By the tone of her voice, nothing would have mollified her unless I had a date. Which I did, as soon as I called Charlie's answering service and left him a message to meet me at the Pig 'n Whistle at six.

"Not tonight. I have a date. With Charlie. The reporter." That wasn't a lie, but it wasn't exactly the truth.

"Oh. That's nice," she said in a voice that implied it wasn't nice at all. Reporters didn't cut it as future sons-in-law. Plus, he wasn't Catholic. A total no-go in my mother's book.

"We're meeting at the Pig 'n Whistle, Ma. He likes their chicken pot pie. It's not a proposal of marriage. Don't worry. I'll call you tomorrow." I hung up.

Although she adored Nick, my mother considered being his secretary as nothing more than a placeholder until I met a nice Catholic boy and got married. When I was small, she'd bring the box holding her wedding dress down from the top shelf in her closet and place it on her bed. Unfolding

CHAPTER TWENTY-SEVEN

several layers of tissue paper, she'd come to the dress, lift it out of its box, and hold it in her hands like it was sacred. She'd stand in front of her mirror, pinning the dress to her shoulders and remembering her wedding day, I guess. Then, she'd have me stand on her bed, hold it up to my shoulders, and whisper, "You'll make a beautiful bride." It was something only the two of us could share.

I'd never wear that dress. By ten years old, I was taller than her by a head, and by eighteen, I towered over her. My arms were much longer than hers, and the years of golf and swimming had bulked up my shoulders. Even though I was as skinny as a lamp pole, I'd never be able to zip that dress closed. Also, I wasn't a looker by any stretch of the imagination.

But that wasn't the real issue.

Working for Nick introduced me to the world of thieves, hustlers, two-timing dames, bunko artists, gunsels, adulterers, and murderers. I found each one of them fascinating. I hadn't met anyone yet who was worth trading my ringside seat in Nick's world for domestic bliss. I'm not saying never, but I'm saying not now.

I grabbed an old newsboy cap that had been hanging on the coat rack ever since I'd started working for Nick. It must have belonged to him, but I never saw him wear it. Although a bit large, it would do. I tucked it in the space between my shirt and the back of my pants and pulled down the back of my cardigan for good measure. I took the kerchief from around my neck, tied it over my hair, and went looking for a barbershop. I had just enough time to get a haircut, visit Catherine, and, if I were lucky, waylay Janie Morris, the secretary at the law firm, when she got off work.

Three barber shops turned me down before I found one that would cut my hair as short as a boy's. This shop fronted Bush Street, right on the border between Chinatown and downtown. The aroma of bread baking wafted through the shop, reminding me I hadn't eaten lunch. If this barber refused me, then I'd cut it myself. I was running out of time.

"What youse want to do that for, Miss?"

He did not approve. The old Italian barber stood there frowning at me, his hairy arms resting on a considerable pot belly. The frown accentuated his jaw, which had the puckered look of someone missing most of their molars. Short and bald, like many Italian men, he made up for the lack up top with a mustache as bushy as an otter's pelt. Waxed and shaped, it must've been his pride and joy. In his youth, I'd bet he'd been diminutive and attractive in that dark Latin way; he still had remnants of the doe-eyed charmer he'd once been.

"I was in a fire, and my hair got singed. I want to cut it off and start fresh." All true, but it wasn't why I wanted my hair cut. I took off the kerchief and pointed to my hair, singed around the edges.

He narrowed his eyes. "What fire?"

Fires have always been front-page news. But since the earthquake and subsequent fire had gutted the downtown and the Mission, anything bigger than a lit match gets huge headlines.

"The one last night at the St. Francis Yacht Club."

He came closer to me and sniffed at my head, lifting a few strands with a fat finger.

"You?" He pointed at me.

I nodded.

He picked up his shears and, with the pointed end, motioned toward the cross around my neck. "The Mother Mary protects her daughters. You one lucky girl. Sit."

While the sharp clipping sound of his scissors maneuvered all around my head, I kept my eyes glued to a bad rendering of the Madonna and Child torn out of a magazine and put into a cheap frame.

When he'd finished, he proclaimed, "Basta!"

My reflection in the mirror showed a slim-hipped young man in a pair of dungarees and a white shirt, with a touch of the feminine he'd outgrow in a couple of years. I'd never given much truck to my femininity—valuing my swing more than I did my form—but to have it stripped from me... My hair had softened the strong jaw, the distinctly Gallic nose, and my high forehead. Without my hair to complement their color, my normally dark brown eyes looked preternaturally too large for my skull. The only part of my face that hadn't morphed into caricature was my mouth. Wide and full,

CHAPTER TWENTY-SEVEN

it was my best feature. I had never realized how French I looked. No trace of the bog here.

This is what I'd wanted, but it was all I could do not to burst into tears. I paid the barber with shaking hands.

He patted me on the back.

"It will grow back, Miss. It will grow back."

Chapter Twenty-Eight

My hands were shaking so badly, that it was several minutes before I could retie my scarf over my head and thread the buttons of my cardigan through the buttonholes. Finally, I told myself to buck up; it was only hair.

I took the "D" streetcar out from Geary to Van Ness and got off at the Presidio Parkway. It was a short walk from there to Letterman Hospital. I needed to talk to Catherine about what she remembered from the previous night. Probably nothing, she was so doped up, but I had to make sure.

She was sitting up in bed, staring out the window, the only patient in this small ward. Crumpled-up tissues littered the bedclothes, and her eyes were that scratchy pink when you've been crying for a good while. Still, she smiled and sat up straighter when she saw me.

"How are your hands?" she asked.

I held them up for inspection.

"Tight but okay. You all right?"

I left it at that, ignoring the telltale signs of her weeping, and noticed she began to shove the used tissues under the bedclothes.

"Unfortunately, not tight, and like I've been beaten up. I think I'm getting a cold. Can you tell me what happened last night?"

I hesitated. There were some facts and a lot of guesswork. I didn't want to alarm her, but maybe I should alarm her so she'd watch her back.

"I think someone tried to kill you last night."

"Oh?" She didn't look the least bit surprised. Afraid, yes, surprised, no. That wouldn't have been my reaction.

CHAPTER TWENTY-EIGHT

"Someone doctored up your booze. This is a bit of a guess on my part, but I couldn't wake you up when the cabin began to catch on fire. And believe me, I tried."

"My jaw bears witness." The tone of her voice was light, but her eyes were dead serious. "I've told myself a million times I shouldn't smoke in the cabin. Maybe it was my cigarette."

I shook my head.

"Not unless your cigarette had feet and could wad up newspaper. I'd just fallen asleep when someone kicked in the door and threw a wad of lighted newspaper into the cabin. Then, they littered the deck with more fireballs. We're lucky we got out in time."

"You're sure?"

"Yes." There was no other way to say it.

Eventually, she said, "Lucky for me. Not so lucky for you. Your hair…" She raised her hand to touch the scarf.

I shrugged. "It's just hair. Do you remember anything?"

She shook her head. "We had lunch, went back to the boat, talked, read for a bit, and then I fell asleep. When I woke up, I was getting my stomach pumped."

"Who gets your uncle's shares in the bank if he dies?"

"Me. My uncle never married."

I sat there waiting for the shoe to drop.

"You think?" she said in a small voice.

"I don't know."

"He's my brother!" she protested.

I didn't say anything.

"We don't get along, and he's a creep, sure, but…"

That word hung in the air between us until I broke the silence.

"Are they springing you tomorrow?"

She nodded.

"How about you come to my house for a few days until you decide if you want to live at your uncle's house or somewhere else. My mother would love to have another mouth to feed. I'll come pick you up. Around ten?"

171

"The docs want to listen to my lungs one more time before releasing me. That would be good."

"I'll bring you some clothes. We're probably close to the same size."

"You're a brick, Maggie. See you tomorrow."

I wish I could say she looked a lot happier when I left than when I arrived, but that would be a lie.

I caught the streetcar back to Market Street. Just as I reached Powell Street, the clock at the Ferry Building chimed five-thirty. I might be able to catch Janie Morris as she was leaving the Flood Building. She might know something about Washington's original will. I didn't need more than five minutes of her time, and then I'd race to meet Charlie.

I got lucky. Janie had worked late and had just exited the Flood Building as I reached its entrance. She was walking slowly as she fished in her purse for something. With a big smile on her face, she pulled out a package of cigarettes and headed up Market Street until she ducked into the doorway of a greasy spoon with a closed sign on the door.

"Hey, Janie?" I acted all surprised to see her. She looked up, her face a little wary. "It's Maggie Laurent. We met the other day at the law office. Remember? Your supervisor threw me out on my caboose."

She eyed my scarf and then my face. "Oh, I remember you. Do you mind if I have a smoke? I've been dying for one all afternoon." She shook a package of cigarettes in my face. "Do you smoke?"

I liked this girl. On her salary, every cigarette must be precious, and yet she waved the cigarette pack around like there were plenty more where they came from. I doubted it.

"No, thanks, but nice of you to offer. Say, still no work?" It was the only opening I had.

"No, afraid not." She looked sad for me. "What happened to your hair?"

I needed to pick one story and stick with it. For the next two months, it'd be the first question on everyone's lips, and if I told them I'd lost my hair in a fire, it would only open the door to a zillion questions I didn't want to answer.

"I had to cut most of it off. Isn't it terrible? That'll teach me to try to

CHAPTER TWENTY-EIGHT

imitate Jean Harlow. The chemicals ate half my hair before I rinsed the peroxide off. Any more drama on Washington's will?"

All the exhaustion along the set of her shoulders disappeared. So excited, she even forgot about the cigarette in her fingers. Her blue eyes grew to the size of a half-dollar.

"Oh, my yes! I told you that Mr. Washington came stomping into the office demanding to see Mr. Hardesty about changing his will and then was murdered that very night. This morning—I swear, the man wasn't even cold in his grave—Mrs. W. came in with the son, waving a new will in the air, claiming the old will was void. The day after his funeral! I thought Mr. Hardesty was going to have a stroke!"

I'd forgotten that she was the type of girl who spoke in exclamation marks.

"Do you know who was the beneficiary in the first will?"

"Do I ever! I typed it up. It divided his estate into three equal bequests among his wife, his daughter, and that slimy son. But from what I gathered with all the hoopla, while he and Mr. Hardesty were eating dinner, Mr. Washington had added a hand-written addendum an hour before he was killed, removing his wife and son from the will! Office gossip is that Mr. Hardesty had the *maître d'* and the wine steward witness the codicil. And with all the shouting, I gather that the will Mrs. Washington was brandishing in Mr. Hardesty's face left all of Mr. Washington's simoleons to Mrs. Washington!"

"He cut out the son? Wasn't he upset?" I had to be careful. I couldn't ask too many questions, or she might get wise. I had a hard time seeing Junior standing there, letting his stepmother take the whole shebang.

"Him?" she snorted. "Hardly! He just stood there, cool as you please. Didn't make any fuss at all. Just smoked a bunch of cigarettes."

"You think..." I paused. How to put this? "I mean, being in public at his lawyer's office, you'd think he had the smarts to at least pretend he was upset at his father's death. I mean, if only for decency's sake."

Not that he'd shown even the smallest hint of being upset during that strange confrontation at Washington Senior's house. Of course, what does it matter if a nobody secretary notices your utter lack of affect?

"Yes, you would, the slimy so-and-so. He used to come in with his father a lot. Leered at the typists the whole time. He's the type of guy that you know is imagining what you'd look like without your clothes on."

"Oh, that's awful when that happens! I hate mashers!" I agreed and added a few exclamation marks of my own. "And the funeral only yesterday. I read about it in the papers!"

"I know! They marched in just as we unlocked the doors. This morning! Imagine! And her miles deep in widow's weeds!" From the scorn in her voice, there was no mistaking Janie's opinion of Mrs. Washington. "They sat in Mr. Hardesty's office for two whole hours, yelling and screaming. The entire typing pool heard them. Something about there being two wills."

While I was snooping through his apartment, Phil was lounging around Hardesty's law office after having made a deal with the stepmother.

"Was the sister there?"

"Tall. Blonde. Looks like the brother, but a woman?"

"That's her."

"Nope. Saw her for the first and last time when they settled her mother's estate."

How did Catherine fit into this? I wondered what Philip's cut would be. Enough to start a new life in Paris? More important, his presence at Hardesty's made him an unlikely suspect in Velma's murder. He wouldn't have had time to kill her and empty the office before the cops discovered her body.

"I don't mean to keep you, Janie. If I don't find work soon, may I stop by next week and see if there's something? Even a part-time job would be great."

"Sure bet, Maggie! I'll keep my ears open for you!"

When I reached the Pig 'n Whistle, the young woman at the podium asked if I were Miss Margaret Laurent. I acknowledged I was. Mr. Stein sent his regrets, but he would have to postpone dinner until tomorrow night. I thanked her and left the restaurant. I wasn't too disappointed. I could go home, have dinner, placate Ma, see how Nick was doing, and grab some clothes for Catherine.

CHAPTER TWENTY-EIGHT

The "N Judah" streetcar was packed, and I had to stand the whole way. As we lurched from stop to stop, I couldn't help but admit to myself that I was out of my depth here. Up until now, the Moore Detective Agency largely dealt with insurance swindles, divorce beefs, the occasional political debacle, and the minor criminal underclass of the City who plied their grift rain or shine. Murder was usually limited to a bank heist gone bad. This was different, and despite my boasts to my family, I wasn't sure I'd get to the bottom of all this without Nick's help. But I had to solve this if I ever hoped to have a chance at ditching that typewriter once and for all.

I began reviewing the whereabouts of the most obvious suspects in the Washington, Reade, and Jackson murders. Velma had killed Reade, but what did this have to do with Washington? I was beginning to think that the Washington killing was a separate job, maybe peripherally linked, but how wasn't obvious. Say, the widow mistakenly thought she'd benefit if Washington were plugged, but why not wait and pull her usual M.O.? Feed him digitalis until his heart gave out. If she were guilty of having him killed, something must have happened to push her over the edge. She couldn't wait. That forged will told me that she was desperate enough to try to hoodwink Hardesty, not realizing that Washington had beaten her to the punch with that codicil.

Until now, I couldn't completely discount the possibility that Washington's death had been due to a random robbery. When they waylaid me at my front door, the cops must have searched his pockets and found the receipt in his pocket. Shoving a gun in my face would have had me handing over my purse pronto. I agreed with Murphy. A thief would have demanded his wallet and then fled the scene as soon as Washington handed it over. There was no reason to kill Washington. It was a pretty bold move to kill someone right outside the Pacific Union Club, which was a high-class neighborhood and not the usual stomping grounds for your common thug with a gun. Increasingly, it was looking like a targeted hit. Mrs. Widow couldn't wait for him to pop off from an engineered heart attack. She needed him dead and fast before he changed his will. The joke's on her.

By the time I reached home, my head ached with all these thoughts crashing around in my brain as I tried to make sense of it. So ecstatic to see me, Ma served me double helpings of everything. She didn't even give me too much grief about my hair, accepting my lie that I only cut off those bits singed by the fire.

"Hey, Herman," I said around a mouthful of peach pie, "Can Al borrow your cab tomorrow morning while you nap after your shift with Nick? I need to pick up Catherine Washington from Letterman and bring her back to our house. They're releasing her tomorrow morning. She's going to stay here for a few days until she decides where she wants to live since her boat is lying on the bottom of the Bay."

"Sure, Miss."

Herman was a brick. If I asked him to swim the shark-infested waters to Alcatraz and bring back an inmate, he'd do it.

I turned to Al. "Pick me up at nine-thirty?"

On our way to the Presidio, I'd tell him about what had happened at the yacht club.

"You bet!"

If the sound of his voice were any indication, the thought of seeing Catherine Washington again would have him doing cartwheels down the hallway. My appearance at dinner had mollified my mother enough that she didn't make much of a fuss when I asked Herman to drive me to Nick's place to spend the night.

Things were happening. I felt it in my bones. I scrounged through Nick's closet and found an army-issued pea coat in a navy so dark it might as well have been black. It hung on me, and the sleeves were too long, but it was dark and warm; I'd need that warmth tomorrow night. If the fog were as thick as it was tonight, it would hide the moon. Where I was going, I'd need that cover. I found a flashlight in one of the drawers in the kitchen. I flicked it on. The light was strong. I shoved it into the inside pocket of the pea coat and hung it on the back of the door.

I used to wonder at the change in Nick's face when a case began to pop wide open: his eyes would narrow, giving them a feral slant, like a cat about to pounce on a mouse, and he radiated an energy that at the time I didn't

CHAPTER TWENTY-EIGHT

understand. But I'd always been on the sidelines, taking notes, answering phones, and lying to clients, always wondering what made that shine in his eyes, that nervous grin. Now that I was in the thick of it, I got it.

And I liked it.

When Nick got back to the office, I'd ask him to hire another secretary and have him show me the ropes. I never wanted to sit in front of a typewriter ever again. I needed to solve this case to prove to him I was worthy of being his partner. Between Al, Ma, Herman, Dickie Vance, and me, we'd get him back on his feet and back to the business of being the best gumshoe on the West Coast.

Chapter Twenty-Nine

Even though it was after midnight before I fell asleep, I was up at six, raring to go. I washed my face, and to appear more like myself, I put on some lipstick, which only made me look more cartoonish. I scrubbed my lips clean with Nick's rough soap and planned to avoid mirrors for a couple of months. I tucked the tiny bit of hair I had left under my scarf and tied it under my chin. The scarf didn't hide much, but I hoped it hid enough so people with manners would ignore that I'd just chopped off ninety percent of my hair. A quick breakfast of ham and eggs, followed by a gallon of coffee at the greasy spoon down the block, and I was ready for Al to pick me up.

I hadn't been standing on the stoop for more than a couple of minutes before Al tore down the block, at least fifteen minutes early.

"Hold your horses, Mister," I said after I'd climbed in. "If Herman's cab gets a ticket, he'll get in trouble, not you."

"Yeah, you're right." He pulled away from the curb at a snail's pace. "Your hair looks terrible."

"Thanks for the memo. Do you want to continue to harp on my hair or hear what happened yesterday?"

I didn't want to tell him because he'd get all big brother-ish on me, but if the Washington case was about to blow, he needed to make sure that nothing happened to Ma or Catherine. I hadn't been able to connect the threads, but it didn't take a genius to figure out that these three murders were somehow related. He didn't say anything when I told him about finding the gun at Junior's place, but he exploded when I told him about Velma meeting that

CHAPTER TWENTY-NINE

ice pick.

"Maggie! What in the name of all that is holy are you doing? Breaking into apartments, discovering dead bodies everywhere, I mean—"

I knew he'd go all crazy like this. I interrupted him.

"I didn't break into Washington's apartment. The door wasn't locked. And finding Velma just happened."

"And Reade?"

"No need to be snide, Al. Would you rather that Catherine found her dead uncle by herself?" I didn't wait for an answer. "I've got everything under control. That's why we need to pick up Catherine. She's in the middle of this. I'm not going to do anything stupid. Doyle's got a couple of buttons watching the house, but I need you on your toes. No one is going to hurt me. I'm a nobody. The fire wasn't meant for me. It was meant for her. Got it? Please don't tell Ma. Okay?"

He gave me a short nod, but he wasn't happy.

Once we reached Letterman, I asked Al to wait in the car. I'd bring Catherine down. With a spare set of clothes under my arm, I found the ward where I'd stayed the night before last. The front desk was manned by an older nurse wearing pince-nez, whose bun was so severe it was a wonder she could move her head. She reminded me of the nuns who'd taught me in school: big on piety, skimpy on humanity.

"Hello, I'm Margaret Laurent. I'm here to pick up Miss Washington. I assume Mr. Doyle called to tell you I was coming?"

She looked up from the chart in her hand and sized me up in one glance. The nuns used to do that, too, and their brows would furrow as if anticipating trouble. They were seldom wrong.

"Yes, I spoke to Mr. Doyle myself. Unfortunately, Miss Washington has already checked out," said the nurse, her shoulders quivering with disapproval.

I stared down the row of empty hospital beds, now all starched sheets and scratchy wool blankets made up with impeccable hospital corners. No Catherine.

"This morning? What time?" My neck seized up with an ugly foreboding.

The nurse blushed. "Well, it's a little unclear."

Unclear? She either checked out or she didn't.

"What do you mean by unclear?"

The temperature in the room dropped by about forty degrees. I half expected it to start snowing.

"She asked to use the phone right before dinner. Naturally, we complied with her request. Later, I noticed that she had disappeared."

"Disappeared," I repeated. "Have you searched the grounds? Maybe she's suffering from some brain thing?"

"She did not suffer a brain thing, as you called it," said the nurse, throwing a bunch more arrogance my way in a move to deflect any hint of negligence on their end. Doyle would not be pleased. "We searched the grounds the second we realized she was missing. We found her hospital gown and a blanket thrown in the bushes at a back entrance to the base." She sniffed with yet more disapproval.

"What time did she ask to use the phone?"

"Five o'clock."

"When—"

She cut me off. Dots of embarrassment flushed both cheeks. "Someone tripped the fire alarm last night. Of course, the staff all rushed to get the non-ambulatory patients into wheelchairs or gurneys, and that was the last time anyone saw her." She lowered the pince-nez. "All according to protocol." She said "protocol" with the maximum amount of officiousness possible.

Catherine pulled the alarm, no doubt about it.

"Do you know when the fire alarm was pulled?"

"At seven-twenty p.m."

"She was your only patient?"

She nodded. "This is the female ward. You and she were the first patients I have had in months. I usually run the male wards. I am here waiting for Mr. Doyle or one of his emissaries. Frankly, Miss Laurent, I fail to see how this is any of your business."

I'd been taught by nuns. I was immune to any stare-down this woman

CHAPTER TWENTY-NINE

could throw my way, pince-nez or no. She was a rank amateur with her charts and her pince-nez. If you want to terrorize someone, go to the professional wearing a habit.

"It's Mr. Doyle's business. He sent me here personally." Her mouth puckered in response. "May I use your phone?"

While she debated my request, the foreboding now reached my neck and curled around one ear. I liked Catherine a lot, but she was mixed up in this in ways I didn't understand. I remembered that fear on her face. Did she escape because she was afraid they'd try again? But what could be safer than a hospital bed on a military base? Who did she call, and who picked her up? It made me ask once again: why was she at the speak the other night if she hated her brother? You'd think she'd put as many miles between them as possible. Even wearing that wig, the waiter knew who she was. He called her by name.

You can like someone, but not trust them. I liked Eileen Taylor, too.

"Ahem. The phone?"

A frown so deep it hit her jawline told me she was on the verge of saying no.

"To call Mr. Doyle? The District Attorney?" I pronounced every single "T" in "district attorney." I admit that I sounded miffed.

"As you wish." More sniffing.

She shoved the phone on her desk toward me. And sat there to monitor my phone call.

Doyle's secretary put me through right away. I was back in her good graces.

"Doyle, Maggie Laurent here. Why didn't you tell me Catherine Washington checked herself out already?"

I could hear the strike of a match as he lit a cigarette. I'd have to ask him one day if being around me had increased the number of smokes he went through in a day.

After a loud exhale, he said, "What are you talking about?"

"She's not at Letterman. Gone. I just arrived to take her to my house, and she's already checked out."

Silence and then he said, a wee bit peeved, "What do you mean she checked out? I talked to the hospital this morning."

"Bet they were still combing the grounds, looking for her. Looks bad when you lose a banking heiress on your watch." I ignored the salty "I beg your pardon!" in the background. "She took a powder sometime last night. Asked to use the phone around five p.m. I'm guessing she set up some sort of rendezvous. Someone tripped the fire alarm around seven-thirty, and in all the hubbub, she snuck off. They found her hospital gown and a blanket just inside the grounds."

More silence on the other end until Doyle said, "I'll send Murph out to interview the staff."

"Tell Murph the nurse here is a dead ringer for a nicer, but not that much nicer, Sister Hilda. He'll know who I'm talking about." The scars on my psyche from that fifth-grade class would never go away.

There was more silence, and then he said, "I'm going to increase the patrol at your house and station a beat cop on your front porch." Like me, Doyle had the heebie-jeebies about this case. "Do you think she's in on all of this?"

I wanted to say no, but I didn't.

"Yeah. How deep, I don't know, but deep enough."

Chapter Thirty

Al didn't even wait for me to close the car door before he began yammering at me. "Is she still sick? Why are they keeping her? We should demand that they transfer her to S.F. General. I mean, Letterman is a military hospital. I hope to God she's not—"

I threw the clothes in the back seat and held up a hand. "Stop. She must be feeling fine. She asked to use the phone around five. I think she set up a rendezvous because someone pulled the fire alarm after dinner. I can't prove it, but I'm betting she activated the alarm so she could skedaddle unawares. They found a blanket and a hospital gown near one of the exits."

He didn't say anything else, but his hands gripped the wheel, his knuckles white.

"She wasn't kidnapped, Al. Someone picked her up. She planned it."

His knuckles turned even whiter.

"You okay?"

He nodded. We both knew he was lying.

"Drop me off at Nick's office, would you? And tell Ma I'm meeting Charlie again for dinner and spending the night at Nick's."

"She won't like it."

"No, she won't. If you can, soft-shoe Catherine's disappearance. Otherwise, she'll worry. I'm sure she's okay, Al. She wouldn't go with someone she didn't trust." I gave his shoulder a squeeze, which he ignored.

He was silent the rest of the drive and didn't even bother to say "good night" before I hopped out of the car.

I hope I never fall in love.

I spent the rest of the day in the morgue of *The Call-Bulletin*, a newspaper that had been gobbled up by bigger papers so many times that I had trouble remembering its current name. It was the paper you reached for when you wanted the dope on the latest business deals and when the newsstands were out of *The Examiner* or *The Chronicle*.

I needed to widen my net. See who in the business community might have had a reason to bump off Washington, other than his family. If Dickie knew about Commerce Bank's pending bankruptcy, then all the major bankers did as well. Combing through ten years of the business section line by line made it clear to me that Washington might have been high on the social ladder, but he wasn't considered a major player as far as the monied types were concerned. His shipping line wasn't among the prominent players operating out of the port like the United States Line, which had been originally made up of ships confiscated during the war. The stock for Commerce Bank did middling well, but it's not the place I'd put my money. They dealt primarily with mortgages, which might explain why it was going to go bankrupt in the aftermath of the crash. Washington needed a lot of capital he didn't have to stay in business until real estate regained its value. Based on Dickie's opinion, he didn't have the smarts or the capital to weather the crash, which didn't make him worthy of murder in terms of his business acumen. I was back to square one.

Charlie was waiting for me in front of the Pig 'n Whistle, slouched against the large plate-glass window.

"Sorry, I'm late," I apologized, a bit winded after my jog down Market Street.

"No sweat. I just got here," he lied. He must have smoked a couple of cigs while waiting for me because I smelled the smoke off of him. He didn't say anything about my hair, which, in some ways, was worse. Like the elephant on the sidewalk.

I began to walk toward the door to the restaurant when he hooked his arm through mine and began walking me down Market.

"I got somewhere else in mind," he said and gave me a wink. "I need to apologize for standing you up yesterday. Something came up on the paper."

CHAPTER THIRTY

"Don't be silly. It was fine." I kept up with him but wasn't sure where we were going.

"I wanna take you someplace special," he assured me. "Someplace nice."

"Oh, Charlie, you don't have to take me anywhere spiffy," I protested. "I love the food at the Pig 'n Whistle."

I slowed down, intending to turn around.

He stopped and gave my chin an affectionate twist with his free hand.

"You've had a tough couple of days. Hey, let me treat you. I want to."

I was starving, but I also didn't want to give Charlie any false expectations, which him treating me to a nice meal would do. I liked him okay, but I didn't *like* like him. Not yet, anyway.

When he turned right onto Ellis, I stared at him. No, he couldn't be thinking...

Then he steered me inside John's Grill, and I was too shocked to protest. At Charlie's "Stein, party of two," the waiter led us to a table in the very back, where the fewest number of people could see us.

Once we were seated, I said in a low voice, "Charlie, I'm not dressed for a place like this. How can you possibly afford—"

He put his finger to his lips and then said, "Shush. I got a bonus for that story about the Reade murder. And I heard through the grapevine that it was you who put a bug in Doyle's ear about Reade being left-handed, so maybe not a suicide after all. Smart girl," he cooed.

I know he thought he was being kind and wonderful and magnanimous, but I wanted to crawl underneath the table and hide. You don't walk into a restaurant like this wearing this stupid scarf because you've cut off your hair, a pair of dungarees, a cardigan over five years old, and scuffed loafers that hadn't been shined in a month of Sundays. I kept staring at the tablecloth, praying for God to make me disappear.

"Not so smart," I managed to get out without a stammer. I felt rather than saw a shadow to the side of me and realized it was the waiter waiting to take our drinks order.

"I'll have a," he coughed twice, "lemonade," and the lady will have tea?" He looked at me for confirmation. I kept my head down as I nodded. "Tea, please."

We sat there in silence for a few minutes until he said, "I'm sorry. I'd hoped this would wow you. I'm kinda sweet on you if you haven't noticed."

Yeah, I'd noticed. Hard not to. But I didn't want to think about that now. Everyone would be staring at me. If the dungarees weren't bad enough, I wasn't wearing a proper hat and no gloves.

"No one is looking at you. Not a single person. Except me," he said in a light voice, which made it a thousand times worse.

I managed to cobble together: "It's all right. A nice thought."

"Here's your tea, and, boy, do I need my lemonade," he joked.

"It's all right," I insisted and slowly raised my head. He was right. No one was looking at me, laughing or pointing. The diners were far more interested in their food than me.

I'd never eaten at a restaurant with no prices on the menu. I chose the chowder and a small salad. Charlie ordered a steak. That would set him back a few clams.

"Anything happen yesterday or today that I should know about?"

I started laughing. He raised an eyebrow because it wasn't a carefree guffaw but strained and a little hysterical. Because what hadn't happened would be more accurate.

Chapter Thirty-One

When I got to the part about seeing Velma with that ice pick in her chest, he stopped eating and placed a hand over mine.

"I'm sorry you had to see that."

I lowered my head and swallowed a few times. After a minute or two, I looked up and faced him with clear eyes.

"It was pretty grim," I admitted and then said a small prayer for her soul as I crossed myself. "I'm surprised it didn't make the afternoon papers."

"Embargo. She was just a junkie who worked in a speak. They're a dime a dozen. Not news. And we can't print it because then we'd have to publicize that Washington owned the speak and that they were living together."

I didn't bother to hide my anger. "Please. The embargo has nothing to do with saving Washington's reputation. Half the town are members of that speak. The mayor and police chief didn't want their favorite watering hole exposed. Both of those men should be ashamed of themselves. She wasn't just a side piece! She was the most amazing singer I've ever heard. Lots of people like their pipe, and lots of people like their hooch." I stared at his coffee cup. "Let's not cast those particular stones, Mr. Stein."

"Hey, calm down," he admonished. "I agree with you. An amazing singer. But I don't make the rules. Take it up with the mayor."

As if I could. "Don't patronize me, Charlie."

He blinked a couple of times and held up his hands in surrender. "I'm sorry."

We sat there for a few minutes in silence, me pushing the last of my pecan pie around my plate and Charlie drinking his "lemonade" in a rush and ordering another. I should have said something like, "Point?" I didn't, but I sure thought it.

Finally, he said, "I'm sorry. It must have been horrible, and I don't mean to say that her death wasn't tragic. I wish I'd been there for you."

"For the story, you mean," I snapped.

"Noooooo," he countered and put a hand over one of mine. "For you. Like I said, I couldn't file anything even if I wanted to."

Nick has always advised me to hold back something so that you'll have something to play later. Never let anyone see all your cards. I didn't tell Charlie that I'd been to Washington's apartment twice. I told him that when I arrived at the apartment, the front door was ajar. I called out hello but didn't get an answer, and worried, I pushed the door open and saw Velma dancing with the ice pick. I didn't say anything about Washington cleaning out the apartment as a prelude to him and Velma sailing to France. Nor did I say anything about wheedling information about the original will from Janie or the scene in Hardesty's office with the widow and the son.

"Why did you go to Washington's apartment in the first place?"

"To tell Junior that his sister was in the hospital. I thought he should know. Nobody else seemed to care." I tilted my chin up in defiance and pulled my hand away. I counted to ten, still angry about his cavalier comments about Velma's death, counted to ten again and swallowed my anger.

"You're a good person, Maggie Laurent," he said, but not in an admiring tone, but more thoughtful and half to himself.

"You run around with some pretty cynical people if letting someone know their relative is in the hospital is considered halo-worthy. Anyway, Doyle was all hopped up about Catherine Washington not being by herself, so Al and I went to Letterman to take her back to my house. When we got there, she'd checked herself out already."

"What?" His eyebrows hit his hairline.

"Yeah, I thought Doyle was going to have kittens. Catherine escaped from the hospital by pulling the fire alarm last night and skipping out in the confusion. As near as we can figure, she met someone at the back gate. They found a blanket and her hospital gown in the bushes."

CHAPTER THIRTY-ONE

As he lowered the coffee cup, I noticed what large hands he had. His hand engulfed the cup. "Wait a minute. Was Doyle planning on parking the Washington dame at your house because he was worried about her safety? Does Doyle think that fire was deliberately set?"

"He sure does because it was deliberately set. I told you. Someone ignited a bunch of newspapers, kicked in the door to the cabin, and tossed them in. I saw it with my own eyes."

Charlie finished off his drink and motioned the waiter for another.

"Could you identify who it was?"

"Nope. It was too smoky, but it was definitely a guy. It would take some strength to stave in that cabin door. Phil Washington certainly has motive. I'm assuming that if Catherine dies, he inherits her shares in the bank. He had plenty of time to sabotage the boat and then hightail it back to the speak in time to escort Velma to the stage."

Charlie sat very still, staring off into space, the hand that had been clutching the cup now slack on the tablecloth. I sat there for an uncomfortable couple of minutes and then said, "Charlie?"

He snapped his fingers and faced me. "Sorry." He gave a nervous laugh. "Does Catherine have an idea who did it?"

"Not a clue. I saw her yesterday afternoon, just to see how she was doing, and she can't remember a thing from the time she fell asleep in the boat until they were pumping her stomach at the hospital. By the time I got to Letterman this morning to take her back to my house, she'd taken a powder. After her father's funeral, we had a late lunch at the yacht club, and she was pounding them back the whole time. There's no way to prove it, but I'm speculating that someone snuck on the boat and doctored up her booze. Had she finished her drink in the boat, she'd have overdosed. As it was, all that alcohol at lunch made her sleepy, and she didn't finish her drink."

"Are you sure? Maybe she'd had too many."

"Charlie, you saw her. She was almost comatose. Would you be passed out on three martinis and four sips of whiskey?"

"No," he admitted. "Who do you think she called?"

I shrugged. "No idea."

"Do you think that Junior is good for Velma's murder?"

I'd deliberately withheld my knowledge of the scene in Hardesty's office with the widow and her stepson playing the not-so-grieving relatives of the deceased. This gave Junior a solid alibi for Velma's murder. Not even Clarence Darrow would be able to shake that alibi. I didn't want to get Janie in trouble.

"No, and neither does Catherine. When I hinted that he might be responsible, she denied it. I got a sense that even though she knows he's a first-class louse, she doesn't think he's capable of murder. There's a shadow person in this whole mess. Washington gets killed, but his entire family, except his brother-in-law Reade, has an alibi for the night of his murder. The entire family is attending his brother-in-law's funeral at the time Reade is killed. Now Velma is iced, and the most obvious suspect is Junior, except all these murders must be linked, and he's got an alibi for both his father's and his uncle's murders." I threw up my hands in frustration. "Who's number four, Charlie? I've been wracking my brains for the last week trying to figure out who it is."

At some point, the mayor's office would have to reveal Velma as Reade's killer. Had Reade been a nobody, it wouldn't even get a one-sentence notice next to the announcements about the latest murders in Chinatown, if that. But Reade wasn't a nobody. They'd have to comment on it, and it would have to be soon, or Reade's rich neighbors would start hiring private armies to protect their ill-gotten wealth from roving bands of killers terrorizing Pacific Heights.

"You need to be more careful, Maggie." He cupped my cheek as he said this, his palm cold from the ice in his drink. I smelled the citrus of his aftershave as he leaned over the table toward me, and for one second, I thought he was going to kiss me.

"You sound like my brother. I'm small fry. No one is going to be interested in me," I insisted, moving away from his hand and fussing with the buttons on my cardigan. "Shall we go?" I said and then smiled so it didn't look like I didn't want him touching me. But I didn't want him touching me. I was still mad about his dismissive attitude when talking about Velma, and I had this

CHAPTER THIRTY-ONE

gut feeling that if it were down to me and the scoop, the scoop would win every time.

"You're smart small fry," he warned. "That makes you dangerous." He finished his drink and signaled for the bill.

Charlie walked me back to Nick's place on Post. I steered our conversation away from the case. I can't say I didn't trust him, but I also can't say I did. He seemed to like me a lot more than I liked him. But I wasn't sure if this was genuine interest, or if he saw this case and my involvement in it as a means of building his rep in this town. I asked him a bunch of questions instead. How did he like living out here? Did he miss New York? Yeah, he missed New York. Had he had a chance to drive up and down the coast? The area around Big Sur was amazing. Not yet. He'd just gotten the car, so when he had a day off, he'd take up my suggestion, hinting that maybe he and I could drive down to Carmel together. I ignored that. We reached Nick's place, and he walked me up to the front door of the apartment building. He waited until I got out my key before he leaned over to give me a peck on the cheek and then stepped back a foot.

"Is that allowed?" he said and grinned.

"Sure," I replied in an equally breezy tone. "Thanks for dinner. It was swell."

"You're welcome. Look, Maggie. Back there in the restaurant, I meant what I said. I'm falling for you, and I don't want you to get hurt. This is getting ugly. We now have three murders." He held up his hand to show me three fingers like I couldn't count. "Why don't you let the police handle it from here?"

Aside from the fact they were doing a lousy job of it, I had no intention of walking away from this case. I had a couple of hours before the sun went down, and I needed to get down to the docks.

"I'll be careful, I promise. Talk to you tomorrow?" I began to walk up the steps, hoping he'd take the hint.

"Sure," he called after me. "Lunch tomorrow? Noon?"

I waved a hand, neither a yes nor a no. It all depended on what happened tonight.

Once inside Nick's apartment, I phoned Dickie. His mother answered the phone and screamed at me, "He's not here!" and then hung up on me.

Given his gang of Powell Street Irregulars, Dickie must know about the codicil to Washington's will. Nothing happened in the hotels along the cable car line that he didn't know thirty minutes after it happened. But did he know about Mrs. W's fake will?

I called back and asked for the front desk.

"May I leave a message for Mr. Vance in Suite 895? 'New will ginned up but before dinner at PUC. Hard luck to them.' Can you repeat that back to me?"

It was subtle and anonymous, but I trusted Dickie would know whom I was talking about, and if not, I'd waylay him at lunch tomorrow.

Chapter Thirty-Two

I changed my clothes. Fortunately, I was tall and slender, and most of Nick's clothes fit me. More or less. I ruined a pair of expensive white-calf tennis shoes by blackening them up with some shoe polish I found in Nick's closet. I'd saved for weeks to buy those shoes. Darn it. But they had crepe soles to muffle the sound of my footsteps, and if I had to run, they would be the best bet. I studied myself in the mirror. With the flat cap over my hair, a dark sweater under the pea coat that hid what little figure I had, a pair of Nick's dark trousers cinched tight with one of his belts, and a black wool scarf wrapped halfway around my face, I looked like a teenage boy who hadn't grown into his shoulders yet.

I shoved the flashlight, a packet of matches, the key to the apartment, and a small penknife filched from Nick's dresser into my pockets. I had one foot across the threshold when the phone rang. I had half a mind to ignore it, but what if Nick wanted to talk to me? I pulled down the scarf from my mouth.

"Hello."

"Maggie, it's your mother."

My hand tightened on the receiver.

"Hey, Ma, what's—"

"You come home right now, young lady. Al's told me what's been going on, and I'm not going to have you gallivanting all over San Francisco. I want you—"

I didn't let her finish her sentence. I didn't even hesitate for a second before replying, "I'm not coming home just yet. I'm working this case until Nick gets better and that's flat."

"Margaret, listen to—"

"No, Ma. I'll come home when I'm done."

I hung up and waited. Sure enough, the phone rang again.

"Maggie, you need—"

Al. As I knew it would be.

"You need to mind your own business. I told you I was handling things. Why'd you have to be such a rat?"

"You don't know—"

I hung up a second time and didn't wait this time for the third phone call. The phone began to ring again as I made my way to the staircase to the street.

I was so tired of people telling me what to do. Ma, Al, and now Charlie. This was my chance to get out from behind that desk and typewriter. To use the smarts God gave me. I might find a fella one day, and maybe we'll buy a house near Ma and Al and raise a family just like she had, but I hadn't found him yet. And until I did, I liked being front and center and not in the background, hearing about it all secondhand or after the fact. I wanted to be there while things were popping.

Maggie, you can't do that. Maggie, stop that. Maggie, good girls don't do those sorts of things. I'd heard that all my young life. I didn't want to hear it anymore. I was a good girl. I said my prayers and confessed my sins every week. I hadn't missed a Sunday mass in years. And I honestly didn't think God saw me trying to solve this case as a sin. I guess my definition of what good girls did and what they didn't was different from most people's. The only ones who might agree with me were, ironically, Nick Moore and Dickie Vance. I was an adult, and I planned on ignoring all those "you can't's" for as long as I could get away with it.

La Chanteuse had already docked by the time I arrived at Pier 29. The dockhands had begun unloading her, taking advantage of the summer light. I stood in the shadow of the warehouse, watching the men shift as much of her load as possible until it got too dark to work. The cargo was being hauled into the large warehouse through double doors tall and wide enough for a large truck to pull in. A smaller door was next to it, so you didn't have

CHAPTER THIRTY-TWO

to winch open the double doors to get into the warehouse. A couple of bulls patrolling the docks came up to me, asking me what I was doing hanging around.

I pointed to the ship and said in a gruff voice with a fake Irish accent. "Waiting for me Da. He's working that ship." They left me alone after that.

Most of the crew were French. I listened to the chatter of the men working the load, only understanding half of what was said. Fortunately, I was bilingual because of my father, but dinnertime conversations at the Laurent house had been limited to topics like the newest French bakery over on Geary, as opposed to which brothels had the best whores. The rest of the back-and-forth seemed to be dockyard slang so base, I considered it a blessing I didn't understand much.

Suddenly, the fog came in, fast and thick, the type of damp fog where you can't see more than four feet in front of you. Within a minute, your face and hair are so wet it's like you dunked your head into a bucket of water. In weather like this, you double-check that you closed the curtains tight and triple-check the locks on all the doors and windows because who knows what's out there. Men drink too much, and their wives brace themselves for the inevitable black eye. Children huddle in their beds, their feet cold, but they're too afraid to cross the room to get a pair of socks because their dresser is against a window and faces all that wet, gray dark. Cars hit the barflies as they weave in the crosswalks at closing time. And it seems like the only sound in the city is the sad moaning of the foghorns.

The foreman blew a whistle and locked up the warehouse, and the dockhands knocked off for the night. I waited until it was fully dark before sliding out from the shadows to check if the smaller door was unlocked. Not that I thought it would be, but I had to make sure. No dice. Locked up tight, as I suspected. Then I ran across the Embarcadero to the front of the speak. By that time, the fog had surrounded everything like a shroud, and the visibility had decreased even more. I couldn't have asked for better weather. I shrank into Nick's pea coat, grateful for the thick weave.

The cops had nailed a slab of wood over the front door of the speak that they'd busted open while investigating Velma's murder. I wouldn't be able to get in that way. The front door to the apartment had been similarly boarded up. Fortunately, the windows next to the door of the speak had been left untouched. Plan C. Walking quickly to the corner, I looked left and then right. All clear. It would be sheer madness to drive in this pea soup, but I didn't count on that. I shoved my elbow into a pane of glass closest to the latch. The first and second times I tried, it didn't work, but then I gave it some muscle. The bright sound of glass shattering sounded to me like it was being broadcast all over the docks, and I poised myself on the balls of my feet in case I'd have to hoof it. I waited for five minutes. Aside from the inevitable foghorn, it seemed all clear. I undid the lock, hoisted up the sash, and climbed in.

I turned on the flashlight but doused most of the light with the flat of my hand. The office looked roughly the same as the night Al and I had crashed the speak, except the one lone desk had had all its drawers removed and tossed on the floor. The cops had either scooped up all the contents or the drawers had been empty, probably the latter. I took each step down to the speak as slowly as I could, being careful not to make a sound. My fears were groundless. The secret door hung off its hinges, and the room was empty except for a few random chairs scattered around the room. Even the pint-size piano had been moved out. I peeked into the room with the Employees Only sign above it. It turned out to be Velma's dressing room. As disordered as the apartment upstairs, used pots of makeup and tubes of lipstick vied for space on her dressing table among the tumblers half-filled with whiskey and used coffee cups. Dresses had been thrown in one corner, her shoes in another.

As I expected, the other door in the room contained the staircase that opened onto the kitchen of their apartment. Velma and Philip could have entered the speak from that door, but where was the drama in that? Not half as exciting as making a grand entrance on Washington's arm, walking through the room in that languid, sexy saunter, and greeting her fans with the occasional nod of the head and a sultry smile. It also explained why we never saw the two of them exit the speak that night. After the floor show, they'd take this staircase up to their place.

CHAPTER THIRTY-TWO

No one in the neighborhood had seen Junior loading boxes into a truck out front; there must be a secret way out of this joint. The more I thought about it, the more I realized he didn't have time to burn all that paper. He must have carted some of it out of the apartment. I wasted an hour going over every single inch of wall. Nothing. I stood on a nice Persian rug running the length of the bar behind it, hoping I'd get some perspective. Seemed stupid. Wouldn't it be ruined if... Jeepers! What an idiot.

They'd nailed the rug to the floor. A hammer and a fresh box of nails sat next to a stack of glass tumblers. It took some tugging, but eventually, I brought up enough nails to shove the rug up against the bar to reveal a trapdoor right in the middle where the barkeep would stand. Of course, they'd need an escape hatch in the unlikely event of a raid. If the cops had found it, they wouldn't have bothered to nail the rug back to the floor.

The trapdoor was well-oiled. I didn't raise even the hint of a sweat as I pulled it open to reveal a short ladder leading to a tunnel that must connect to the warehouse across the street. I debated closing it behind me, but then realized, why bother? I couldn't pull the rug over the trapdoor to conceal my tracks. Plus, I wanted a clear line of escape.

Water had seeped in at certain points along the length of the tunnel, and I found myself trudging through freezing seawater deep enough to cover my ankles. Ruined shoes were the least of my worries. I'd have to bathe my feet in bleach when I got home. I didn't need the flashlight. A string of lightbulbs hung from the ceiling of the tunnel, and I could see pinpoints of light that went on forever. Rats the size of small dogs scurried in front of me, squealing in terror as I sloshed along this makeshift corridor. It seemed a million miles long, even though, rationally, I knew it was only as long as the traffic lanes overhead.

The smell of damp and decay was so overpowering that several times I had to push a hand against my stomach to hold back the heaves. I kept walking, my eyes straight ahead, praying for the sight of another trapdoor. As I neared the end of the tunnel, the rats that had fled ahead of me did an about-face and rushed back toward me, crowding against my trouser legs as they tumbled over one another in a frantic bid to escape. I bit my lips to keep from screaming.

Finally, I reached the end. If the trapdoor on the other side was locked, I'd probably go full bughouse nuts as there was no way I'd be able to do that walk back to the speak. I pushed. The door went up easily and without a sound. The rats must have smelled the fresh air because droves of them scurried up the ladder to flee into the warehouse. I stood on the small ladder breathing in and out, trying to ignore the rats rushing by me while cocking an ear for any sounds. All clear. I climbed to the top of the ladder, eased myself onto the floor, closed the trapdoor, and parked myself in a dark corner as far away from the entrance to the warehouse as possible. I waited. I had a hunch something was going to happen tonight, and my hunches often turned up aces. I'd been wrong about Eileen Taylor, but so had everyone else. Even Nick.

I sat there in a light doze for God knows how long when the screech of the double doors being pulled back woke me up. The hum of an engine filled the room as a car backed into the warehouse. The shadowy light of a flashlight raked my side of the hangar, and I flattened myself against the wall and crouched down. When the flashlight dimmed to a faint glow, I eased my head around a stack of boxes.

Helen Washington manned a flashlight while her butler and Junior loaded boxes into a yellow convertible. That had to be Catherine's car. How did they come by her car? My stomach lurched with fear. Where was she? After filling the trunk, they began to fill the back and passenger seats. A fourth person stood back in the shadows, revealed by the red glow of a cigarette as this person dragged on the butt. Was this my fourth suspect? The one who'd killed Washington and had murdered Velma. The person who was the key to all of this. The one who didn't need an alibi.

"Hand me the next one, Philip," the butler demanded in his Oxbridge drawl. He'd abandoned the silk pajamas for a tailored suit. If I ignored the black braid stark against the white of his shirt, I would have assumed he was a well-bred English gentleman.

I didn't so much hear it as sense it. Someone opened the trapdoor to the tunnel and was climbing out. The rats made a rustling noise as more of

CHAPTER THIRTY-TWO

them escaped into the warehouse.

Helen Washington screeched, "What's that sound?"

The butler replied in a brusque tone, "Helen, do pipe down. It's only rats." This wasn't the submissive voice of a servant. She screamed again, as one must have scampered over her shoe in a mad dash for the dock.

"Helen, shut up," ordered the butler. Definitely not the voice of a servant. "If you keep screaming like this, the police are going to discover us."

The person who'd crawled out of the trapdoor began to make their way toward me. I could only make out the faintest shadow of a body. After easing the trapdoor shut so it wouldn't make a sound when they closed it, they began to make a silent beeline for the very wall I'd plastered myself against, cutting off my escape route.

Given the size of the warehouse and with the flashlight trained on the car, it was impossible to see them, but we're animals at heart. Just as I'd sensed their presence, they'd sensed mine. They stopped. By my reckoning, we stood only about six feet apart. I slowed my breath to something like three breaths a minute and reached for the penknife in the pocket of Nick's coat. That tiny movement gave away my location. Suddenly, they were on me and had me pinned in their arms. I knew immediately it was a man. He was too bulky and strong to be a woman. He covered my mouth with his hand, wrapped one arm around my torso so tight I couldn't breathe, and then corralled my legs between his own. Then he removed his hand from my mouth and began to choke me with a hand that felt like it was the size of Golden Gate Park.

"Who are you, and what in the hell are you doing here?" he whispered in my ear. I smelled lime and knew the voice.

Around the vise crushing my windpipe, I managed to whisper, "Charlie?"

Chapter Thirty-Three

His grip slackened, but he still held me. The hand that had threatened to choke me to death slid down to my collarbone and rested there at the base of my throat. Both of us struggled to control our breathing. It was several minutes before my heartbeat stopped racing, threatening to burst through my ribcage.

"Shh," he whispered. As if I needed reminding. He let go of me only to grope for my hand and pull me forward. We skulked our way behind a stack of boxes to watch what was going on without being seen.

"Okay, that's the last one. Jesus, I need a drink," said Philip Washington.

"Stop your whining, Philip." Although the butler said it in a quiet voice—I had to strain to hear what was being said—there was no mistaking the threat behind it. "You have lost the luxury of complaining. Someone will place that floozy of yours at Reade's house, and now we're all looking at the hangman's noose. We need to keep calm and then sail out in two days. You and your whore might have jeopardized everything. Was that your idea or hers?"

Philip's face hardened, and he reared up on the balls of his feet to lunge at the butler.

"Do not even think about it," said the butler. The flashlight caught the gleam of a knife in his hand. "I will cut you into ribbons before you even have a chance to scream."

Philip came down on his feet, and his shoulders relaxed. He pulled out his cigarette case and lit one with the lighter that looked like a twin to Catherine's lighter. Come to think of it, it might even have been Catherine's lighter. The yellow of the flashlight bathed the three of them and the car in

CHAPTER THIRTY-THREE

a surrealistic spotlight, as the rest of the warehouse faded slowly into the blackness. The fourth man in the shadows must have finished his cigarette because I couldn't see the red glow of the butt end anymore.

"Wai-Ling, you're looking at the gallows. And maybe you as well." Philip pointed at Helen. "I had nothing to do with my father's death. Neither of you can say the same."

"As if you shed one single tear, Philip," said Helen. "Calm down. We'll sail out of here with no one the wiser. I've left Hardesty instructions to sell the house and sort out the will. Our solicitor in London will handle the rest. Once in Hong Kong, we'll lie low for a bit."

Philip spat on the floor. Both Charlie and I jumped a little.

"As if I'd ever touch you again," he snarled.

She went for him and slapped him across the face so hard it would have left most men reeling. It said to me that he half expected it, and it wasn't the first time she'd hauled off and smacked him. He reared back his fist and would have decked her if Wai-Ling hadn't moved toward Philip at an astonishing speed and pushed a knife against his neck.

"Think again," said Wai-Ling in a calm voice. "Whatever she dishes out, you will take it. Do you understand?"

Philip flinched as the blade of the knife bit into his neck. Even in this dim light, I could see a trickle of blood darken the collar of his shirt.

Helen then grabbed Philip by the tie and brought his mouth to hers. He didn't fight her but stood there as she mauled his lips and then bit down hard enough to draw blood. "You are mine, and don't you forget it." Then she pushed him away and stood back to admire her handiwork as the blood from his torn lip ran down his chin.

She might have won that round, but based on the look of hatred on Philip's face, it was the last round she was going to win.

"Why'd you kill her, Helen?"

She laughed. If anyone ever asked me what evil would sound like if it laughed, I'd point to Helen Washington.

"As if I would sully myself. She was trash, pure trash."

"Enough. All of you shut up," said the smoker and stepped into the light from the flashlight.

It was Catherine Washington. I flinched. Charlie brought his hand up to my mouth to stifle any noise I might make. In that cool voice of hers, smooth, cultured, and unruffled, she said, "I'd like to get some sleep at some point tonight. Meet me at Shan-Shan's."

"I'll make the drop. Give me the keys, Catherine," said Wai-Ling.

"Like hell, I will. It's my car, and it's my drop." There wasn't even the tiniest quiver in her voice. "Shan-Shan trusts me. Unlike you. Cutting him out of the last shipment didn't go over very well. I'm making the drop."

"Use the Stockton Street entrance," ordered Wai-Ling.

She ignored him. Before Catherine climbed into the car, she slipped a handkerchief into Philip's breast pocket, drove forward onto the dock, and drove away.

Not another word was spoken as the three of them made their way out of the warehouse and closed the double doors. Charlie and I stood there for another few minutes and then slipped out through the smaller door onto the dock and into the night.

Charlie's car was parked a couple of blocks away. We didn't speak until we'd put several blocks between ourselves and the waterfront, and then he pulled over and stopped the engine.

"What in the hell were you doing there?" he yelled.

"I could say the same!" I shot back, with an equal amount of volume.

"I might have killed you back there!"

"Another second, and I would have sunk my teeth into your hand—like through your entire hand—and taken my chances with the Washingtons."

"I need a drink." He pulled a bottle out from under his seat and drank straight from the bottle, shuddering as the whiskey hit his system. He held up the bottle in a "want-some?" gesture. I shook my head. He took another couple of swigs.

When I'd calmed down enough to speak in a normal tone, I asked, "Charlie, what were you doing there?"

"To see if I could find anything at the speak that I could turn into a story. Someone had bashed in a windowpane, and I threw up the sash and entered

CHAPTER THIRTY-THREE

the building that way."

I didn't comment one way or the other.

"It'd been cleared out except for a few chairs. I figured one of the doors was the staircase leading to the apartment upstairs. I was about to check it out but saw the trapdoor hanging open that had been previously hidden by the carpet. I'm betting you opened it. Why were you there?"

Something niggled at me, trying to pry its way around the exhaustion, but every time I tried to nab it, it slithered away.

"*La Chanteuse* is another of Washington's businesses. I read in the newspaper that it would dock tonight and then leave in two days for Marseilles. The police are slow, but Doyle's smart. With Velma's murder, at some point, they'd have to search the warehouse. I figured there must be a hidden passage from the speak to the warehouse."

I kept mum about Junior and Velma planning to hightail it out of town and how Junior was clearing out the office. All that furniture and booze had to go somewhere since the neighbors hadn't seen any trucks or vans moving boxes out of the building. I had no intention of telling him that.

"Reade was a big wheel at one point in the city," I pointed out. "The mayor can't hide his murder under the rug. All the prime suspects were at Washington Senior's funeral except for Velma. It's common knowledge that Junior was sleeping with her. I heard it from both Dickie and Catherine. Who else is left but Velma?"

"Based on what we heard back there, she's good for it."

"And if there was something illegal on that ship, like an entire hull devoted to cases of alcohol, there's only so much they could ignore."

"Or confiscate."

"Yep."

"What do you think is in those boxes those three were hustling to get out of the warehouse?"

"Catherine was driving to Chinatown." I choked a bit on her name. I needed to think about the implications of her being in cahoots with the rest of them, but not now. My brain was mushy from exhaustion. "Opium? Dickie hinted to me that the speakeasy wasn't just pouring shots. And given

Junior's well-known drug habit, it makes sense."

"Makes a lot of sense. Do you think Washington Senior was in on this grift?"

"I don't know. Seems a little far-fetched. Tax or stock fraud? Sure. His high-class lawyers would save him from prison on those beefs, but smuggling booze or drugs? Another kettle of illegal fish. Hardesty wouldn't touch something like that with a ten-foot pole. Still, while all the big-money heavyweights loved to be a fourth at his bridge parties, they didn't seem to be itching to rub financial elbows with him. Catherine thought he was the anti-Midas. Everything he touched turned to dross. Maybe he was drug running, trying to keep the bank afloat."

We sat in his car, with him drinking and smoking, and me mentally running through a bunch of scenarios in how Catherine figured in all this until I began to shiver.

So beat I could barely form sentences, I said, "I'm freezing. Would you take me to Nick's place now? I'm tuckered out."

"Sure." He capped the bottle of booze, shoved it under his seat, and started up the engine.

I'd said enough that he'd have a million questions, none of which I had any intention of answering. The last of the adrenaline that had coursed through my body in the warehouse had finally leached out of my system, leaving me with all the energy of a rag doll.

We crossed town to Post Street in less than six minutes.

He walked me up to the front door of the apartment building.

"Night," I said.

"You owe me lunch," he teased.

"I'll have to take a rain check on that. The way I feel right now, I might sleep through dinnertime."

"Call my answering service when you wake up."

"Will do. Now get some shut-eye yourself." I shoved at his shoulder hard enough to make my point. No way was he coming up to Nick's apartment. I didn't wait to see him drive away. I was so tired even my eyelashes were yawning. For once, I took the elevator up to the third floor. Normally, I'm

CHAPTER THIRTY-THREE

too impatient and take the stairs. As I got out of the elevator, I saw Al lying asleep on the carpet in front of Nick's door.

I shook him awake and braced myself for the inevitable lecture.

"What are you doing here?" I demanded as I opened the door.

Al rubbed his eyes. Once fully awake, he glared at me.

"You need to call Ma. She's going nuts. What's that God-awful smell?" He pinched his nose shut.

"Charlie and I were playing in the surf near Fort Point." This was sort of true because, technically, the surf was sloshing into the tunnel. "Get in," I said and held the door open for him.

I dialed. It didn't even trill before she picked it up. She must have been hovering over the phone. "Margaret Mary Laurent. Where have you been? I've been calling and calling, and no answer. Listen to me, young lady—"

This was exactly why running the office from my house was a bust. She'd be standing over me constantly, interrogating me every time I put on my coat.

"Ma," I interrupted. "I was on a date with Charlie Stein. He took me to dinner at John's Grill, and from there, we drove to Fort Point to watch the tide come in. After that, we sat on benches near the Palace of the Legion of Honor and talked until about fifteen minutes ago. That's all. Nothing more."

She was silent for a bit and then said, "Is Albert there?"

I handed him the phone. "She wants to talk to you."

My body ached everywhere—even in places I didn't know existed—purely from the tension of that scene in the warehouse. Although what I needed was a scalding bath, it'd have to wait until morning. I had no hope my mother would ever understand my desire to become a detective, but maybe I could square it with Al.

Nick had an extra blanket in the closet, and I got that out and spread it on top of the bed. I rummaged in my suitcase for my dungarees. Once in the bathroom, I pulled off the trousers I'd borrowed from Nick, toed off my shoes and socks, put on my dungarees, scrubbed my feet with a washcloth, wrapped the shoes up in Nick's trousers, and threw them in the garbage can in the kitchen. I put the can outside the front door. There was no way any dry cleaner would be able to get the stink of dead rat and putrid seawater out of those pants. I'd have to buy him a new pair. Once that was done, I lay on top of the bed, fully clothed, punched the lone pillow into a big lump, and closed my eyes.

Not that I had a hope in hell of getting to sleep until Al and I had words, but I couldn't keep my eyes open any longer.

From the bedroom, I could hear Al's conversation with my mother: "Yes." "Okay." "I'll try." "No." "No." "You know what she's like." "About ten." "Yeah." "Good night, Ma."

When he entered the room, I said, "Turn out the light, will you?"

"Maggie—"

"My vocal cords work in the dark. Please turn out the light and get into bed. We can share the bed. You'll never get a cab at this time of night. I'm not sharing the pillow. Get a towel from the bathroom and roll it up if you want."

Finally, he turned out the light.

"Where were you tonight?"

"You heard me tell Ma. I was with Charlie." It wasn't exactly a lie.

"Until two in the morning?"

"Yes. I'm going to remind you, Albert William Laurent, that I'm an adult. I don't have a curfew, and I can take care of myself."

"Yeah, like you did on that boat?"

"Exactly like that. I saved Catherine's life!" I hoisted myself up on my elbow to look at him. The blinds had been pulled, but tonight's full moon had weaseled its way in through the slats just enough so I could make out his face in the dark. "She'd be dead but for me."

"Decent young women don't go around pretending to be gumshoes, Maggie. That's all I'm going to say."

"Good, because that might be your and Ma's definition of decent, but it's not mine. And for the record, if you'd been out on a date with that Katie O'Meara or anyone else, would Ma be waiting up for you, ready to blast you to hell and back because you came back late? You know she wouldn't."

"It's different with you."

CHAPTER THIRTY-THREE

"Why is it different with me?"

"Because it is. You're a girl," he insisted.

"Al. Listen to yourself. 'Cause it is. You're a girl,'" I mimicked in a snotty tone. "I'm finishing this case. Don't try to talk me out of it. You should know I'm thinking of asking Nick to make me his partner."

There, I said it.

"You're what?" he shouted.

"Keep it down," I demanded. "The walls in this apartment are paper thin. You heard me. I'm not going to go back to that typewriter if I can help it. And another thing. You loved being part of Catherine's orbit for just a little while. Sitting at a table in a speak, drinking expensive hooch, and lighting a cigarette for a beautiful woman wearing a mink coat. Don't tell me different. That's a bunch of window dressing. But what isn't, is that every day in that world is different. There isn't a lot of shouldn't do, must do, or can't do. You use your own moral compass. It hasn't steered me wrong yet."

"Yet," he said with a sneer.

"I'm going to sleep now."

"Do you know why I'm here?"

"To yell at me on Ma's behalf?"

"No, well, yeah, that too, but to tell you Nick's disappeared."

"What? You were supposed to be—"

"Snuck out when Ma was at bingo. Herman was taking a nap, and I was making dinner. When I checked on him, no Nick. He left a note on a pillow thanking me, Ma, and Herman, but with no clue as to where he went."

"He's probably staying at a hotel downtown," I replied.

"Or getting blotto down at the Hotel Utah."

"I'm not worried about him," I said in a calm voice.

And I wasn't. In my morning prayers today, I asked for Mother Mary's intervention on Nick's behalf, and the answer I got was that only he had control over his destiny. *Maggie, you can't stop him from drinking himself to death. You've given him the chance to have a choice. That's all you can do.* As hard as this was, I had to live with his choices.

"All that Ma has done for him, she did it for you, you know. And here you are—"

When we were kids, Al and I rarely fought. But when we did, it was no holds barred because both of us had inherited that Irish stubborn gene.

"I'm going to sleep. You can pile on more guilt in the morning."

I turned over and drew the blanket over my shoulder because if I didn't, I'd start hitting him. Were these my choices? Living Ma's life, raising a family, which has its rewards, but she found herself nearly helpless when her husband died, leaving her with two kids to support and feed. Or becoming like that witch at Hardesty's office, typing my way to become head witch, whose only pleasure in life is to berate the typing pool under my thumb for minor typos and wearing their skirts too short?

Chapter Thirty-Four

"I'm going home," Al said in my ear.

I needed another couple of hours more sleep before I'd feel even remotely human.

"Fine," I mumbled. "Give Ma a kiss for me."

"Not your damn errand boy, Maggie."

I pulled the blanket over my head. He slammed the door so hard on his way out, I thought it was a gunshot. I leaped out of bed and realized Al was just being petty. I raced to the door and shouted at his back, "Jerk!" and added, "Rat!" for good measure.

Now awake with no hope of going back to sleep, I made the bed, ran a bath, and soaked away my aches. I needed to dress, eat, and see Doyle, in that order. By the time I got dressed, it was midafternoon. I had ten cents in my purse, so I raided the safe at the office to pay for an early dinner and headed for the closest diner.

Once I'd worked my way through my third cup of coffee, my brain began to work again, and it worked in the direction of Catherine. Who'd picked her up from Letterman? Where was she staying? Why, after making it damn clear that she hated her brother, was she in some skullduggery operation with him? Based on the consensus that she hated him, I suppose no one would suspect her working with him, given his reputation as a hophead and a thief. Had they actively cultivated this alleged animosity? But why? Was the storied Washington wealth nothing more than fiction? A trust fund with enough money in it to buy a nice sailboat and a ton of books, but little else? According to Dickie, the bank was about to go bust, making her shares worthless.

She might have been lying about her relationship with her brother, but I'd bet my neck that her antipathy toward her stepmother was genuine. Had the smuggling scheme been going on for a while, something the twins concocted, given Philip's penchant for the pipe? Or given Helen Washington's contacts in Hong Kong, did she set up the whole operation in collaboration with Philip and his association with the opium dens in San Francisco? And what about Catherine? What if Catherine and Philip worked the grift, with no choice but to continue when Philip brought the stepmother in on the operation?

The only place that I could think of that she might have escaped to would be the Reade house.

I walked back to the apartment, yawning the whole way, and called the Reade house. The housekeeper answered the phone, and no, "Mrs. Washington and Mr. Philip picked up Miss Catherine this morning. Shall I tell her who called when she comes back?" I told her no; I'd call again.

Someone had tried to murder her. No shortage of suspects here. Philip might be at the top of the list, but Helen was running a close second. So why would she leave with them? Unless she was coerced. I needed to see Doyle. I also needed to lie down. Just thirty minutes of shut-eye…

I woke up to the loud ringing of the telephone. The discombobulated mental fog that always accompanies a long nap had me fumbling for the bedside lamp. Already dark outside; what time was it?

It would be Ma, and I didn't want to talk to her right now, which wasn't very dutiful of me. I'd add it to the list the next time I went to confession. The sins were piling up.

They hung up. Then tried again. And again. And again, breaking my resolve.

"Ma, I'm—"

"It's Helen Washington." All remnants of mental fog disappeared.

"Hello, Mrs. Washington."

"We have some unfinished business, you little busybody. Meet me at the speakeasy in an hour. Don't bring anyone with you and don't tell anyone

CHAPTER THIRTY-FOUR

you're coming here. Is that clear?"

"Yes, but how will I get in, and why this meeting?"

"The wood over the door to the upstairs apartment has been removed. There's a door in the kitchen that leads to a staircase down to the speak. You'll find out why when you get here."

A voice in the background shouted, "Maggie, don't come! It's a—"

There was a scream and then a dial tone.

I called the Doyle residence.

The nanny answered the phone. No, Mr. Doyle wasn't home. He and the missus were having dinner with the mayor. I asked for the telephone number, as this was an emergency. I got through right away, but the butler at the mayor's house fought me. No, he couldn't possibly disturb Mr. Doyle. They hadn't served the cognac yet.

"Look, you whisper in Mr. Doyle's ear that Maggie Laurent is on the phone. He'll want to speak to me."

"Miss, I'm sure—"

Lord, give me patience!

"If you don't get Mr. Doyle right now, I will call in a report that the mayor's house is on fire. In five minutes, twenty fire trucks will descend on the premises, and no one will be handing out snifters of booze until after midnight. Got it?"

He might have sworn at me under his breath and slammed the receiver down, causing me to jump, but Doyle picked up thirty seconds later.

"What's going on?"

"Meet me at the speak with a bunch of buttons as soon as possible. They've taken down the plywood from the apartment door. Access the speak from the kitchen. The case is breaking." I hung up before he could say anything.

I put on Nick's pea coat and curled my hand around the penknife. It might come in handy.

Chapter Thirty-Five

The cab dropped me off in front of the speak. The street was deserted except for two cars parked right in front: a black roadster and an equally sleek saloon car that I assume belonged to Helen Washington. I didn't see any sign of Doyle or any cops, which was a little worrisome, but then they'd stay hidden as much as possible, wouldn't they? I didn't bother to muffle my footsteps. First, because I wanted Doyle to know I was here if he'd arrived before me, and, second, if Doyle was just arriving with what I hoped was about four hundred cops, then all my noise might give them some cover.

Helen, the butler, and Philip didn't seem surprised to see me.

"I told you she'd come," said the butler.

"Maggie, run," Catherine said in a tight voice. She was standing behind the bar, with double black eyes rising. Whoever had hit her had struck her across the face and backhanded her for good measure.

"Miss Laurent. Welcome to this little family gathering. Our Catherine isn't cooperating, I'm afraid," said the butler in his perfect English. "We need some information from her. I'm very sad to say that she is not forthcoming. If I, say, cut off one of your fingers, or, say, put out one of your eyes, I imagine that she'll reconsider her current stance."

His calm voice, so much more terrifying than if he'd screamed these threats at the top of his lungs, was the sound of true psychopathy.

"If I tell you where the car is, you'll kill me. It's only because of her," Catherine pointed in my direction, "that I'm still alive."

She didn't make the drop at Shan-Shan's in Chinatown as they'd planned.

CHAPTER THIRTY-FIVE

She'd ditched the car somewhere and then taken a cab to her uncle's house. They lured me here as bait to force her to tell them where the car was located.

The manservant turned to look at Helen with an expression of extreme disapproval. "I told you that the fire was a stupid idea, Helen. It shone too much attention on the family." He turned back to face Catherine. "When you refused to play ball regarding the will, Catherine, we should have shot you. However, that's water under the bridge at this point. Philip, tie Miss Laurent to a chair. Use your tie and tie it very tight. If it hurts her a little... Oh well."

Philip grabbed my wrist, dragged me over to a chair near the wall, and shoved me back into it with such force it threatened to topple backward.

"Bitch, put your hands behind you," he ordered. I braced myself for the silk of his tie to cut into my wrists, but he didn't tie it very tight, and I had a lot of play with my wrists. He unbent the fingers of my fist and saw the penknife. I swear he smiled. He flipped open the knife and gently curled my fingers into a fist again. He leaned toward me and tilted his head so that Wai-Ling and Helen couldn't see his face.

"It's as loose as I can make it," he whispered. It was certainly loose enough for me to start sawing away at the silk. He stood up and gave Catherine a look—the sort of expression a brother gives his sister and a sister understands. He leaned over and pretended to check on his handiwork.

"Nice and tight," he said to Helen and the butler with a big smile. Catherine was too smart to react, but her shoulders eased a fraction. Philip had no intention of letting Wai-Ling kill either of us if he could help it.

I didn't question why he'd switched sides. I doubt he gave a tinker's damn about his father, but he'd loved Velma. Her death must have made him realize that any collaboration with these two would have him dead at some point soon, either by their hands or the hangman's noose.

"Wai-Ling, don't do this," begged Catherine in a small voice. "She has nothing to do with it."

"No, she doesn't, but you do. Unless you tell us where you stashed the car, I'm afraid Miss Laurent will not survive the night."

Catherine didn't reply because neither of us would survive the night, regardless.

Wai-Ling came up to me and with a hand so fast it was only a blur, he backhanded me with such force that the chair fell to the floor. I screamed. Oh my God, my cheek felt like someone had shoved a hot poker against it. Somehow, I managed to keep the penknife in my fist and elevated my head and neck enough that I didn't bash my head into the floor.

"Pick her up," he ordered Catherine.

Catherine came out from behind the bar, righted my chair. and scurried back to where she was originally standing. Right above the trapdoor.

He backhanded me on the other cheek. I screamed again. As much as I didn't want to give him the satisfaction that he'd hurt me, I needed all my concentration to keep that penknife in my fist. The chair fell over again from the force of his fist.

"Pick her up," he repeated. Like before, she obeyed him and scuttled behind the bar again. "Where's the car?"

She shook her head.

"Now, Catherine, since you are being so stubborn, I think that we need to move on to more persuasive measures. Helen, did you bring that gun I asked you to put in your handbag?"

Helen reached into her handbag and brought out a small ladylike pistol, but she held back from giving it to him. The grim expression on her face told me she wasn't happy with the way things were going.

"Do we have to—"

"Yes, sister dear. We do. Until Catherine cooperates and tells us where she stashed the car with all that precious cargo, we most certainly do."

Oh. The illegitimate half-brother. Her partner in crime. My fourth person.

"First off, I will shoot out your right kneecap." He came close enough to me that I smelled the pomade of his hair. Things began to click. He pressed the gun against my knee. "You won't be able to walk again, but there you are. Then your left kneecap, leaving you a total cripple. Next, one elbow and then the next. I doubt you'll be able to hold a spoon ever again. Next—"

"Stop!" screamed Catherine. "It's parked behind Grace Cathedral on Jones."

He removed the gun from my knee and stood back.

CHAPTER THIRTY-FIVE

"Are the boxes still there?"

She nodded.

"Good. Philip, you and Helen shall take our car to retrieve Catherine's car. I will deal with the Misses Washington and Laurent."

Catherine and I shared a glance. We both knew what that meant. She began to push back the carpet with her foot.

"Why did you kill my father?" demanded Catherine. She was giving me time to free my hands.

"He found out about me and Helen," Philip said in a deadpan voice. "She was indiscreet. Dad made a lot of noise about changing his will and getting a divorce, so these two decided to kill him."

"You don't know that," screeched Helen.

"That's exactly what happened," I said. "The day your father was killed, he marched into Hardesty's office screaming that he wanted to change his will right there and then, and drive down to Mexico the next day to get a divorce as soon as possible. Hardesty was out of town that day, but due to return that evening. They had dinner together that night at the Pacific Union Club. While they ate dinner, Hardesty wrote an addendum that Helen was to receive nothing because she was two-timing him with his own son." I turned to face her. "He cut you and Philip out entirely. Hardesty had it signed and witnessed by some of the staff at their club. You didn't realize that your husband had already gotten to Hardesty and made his demands known. Wai-Ling didn't get to Harold fast enough."

She flushed, an ugly, blotchy red that covered her whole face.

"You thought you'd waltz into Hardesty's office with the fake will and walk away with the goods, no one the wiser. No wonder there was a lot of screaming and yelling at Hardesty's office when you two turned up. Hardesty had the real will, and you had the ginned-up one."

They all froze. I had only a few more strands to slice through. The knife threatened to slip out of my hand, as it was sweating from both fear and exertion.

"How do you know all this?" asked Philip.

"I get around."

Ten seconds more, and I was free.

Philip turned toward Wai-Ling. "Did you have to kill him?"

The man shrugged. "I didn't see you shedding any tears at the time, my young man. You will get your share of the money once we liquidate the bank shares."

"Bank sh-shares?" Catherine started to laugh, an edge of hysteria in her laughter. "You must be joking. I was at the bank yesterday. It's a week from declaring bankruptcy. All those shares you thought were worth incinerating me for are worthless. And because Daddy was such a fool, he'd mortgaged both our house and Uncle Dill's to the hilt to prop up the bank. There's no money to be got from the sale of either house."

"Worthless?" Philip spoke like it was two words. Worth. Less.

"Yes," she confirmed. In a malicious voice, she added, "You'd better hide all your jewelry, Helen. The stockholders are going to demand they strip the house bare. I wouldn't be surprised if Daddy hadn't put liens on all that glitter of yours as well."

As if he hadn't heard a word of what Catherine had said, Philip muttered, "So you didn't kill Velma."

I don't think anyone took a single breath for at least twenty seconds.

Catherine stared at him like he was crazy. "Why would I kill Velma?" She pointed at Helen. "Her, I'd seriously consider, but Velma?"

Philip turned toward Helen.

"It was you. You stood there and plunged that ice pick into her over and over until—"

"No, Philip," I said quietly. "It was him." I nodded in the direction of Wai-Ling. "The pomade he wears on his hair. I smelled it when I returned to your apartment the second time. He'd been there."

They all stared at me.

"What were you doing at my place?"

"The first time I came to tell you about the fire and that Catherine was in the hospital. I knocked several times but didn't get an answer. The door was unlocked. I went in, thinking that maybe you were sleeping off a hangover. Velma was high as a kite, and her face was badly beaten. I asked for you, and

CHAPTER THIRTY-FIVE

she told me you'd gone to see Helen to get some money for your trip."

"What trip?" said Helen.

"It doesn't matter now," said Philip dully.

"What trip?" asked Wai-Ling in a much more menacing tone. He turned the gun on me and repeated, "You seem to know everything. What trip?"

"They had passage on *La Chanteuse*."

"You said you wanted money to buy a new car." The color in Helen's cheeks flared again, and her eyes narrowed.

Philip shrugged. "But I don't understand, Maggie. Why did you go back to my apartment the second time?"

"I found a gun underneath the sofa, next to her pipe. I thought it might have been the gun that smoked your father. I took a cab straight to the D.A., told him about the gun, and he sent some bulls over there to retrieve the gun. They found her body. Doyle had me come back to your apartment to see if anything had changed from before she was killed compared to after. The gun was gone by that point, but we both know it was the gun she used to kill Reade."

He didn't move.

"She'd stashed the money from your uncle's safe in the lining of her fur coat."

"Velma killed Uncle Dill? For the money in the safe? Philip, you absolute bastard!" screamed Catherine.

"It was an accident!" he shouted back. "He was supposed to have left for the funeral already. They fought for the gun, and it went off."

"That tramp!" Helen shrieked. "You were leaving me for her?"

Philip, Helen, and Wai-Ling began circling each other like jungle cats. The three of them were so intent on each other that they didn't even notice Catherine running over to me, grabbing my wrist, and dragging me behind the bar. She raised the trapdoor and began to climb down the ladder.

Time began to distort, moving forward at a glacial speed. It was like watching a movie in slow motion. Suddenly, Helen lunged for Philip with a small knife in her hand. She raised her fist to stab him, and he struck her. Before she had even reached the floor, Wai-Ling began to shoot. Helen screamed, "No!" as Wai-Ling emptied his gun. In a futile gesture, Philip Washington brought his hands up in surrender. As the bullets hit him, he started to fall backward, but not before red stains began to blossom on the white of his shirt. Helen caught him in her arms before he hit the floor.

Catherine stopped and made to go to him.

I grabbed her wrist and screamed, "Leave him. He's done for! Go!" As I pushed her again toward the trapdoor, I heard voices and several guns going off. I made for the trapdoor and pulled it closed behind me.

Catherine raced down the ladder, with me close behind her. Someone had either disabled the lights or had turned them off. "Catherine, take this." I handed her the flashlight. She charged ahead, running down the length of the tunnel. The squeal of the rats as she made her way to the warehouse filled my ears. As she moved farther and farther away, the weak beam of the flashlight left most of the tunnel in darkness. There was no way I'd walk that tunnel in the dark. I stopped at the bottom rung of the ladder and sat there, clutching its sides for some sort of comfort. At some point, someone opened the trapdoor.

"Come on, Maggie. I'm taking you home."

Murphy.

I shook my head. Then I realized that once she made it to the other side, the rats would swarm back this way, desperate for an exit. *Jesus, give me strength*, I prayed and uncurled my hands, a finger at a time. One foot on the rung, then the other foot, then another rung, then another, until I reached the top. Murph gave me a hand and pulled me up. I stood behind the bar, with my arms wrapped around me to stop the shivering, and trying to avoid the bar mirror reflecting Helen, Wai-Ling, and Philip and all that red. I thought the sounds of the shooting would never stop.

"Close the trapdoor, Murph, or the rats will overrun the speak."

After he'd secured the trapdoor, he placed his jacket around me. "Come on," he repeated. "Under orders."

I took several deep breaths and shook my head again.

"Not going home. Nick's place."

"Nerts to that. Let me take you home," he pleaded and placed a hand on

CHAPTER THIRTY-FIVE

my shoulder. "You shouldn't be here. This isn't no place for a lady."

"Little Miss Muffet all right? Doyle's asking." O'Malley sneered at me with a nearly spent cigarette dangling from his mouth.

"Christ, O'Malley," muttered Murph. "It's a bloodbath back there. Give her a break."

"I'm fine, O'Malley." I sneered right back at him, which jump-started my moxie. "Murph? Not my house. Take me to Nick's apartment. I'll be okay," I insisted.

I remembered how condescending Al had been. How in his mind, tonight's carnage would prove him and Ma right. In my mind, I'd handled it about as well as anyone could have.

"Like hell," said a different voice. "Murph, take her to my house. I'll phone Moira. Maggie's spending the night at my place. She can bunk with one of the kids." Doyle pointed a menacing finger at me. "No arguments."

We had a bit of a stare-down, stubborn Irish to stubborn Irish. Eventually, I conceded with a reluctant "Okay." Anywhere but home, where Ma and Al would lecture me for a solid week.

He came over to where I was standing and whispered in my ear, "Are you okay?"

"Yes," I whispered back.

I didn't look at the bodies sprawled on the floor as Murph led me out of the speak to the sidewalk. I sucked in the fresh air, clearing my nose of the sulfur smell left by the guns and matches as the cops lit one Lucky Strike after another. It was a clear night, no fog. The searchlight on Alcatraz skipped over the water. I hoped Catherine had made it out of the tunnel okay. The first clear night we'd had in ages wouldn't do her any favors.

Chapter Thirty-Six

The Doyles lived in Pacific Heights. Although not as grand as houses in Pacific Heights go, it was swanky enough. The years married to Doyle hadn't quite scrubbed away his wife's Irish accent. Like most Irishmen, he'd been dragged to the altar. She was younger than him, in her early thirties to his forty. Five kids in seven years had given her a plump, roundish figure not yet matronly, but headed there. She'd held on to her good looks, though. Doyle's secretary didn't have a snowball's chance in hell at getting him secondhand.

She didn't ask any questions, merely introduced herself and said, "I'll put you in with Mary. Seamus is younger, but he's a thrasher. Now, do you want anything to drink or eat?"

The thought of food made me gag. I shook my head.

"Let's get you to bed," she said and handed me a nightgown. She led me to a room at the top of a long staircase. The bedroom had bunk beds on either wall; the breathy sounds of sleeping children filled the room. She made room for me in the bottom bunk, gently moving her daughter to one side without waking her. I undressed, put on the nightgown, climbed into bed, and closed my eyes. I buried my nose in the girl's hair and fell asleep to the metronome of her in and out.

The sun was already high enough to be considered midmorning when I finally woke up, the house quiet.

I made my way down the staircase and found the kitchen. There was a note on the table. "Oatmeal's on the stove. Tea is in a canister in the cupboard to the right of the stove."

CHAPTER THIRTY-SIX

I was on my second cup of tea when Doyle came in.

"Just made tea. Want some oatmeal and a cuppa?" I pointed to the teapot.

He loosened his tie with a large sigh. Exhaustion made him look much older than he was. Or he was older, and ambition had made him appear younger.

"No oatmeal and the tea would be grand. Thanks," he said, his voice rough with fatigue. He grabbed a mug from the cupboard and handed it to me. After opening a window, he plopped down in a chair and lit a cigarette, blowing the first puff toward the open window. I raised my eyebrows in question.

"Moira will kill me if she catches me smoking in the house," he confessed.

"Your secret is safe with me. I hope she didn't feel like she had to leave the house because of me."

"Nah. During the summer, she spends most of her days at her mother's house out in the Aves. Your family is probably in the same parish. How are you doing?"

"Okay. Considering. Have you been up all night?" I handed him his tea. He pulled out a hip flask and added a healthy dollop of whiskey into his mug.

"Yes. I hope to catch some winks before the news conference at four." He paused. "I'd rather you didn't attend."

"I'm good with that."

"I'd also like to keep your name out of the papers."

That would make Ma happy.

"That's okay as well, but why?"

"You won't like it, but the mayor is crafting a story that the butler killed the Washington family for money. There's no speak and no dope smuggling."

People would buy it. There was a lot of animosity toward the Chinese. The influx of men coming home from war and who were looking for work saw the immigrants as taking jobs away from them. The crash would turn what was now animosity into hatred. Plus, by eliminating the existence of the speak, the mayor could sleep better at night. No one who'd frequented that speakeasy would say any different.

"Did Catherine escape?"

"Yeah. Even if we found her, we can't prosecute her because then we'd have to admit to the smuggling angle. I'm not putting much effort into tracking her down. She stole a boat down at the St. Francis Yacht Club and sailed away. We have a notice out to all the docks up and down the coast, but I understand she's a hell of a sailor. The owner would like his sailboat back. We'd probably let her walk if she tells us where the sailboat is anchored."

It didn't seem quite right, but I wasn't going to squawk. It wouldn't bring back all those people Helen Washington and her brother had killed, nor would the world mourn Philip Washington's death. This was where the fiction of Wai-Ling being Helen's butler worked against them. No one was going to care about a Chinese butler getting shot up by the police.

"So where were they killed if it wasn't at the speak?"

"In the office above the speak. The butler thought there was a safe full of dough for the shipping company."

"He did, did he? And Washington?"

"Simple robbery. What a tragedy. Doubt we will ever catch the guy."

"Who will, no doubt, be a communist. For heaven's sake, Doyle, no one is going to buy that story. Anyone who peeks in through the windows will see that the office is empty."

"We boarded up the windows. You broke that pane, didn't you?"

There didn't seem any harm in admitting it. "Yeah. Who killed the butler if it wasn't the police?"

He took several drags on his cigarette before replying. "Philip Washington before he died."

I rolled my eyes. "With the gun he wasn't carrying. If all of them are dead, how did you discover the bodies?"

"Someone reported gunshots," he said with a grim smile.

"You?"

"Could be."

"What about Reade?"

"The singer did it, of course. You saw the coat. I didn't tell you, but Reade had defensive wounds on his hands. I think he smacked her several times

CHAPTER THIRTY-SIX

as they wrestled over the gun. I heard Philip confessing that she'd gone to rob Reade's house, thinking he'd already left for the funeral. They fought. During their struggle, her gun went off, which killed him. She staged it to look like a suicide and fled."

I gave that scenario some thought. As an explanation for Velma's busted face, it made a lot more sense than Philip beating her up. "That works."

"The fur coat should be good enough for a judge." His voice was bored. He didn't care about a druggie torch singer. "The butler killed Velma. Huh. We never would have gotten him for that."

"Someone needs to tell Helen and Wai-Ling's mother."

"I'll hand that over to the governor's office, who will hand it over to the Feds." Another shrug.

"How long were you there on the staircase listening?" I brought my fingers up to my cheeks and pressed. Ouch. A glance in the hallway mirror had shown minor bruising and lots of red, like I'd gotten a bad sunburn. Fortunately, he hadn't blackened my eyes. "Did you see me get backhanded?"

He nodded.

"Gee, thanks, Doyle. At what point were you guys going to save me? When he'd shot both my kneecaps and crippled me for life?"

He yawned. "Keep your shirt on. We were hoping you'd get them talking. You did a good job. We wouldn't have let him hurt you."

"My jaw says differently."

"We also saw you working away with the penknife. What would you have done if he'd tried to shoot you in the kneecaps as he threatened?"

He sounded genuinely curious.

"Stab him. Just like he did to Velma." I wasn't kidding. "I knew he'd killed her when I smelled his pomade. I hadn't smelled it the first time I was there, but I sure did the second time. Once Helen found out about Junior and Velma, there was no way that she'd put up with that. Because, well... They were... Helen and Junior..." I blushed.

His mouth turned down in disgust. "Yeah, I heard. No wonder Washington Senior demanded a divorce."

I nodded. "The Reade murder made her a liability they couldn't afford.

They moved a bunch of boxes out of the warehouse to Catherine Washington's car just after *La Chanteuse* docked. She was making a drop in Chinatown, and, no, I don't know what was in the boxes."

"And you know this because?"

"I happened to be in the warehouse while they loaded up the car."

He took a slug directly from the bottle. "What else haven't you told me?"

"None of it happened, remember? Are you going to follow up on the drop in Chinatown? Catherine Washington said she was going to Shan Shan's."

"No, because none of it happened, but if it did, I'm assuming the boxes were filled with opium, given Junior's history. But it could have been booze. Anyway, Chinatown's off-limits. All the public needs to know is that Harold Washington was a victim of a robbery gone bad, the Chink killed Helen and Philip Washington, and the Jackson woman is good for Reade's murder. A neighbor reported someone fitting that description entering the Reade residence around nine on the morning of Washington's funeral. Jesus, these people," he whispered as an afterthought. He said it like he was talking to himself.

"Did you find the car?"

"Nope. Either she moved it, or it was stolen, or she drove to Chinatown to auction off the lot to finance her escape and then stole that sailboat. Depending on the wind, it'll take her about a week to reach Mexico."

Doyle finished his tea and then turned to me.

"Tell me what you know. All of it. I don't want to be blindsided at the press conference by some nosy reporter like that boyfriend of yours."

"He's not my boyfriend."

"Whatever. I want the whole thing, and I want it fast because if I don't get some sleep before this press conference, I'm going to keel over."

I took a deep breath.

"Helen Washington and her illegitimate half-brother, Wai-Ling, were born in Hong Kong to British diplomats. From the exchange last night, I gather he was head grifter. Posing as her butler, they targeted wealthy older men with bad hearts. Once she got enough scratch out of the marriages, they poisoned their marks with digitalis, lived high off the hog until the jack ran

CHAPTER THIRTY-SIX

out, and then looked for another patsy. I don't have proof of the poisoning angle, but it fits. Enter Harold Washington, victim number three…"

Chapter Thirty-Seven

Nick was waiting for me at the apartment when I returned from Doyle's house, standing by the window and smoking a cigarette, with his suitcase parked at his feet and his winter coat flung across the only chair. Now stripped of everything personal, the apartment already bore a forlorn emptiness. No ashtray, no pens or papers on the desk, no alarm clock, no dishes in the sink, and the hat rack empty of hats. The calendar near the front door was gone, and the astringent odor of bleach hung in the air.

"Hey, precious," he said in a steady voice. He hadn't regained any of the weight he'd lost while on his bender, but he looked okay. Not great, but okay. The black eyes from the beating looked worse, but I knew from experience they were healing. Most of the swelling had gone down, and he'd shaved that morning. The chin was pointier, and the cheeks had too much hollow to them, but my Nick was back.

"You heading off?" I said, with a jerk of my head in the direction of his suitcase.

"Heading to Chi-town. I'm taking the Overland Limited out of Oakland in—" he looked at his watch"—a couple of hours. Pinkerton's got a job for me."

"You didn't like working for them in the past," I reminded him.

He shrugged. "I need a new start. Can't stay here, Mags. You know that."

"Yeah, I do." I waited a couple of beats and then said, "I'll miss you."

I don't think I've ever seen Nick blush. I wasn't sure if it was from embarrassment or pleasure. Maybe a little of both.

CHAPTER THIRTY-SEVEN

"You need to go home. Your mother's worried sick about you." He didn't say it to chide me, just as fact.

"I know, but I'm not going home. I was going to suggest that you take me on as a partner. I don't want to type anymore."

He shook his head. "This is a nasty business, Maggie."

"I know that, too, but I don't care. I don't want to marry the boy next door, have five kids in five years, and spend my days doing laundry and cooking. Every day like the one before. I did okay with this case. I liked being in the thick of things, not on the periphery or the sidelines. I'm good at this stuff, Nick. I could be your partner. And while there are a lot of places I can't go to because I'm a woman, there are a lot of places you can't go because you're a man. Stay."

"You got me there," he admitted. "You got the smarts and the gumption to do this by your lonesome. Don't let anyone tell you differently." He refused to look at me as he pulled on the cigarette until he'd smoked it down and then threw the end into the kitchen sink. Without looking at me, he lit up another, the strike of the match the only sound in the room.

Eventually, he said, "You going to change the name?"

Nick was leaving. I took a deep breath and found a small smile from somewhere.

"That would be stupid. I want to keep your name for a while if that's okay with you. I don't plan on broadcasting you've left town. And if you find the Chicago winters too cold, there's still a place for you here."

His smile was sad. "I don't think so. Those days are gone. You think you can pull it off?"

"Yes."

The Nick Moore grin that I hadn't seen in months appeared; no teeth but lots of curve to his lips.

"You're giving me the Maggie Laurent chin of defiance. Hey, did someone rough you up last night?"

With one thumb, he tipped my chin up toward the window and the light to study my face.

"Nothing to write home about," I lied.

He balanced his cigarette on the end of the table and curled his thumb and forefinger around my chin to give it a tiny shake before letting go. "You're becoming a damn good liar, Miss Laurent."

"I went to Catholic school. Comes with the territory."

He barked out a deep laugh. After grabbing his hat, he doffed it toward me in an expression of admiration before placing it on his head at a jaunty angle. Any trepidation I had about him falling off the wagon again vanished.

"You've got plenty of spunk, which is half the battle in this business. I'll give you that for free. Darling, if you can make the agency work, more power to you. Partner with Dickie. He'll steer you right."

"I've already sent him a note. We're having lunch at John's Grill on Friday."

He chuckled, reached for his wallet, and pulled out some bills. "You've got it all figured out. You don't need me. Here's some dough to keep you in business for a while." He left the money on the kitchen table.

"No," I protested. "You'll need that money!" I picked up the bills and tried to shove them in his coat pocket. He batted my hand away.

"You need it more than I do. Is your mother okay with this scheme of yours?"

"No, and it's not a scheme."

"Al?"

"Nope. Would your landlady sublet your apartment to me? From a practical point of view, if I try to run the office from the Avenues, the cab fare alone will bankrupt me, and I can't afford a car right now."

He picked up what was left of his cigarette and inhaled deeply several times, studying me through the smoke. When he'd smoked it down to the end, the second cigarette followed the first.

"Those smokes are going to kill you."

"Sister, don't I know it. I'll talk to her right now. She'll jump at the chance to have a tenant who doesn't have gunsels roaming her hallways every week. Do you want me to give Harvey Cohen a call? You're going to need a lawyer to see how far you can push City Hall without them throwing the book at you. Your mother will hunt me down and kill me if you end up in a jail cell."

"I'll call him."

CHAPTER THIRTY-SEVEN

"Well, that's that," he murmured and picked up his suitcase. "I need to head off if I'm going to catch that train."

"Take care, Nick, and good luck. And if you want to come back…" My voice trailed off.

"I'll be in touch." He gave me a little salute and pulled the door shut behind him. The only thing left of him was the smoke from his cigarette.

I began to cry when I realized that I'd left his penknife on the floor of the speakeasy, and now I'd never have the chance to return it to him.

Chapter Thirty-Eight

I was sitting behind Nick's desk, figuring out which bills to pay and those that could wait a couple of weeks. I had to make Nick's money last as long as possible.

He knocked on the doorframe before crossing the threshold into my office. I'd left both the outer and inner doors to the office wide open in a futile attempt to dispel *eau de bourbon* emanating from the carpet in Nick's office. That was a mistake I wouldn't make again. Better to live with the smell of stale booze than be caught unawares. I'd talk to the maintenance guy about putting in a doorbell.

"Hey, Charlie. What's up?"

"Going back to New York. Hearst wants me back there. Came to say goodbye."

I hadn't seen him since the night at the warehouse. Although he looked a little rough around the edges, like he'd been hitting the "lemonade" too hard, he wore a new suit and hat. He must have been paid off before the shootout at the speakeasy.

"You driving? You have that nice new car. It'd be a shame to leave it behind. Although I've heard you don't need a car in New York." I swept the bills into the top drawer with one hand and grabbed the gun Nick kept there with the other. I'd never fired a gun in my life, but there's always a first time.

"Yeah, I'm driving across. Probably take me a week, give or take a day."

"Have a safe trip."

"I'm sorry this didn't work out," he said and waved his hand between us, all contrite and like he cared.

CHAPTER THIRTY-EIGHT

"Yep, a real shame."

"Maggie, what's wrong? I gotta go. When Hearst says jump, you jump."

My hand tightened on the gun.

"Jump away. Do you honestly think I'm upset because you're leaving?" He didn't bother to hide a cocky little grin. That tore it. "I guess it was too much to hope that you'd just slither off into the night like the lying bastard you are, but since you didn't, let's have a little chat."

I brought up the gun and pointed it at his chest. My hand didn't waver at all.

He straightened up out of a casual slouch and tilted forward very slightly on the balls of his feet.

"Put your hands up. Now. I'm not kidding. Up, buster."

"Maggie, what's going on? Have you lost your mind?"

Even though he was protesting, he still raised his hands. I suppose I should be grateful he had at least a smidgen of scruple. He might have easily killed me in the warehouse and left my body for the rats to feast on, except that I was still useful at that point. He might still have needed me for access to the Washingtons. Now that everyone was dead, it was time to skip town.

"Do you remember that conversation we had earlier about me being convinced a fourth person was also pulling the strings? It turned out I was right. It was Helen Washington's brother, Wai-Ling. What tripped me up was that there was a fifth person. You."

"Oh, come on," he scoffed. "Put that thing down before you hurt yourself."

"Not a chance. You played all of us. I'm just guessing, mind you, but I'm assuming you and Helen Washington knew each other in New York. Probably did nasty odd jobs for her now and then."

He blinked a couple of times. Bingo.

"Helen Washington originally hired you to keep an eye on Junior and the smuggling operation they had going on. She might have been sleeping with Junior, but she didn't trust him. She didn't trust you either, which is why she hired me. Grifters don't trust other grifters. Then you sold yourself to Junior, double-crossing Helen. Then, the triple cross. You sold yourself to Catherine. She called you from the hospital, which is why you couldn't have dinner with me. You picked her up from Letterman and drove her to the Reade house. Then you ratted out her location to Helen and Philip. The housekeeper told me that Philip and Helen had come to Reade's house, and the three of them drove away. No doubt Catherine had a gun pointed at her gut, a fool-proof way of getting her to rejoin them. I'm not sure how she plays in all of this, except that she and Junior concocted this nice little story they fed to everyone over the years whereby she hated Junior and Junior hated her, when all the while, the two were in cahoots. They even fooled Dickie Vance. Had Catherine and Philip been running this smuggling business all along, and then when Helen and Wai-Ling showed up, they took over the grift? Do you know?"

He didn't respond, but his mouth thinned.

"I've got to hand it to you, Charlie. Great footwork. Next came the quadruple cross when you sold yourself to me. Sadly, I didn't have any money, but I had other currency. Tagging along with me was like killing two birds with one stone. You'd get the inside scoop from me to wow your editors and then parlay what information you couldn't print to Helen, Junior, and Catherine. Triple the payoff."

"You're crazy," he said with a hiss, but his body tensed even more like he was going to risk lunging for me.

"Back on your heels right now, Charlie, or I'll shoot. Unfortunately for Junior, he and Velma fell in love and planned on escaping on *La Chanteuse* when it sailed for Marseilles. Junior wasn't above a little double-cross himself. Anyway, when Helen hired you to incinerate Catherine in her boat, you didn't know I was on board, too. And since I don't drink, I put a monkey wrench in your plan. I suspect that Catherine was jake with the smuggling operation, but she had no intention of being party to that fake will Helen was trying to peddle. She didn't trust Helen not to cut her out entirely. Plus, all those lovely bank shares that would go to Junior if she died. Neither Helen nor her brother knew the shares were worthless. How am I doing so far?"

"You bitch," he murmured, with a viciousness that made me tighten my grip on the gun.

CHAPTER THIRTY-EIGHT

"Initially I thought Helen's brother had set the fires, but I can't see him down there at the yacht club without raising a wind. The Chinese don't travel much outside of Chinatown unless they're domiciled at someone's house. He'd stick out like a bowling ball atop a snowdrift, even more so if someone saw him on the deck of the *Aurora* after he'd doctored Catherine's bottle of bourbon. That leaves you. More fancy footwork because you wouldn't have had much time to spike Catherine's booze between the funeral, the reception, hightailing it to Reade's place, and then writing your copy. Or maybe you did it before picking me up for the funeral service. It wouldn't take more than a minute to switch out her usual bottle for a doctored one. Did you wait for her to leave for the funeral and then make the switch? Was it worth the clams you got for risking an attempted murder charge?"

"Have you been hitting some of Nick's hooch?"

My finger tightened on the trigger.

"Why not Junior? He could have done it. You said so yourself." He began to lower his right hand, hoping to grab his hat to throw at me.

"Raise them higher, boyo. I did initially, but it doesn't wash. Sure, he was a slimy so-and-so, but he'd never sign off on killing his sister. All the killing was down to Helen and her brother. And you."

"You've got it all figured out, don't you, Miss Smarty Pants?"

"Keep your hands high, or I'll blow a hole in your chest. A lot of this is guesswork, I admit. Except there are two things that damn you, Charlie, even if my take is a bunch of hooey. I got a call from Ezra Abramson this morning, the Pinkerton op out of New York. Your buddy. Remember?"

The color drained out of his face, and sweat blanketed his forehead.

"Lie number one. When I called the Pinkerton office in Boston and spoke to Ryan about getting the lowdown on Helen, he tasked Abramson with tracking down the dirt on her in New York. Ezra was called out of town on a bank heist job and apologized for not getting back to me sooner. He had the dirt, boy, did he have the dirt. Helen and Wai-Ling's scam of her marrying older men with heart conditions who conveniently die shortly after the I do's goes back years. By the way, he says he hasn't talked to you in six months but sends his regards.

"I have to hand it to you, Charlie. That was pretty smart and a bit of a gamble, but I think you like to gamble. It's part of the grift, the high. You gave me just enough dope on Helen to convince me you were on my side and for me not to follow up with Abramson. You knew he was out for a week or two and hoped that the scam would be over by then and you'd skip town. Like you're doing now.

"Lie number two. Nobody knew where Junior and Velma were living. You said you couldn't print the story about Velma's murder because it would damage Junior's rep. But the only people who knew about them living above the speak were me, Al, and Catherine. The only reason the police knew was because I told Doyle. Junior told you, or maybe Catherine. Finally, only a handful of people knew that Philip owned the speak. But you did. In the end, I guess it doesn't matter."

"You can't prove any of this," he snarled.

The ultimate confession.

"No, I can't," I admitted. "You played all of us like violins. You're damn lucky, you son of a bitch. Philip, the stepmother, and her brother are all dead, and Catherine is God knows where. Also, let's put some icing on this whole pack of lies. I fumbled my way around the warehouse that night, but you knew the layout. You'd been in that warehouse before and knew how the trapdoor worked. You didn't hesitate in the slightest when you climbed the ladder into the warehouse. I kept wondering what was nagging at me at the time, but I was too terrified to connect the dots. You must have unscrewed the lightbulbs as you navigated through the tunnel because I didn't see any light when you opened the trapdoor. And the tunnel was dark the night Catherine escaped. I had to give her my flashlight. You were the last one in that tunnel, so it was you who unscrewed the lightbulbs."

"You won't shoot me." He tried to bluff while simultaneously studying me, gauging whether I'd have the guts to plug him.

"Try me."

The confidence in my voice made him reconsider going for me. He began to back away toward the doorway, his hands still aloft. When he reached the outer door to the hallway, he said, "I am sweet on you," as if that would

CHAPTER THIRTY-EIGHT

win me over at this point, and I'd drop the gun. Fat chance.

"Lie number three. Breeze off and don't come back." I stood up and followed him out into the corridor. He turned around, and with my gun trained on his back, I watched him go down the steps. When I couldn't see or hear him, I ran back to the office, locked both doors and ran to the window to watch him drive away. Only then did I put down the gun.

Chapter Thirty-Nine

With some of Nick's money in my purse, I went to the City of Paris and bought a black suit fresh off the boat from France to replace the one burned to cinders on Catherine's boat. In addition, I bought two pairs of silk stockings that shimmered in the harsh department store light and elbow-length black gloves. I spent a small fortune on a pair of black pumps so comfortable I could have hiked the length of the Alps without breaking out in a single blister. And to my surprise, my boyish haircut was now the height of chic in Paris. The saleswoman clucked at me in approval after placing a stylish hat on my head. I didn't bat an eyelash when they presented me with the bill. One didn't go into battle without wearing the proper armor. I ordered the staff to send my old clothes to Nick's apartment, walked out of the City of Paris wearing all my new purchases, and made my way to John's Grill.

I'd mailed Dickie a personal note two days earlier to inform him that I'd booked his table for lunch two days hence. I signed it, M. Laurent, Investigator. I liked the word "investigator" better than private detective, which always held connotations of something illegal, tawdry, or shady. Someone like Nick could pull that off because you might want to hire someone who's closed-mouthed and not scared of something slightly or massively illegal. Investigator was relatively neutral; it could go either way.

I was early, but he'd already arrived and was sipping his Champagne. He stood up, and instead of the usual flush of pleasure on his face at seeing me, this was more like admiration and even approval. He didn't kiss my hand like he normally did but put his hand out for me to shake. Like I was an

CHAPTER THIRTY-NINE

equal.

I sat down. The waiter shook out our napkins and placed them on our laps. Turning to the waiter, I said, "Mr. Vance will have his usual. I will have the steak, medium rare, with the pommes frites and creamed spinach. Lemon meringue pie for dessert. To drink? Mr. Vance will have his usual lemonade, and I shall have tea. Black."

The waiter's mouth screwed up into a moue of surprise, and he looked to Dickie for support.

"You heard Miss Laurent. Chop, chop, my good man."

With a bow in my direction, the waiter scuttled off to the kitchen to place our order.

"My, my, my. Our little Miss Laurent has grown up. Divine suit, my dear. The *tout ensemble* is lovely. Kudos on cracking the Washington case." He raised his coffee cup in salute. "I know the real story isn't anything like what the police fed us. As if a butler would gun down his employers and their son. Ridiculous. Still, one hears things. I understand it was largely your legwork that cracked the case."

I smiled at him as smug as all get out.

He sighed. "As I suspected. However, sometimes one must live with the crumbs they design to feed us. Was it Doyle or you who insisted on keeping your name out of the papers?"

"We agreed to agree. Ma would have had me kidnapped and incarcerated in the nearest nunnery if my name was anywhere near that story."

"Probably best. At some point, you must tell me the actual story, but not today. Now, what's on your mind?"

I pulled off my gloves, hoping he wouldn't see that my hands were shaking a little. He could only say no.

"This is confidential. Nick has left for Chicago. He's back on Pinkerton's payroll, trying to make a new start." I didn't add that I doubted he was coming back.

Dickie raised an eyebrow but didn't say anything.

"He's left enough money to pay for the office, the phone, and the electricity for the next six months."

He raised the other eyebrow. "You're taking his place."

"I'm taking his place and have sub-leased his apartment as well. I'm not going to tell anyone that Nick's left San Francisco. Let them figure it out. I'm hoping that by the time the shoe drops, I will have established myself so that I won't need the fiction that he's still around."

"Your mother?"

"Doesn't approve."

"Albert?"

"Also doesn't approve."

Al and I weren't on speaking terms these days. I called Ma every day. First to ask how she was, to which she replied, "Fine." Then I'd tell her I was doing great and that I'd gone to mass that morning. She would say, "Good." I would say that I'd call her tomorrow, then hang up. We've repeated this conversation four days running, and until I return home, I suspect that will be the sum of our daily interaction.

"And Charles? I understand he's returned to New York."

"Yes, and he'd better stay there if he knows what's good for him." The tone of my voice left no doubt as to how I felt about Charlie Stein.

"Excellent." Dickie smiled. "I never quite trusted him. Especially regarding you." He peered at me over his coffee cup.

"No worries on that score. I never quite trusted him, either. Dickie?"

Dickie put down his drink.

"Yes?"

"Charlie Stein is very untrustworthy."

Because Dickie's so flamboyant, most people do not give him credit for how sharp he is.

"How untrustworthy?"

"Very," I emphasized. "A wrong gee from the word 'go.' I'll tell you about him when I give you the whole story about the Washingtons. In a nutshell, assume that when his lips are moving, he's lying."

"I am not surprised," he murmured but didn't press me for more details.

"Just for the record, if you didn't trust him, why did you give him an entrée to Washington's speakeasy?"

CHAPTER THIRTY-NINE

Dickie's eyebrows hit his hairline.

"I most certainly did not. Did he tell you that?"

"Yeah," I admitted. "Add that to the hundreds of other lies he spun. He's a very good liar."

"A hard lesson to learn, but valuable. There are very few people I trust in this world, and I can count them on one hand. Now, what are you going to do now with your smart suit and divine hat?"

I handed Dickie a piece of paper with my anticipated expenses written on it.

"I need to bring in enough to pay for the apartment and what I give my mother every month to help her out. I can do both the secretarial and footwork until I get myself established." I had hopes of hiring Janie Morris at some point.

He scanned my numbers. "One divorce case a month will keep you afloat. But just barely. Two cases, and you'll be able to eat three meals a day."

"That squares with what I thought. I need someone to teach me how to fire a gun and basic boxing moves."

"Given your penchant for sports…" He eyed me. "What is your golf score, my dear?"

"Seventy. On a good day, sixty-five."

"I know nothing about golf with the exception that it's played on grass with a lot of standing around and walking. Seems utterly ridiculous to me. That is why God created hotel lobbies and chairs. Is that a good score?"

"Yes. It's considered good."

He frowned. "How good? Don't be modest."

"I could go pro if there were tournaments for women," I admitted. "I leave most men in the dust."

"Excellent. Your hand-eye coordination should make you a natural. The thing with guns is either you have it or you don't. You don't want to shoot someone twice. That allows them to shoot you back. You must shoot to kill. Do you understand?"

I nodded, although I wasn't sure I could kill someone.

"I shall teach you the rudiments regarding firearms myself."

Now, it was my turn for the raised eyebrows.

"Did Nick ever tell you how we met in the army? No? I was part of a sniper team. I saved young Nick's life one day. Interestingly enough, we are related in some obscure way. Did you know he was also part of the Southern aristocracy? His family emigrated north—they saw there was more opportunity in manufacturing than farming—while mine stayed in the south and sold human beings for profit. Anyway, we were in the trenches—God, when weren't we in the trenches—it was pouring with rain, and I was up to my waist in mud. Nick stood next to me, both of us certain we wouldn't see the next day's dawn. As it happened, that afternoon, I drilled a hole in the heart of a Jerry gunner who had Nick in his sights."

"And you both saw the next day's dawn. You never cease to amaze me, Dickie."

"Well, that's natural. Sometimes I amaze myself."

The gourmand facing me couldn't have looked more unlike a military recruit than if he'd carved 4-F on his forehead. The turquoise suit, yellow shirt, and red polka-dotted tie didn't exactly scream regulation.

"Pardon me if this seems out of line, but I have a very hard time seeing you in the military."

"Yes, to say it was a travesty is putting it mildly." He sniffed and took a large sip of his lemonade. "Blame that horrible father of mine. His homage to all things violent was legendary. Naturally, given my penchant for bow ties," he flicked his tie with his thumb and forefinger, "the brass was not thrilled. However, generations of Vances have graced the halls of Montezuma, and they could not say no to him. I imagine numerous bills in very large dominations passed hands. Fortunately, I was president of the sharpshooter club at Princeton, and they made me an officer in charge of my unit's sniper brigade. I'm certain more bills exchanged hands. My hand-eye coordination is somewhat legendary, which saved me from being horribly bullied by the sons of the monied thugs who inhabited my father's world. To date, no one has bested my record. Anyway, Herman will help you on the boxing front, assuming Albert cannot."

"*Will* not is more the case." I kept my face passive, hiding my anger and

CHAPTER THIRTY-NINE

disappointment. Al still maintained that my plans to keep the detective agency alive were, quote, crazy, unquote. "You really think I can make a go of the agency? You're not just giving me a line of hooey to make me feel better?"

"Of course you can. There is only one woman in the world who I think is more competent than you are, and that's my mother. You have my full support."

"No one else thinks I can do it." I tried to stifle the wobble in my voice.

"They are wrong."

My shoulders slumped in relief. I could do this without Dickie, but without his approval, I might as well call it a day. This was the moment to make my pitch.

"I need a partner. A silent partner with no financial support," I stressed. "But someone who has the inside scoop on the social whirl. Who's cheating; who's not? Who's getting divorced? Who's going bankrupt? That someone whose name I can drop on the rare occasion to open doors that wouldn't normally open for me." I lowered my voice. "Now that Nick has left for Chicago, I need someone I can ask for advice now and then. I'm hoping that sort of person is you."

He bowed his head. "I'm tremendously flattered, my dear. *C'est moi.*"

"*C'est vous,*" I agreed.

"Certainly, we are at the *c'est tu* stage."

"*Vraiment.*"

"I must be very, and I mean *trés* invisible. Nicholas and I had a more-or-less identical agreement. We will have to choose our collaborations carefully. We cannot be sighted here more than once a month. Much to my dismay, this must be the last meal we shall share. Coffee," he held up his Champagne and glanced at my tea, "now and then is permissible. Anything else is verboten."

I nodded. "Of course."

"I must have Mother's approval."

"Naturally."

We shook hands.

Our lunches arrived. Before he began eating, he sat poised with his knife and fork in hand and said, "I hope you always retain that refreshing innocence. If you lose it, I will never forgive myself."

"Don't worry," I said. "I've got everything under control."

Chapter Forty

Stuffed to the gills with lemon meringue pie, I waddled back to the office, almost giddy with excitement. I picked up four newspapers from the corner newsstand, intending to read every one from cover to cover looking for opportunities.

A package wrapped in nondescript brown paper leaned against the office door with my name written on it in elegant cursive. Two inches high and about ten inches long, it was too flat to be a bomb. I didn't think Charlie would try to kill me as long as I kept my mouth shut.

I walked by the desk I'd never have to sit behind again, stuck my tongue out at my typewriter, and entered what used to be Nick's inner sanctum. It was now my inner sanctum, all mine. I realized that I'd never really had anything of my own other than my bedroom at home, which was filled with cast-off furniture that had belonged to my parents when they were first married. I hadn't even been allowed to put up the wallpaper I wanted. Too garish, my mother had said, and she then chose something I hated. But this space belonged to me and me alone. I ran a possessive finger over the top of the desk. Although identical to the desk in the outer office, it was nothing like that desk out there.

I sat down in what had been Nick's chair to tear off the paper and open the box. Sitting on top lay a car key, and next to the key was the flashlight I'd handed to Catherine in the tunnel under the speakeasy. Underneath the key and the flashlight was a handwritten note, and underneath the note was a stack of one-hundred-dollar bills. The note said:

Dear Maggie:

Thanks for saving my life. The rest? Well, it doesn't matter now. Will you do something for me? Place flowers on Philip's grave now and then. He wasn't a very good person, but he was still my brother. Sometimes, when he smiled, not his usual smirk, he looked like my mother.

The car is yours. I won't need it where I'm going. The money is to pay you for your services.

Regards, Catherine Washington.

P.S. She's parked around the corner on Hyde. Take care.

I didn't even count the money before putting it in the safe. I owned a car. I didn't have to arrive at clients' homes with a streetcar ticket in my pocket. I raced down the stairs and found it parked exactly where she said it would be. I climbed in. The key slipped into the ignition as if it were made of butter. I put her into gear and pulled away from the curb. With any luck, I'd hit Big Sur before the fog rolled in.

Acknowledgments

First, I'd like to thank Level Best Books for opening that publishing door for me once again. There is the usual crew of fellow writers who have cheered me on along with way, listening to my gripes and whining. Thank you to Sally, Anna, Mike, and Margaret. This series would never have been finished without your insight and expertise. As always, I thank my husband, Mark, for his support over these many decades.

About the Author

Claire M. Johnson's first novel, *Beat Until Stiff*, was set in the restaurant world and was nominated for the 2003 Agatha Award for Best First Novel and was a Booksense pick. Her second book in this series, *Roux Morgue*, received a starred review from *Publishers Weekly*. She has written two Jane Austen pastiches, *Pen and Prejudice* and *Resolution*, which she indie published, *For Thee*, a biographical historical novel of the marriage of Pauline Pfeiffer to Ernest Hemingway won the 2021 Gold Award bestowed by the Royal Palm Literary Award from the Florida Writers Association for genre fiction, and is currently being shopped to publishers. She won the same award in 2022 in the crime-fiction category for *Fog City*, her noir crime novel set in Prohibition-era San Francisco. Ms. Johnson has recently signed a three-book deal for her Fog City Noir series with Level Best Books. *Fog City* will debut in the summer of 2024. She is currently President of Mystery Writers of America's Northern California chapter.

SOCIAL MEDIA HANDLES:
  http://clairemjohnson.blogspot.com/
  https://www.instagram.com/clairemjohnsonwrites/

https://www.linkedin.com/in/claire-johnson-40baa210/

AUTHOR WEBSITE:
https://www.clairemjohnsonwrites.com/

Also by Claire M. Johnson

Beat Until Stiff (Poisoned Pen Press)

Roux Morgue (Poisoned Pen Press)

Pen and Prejudice (self-published)

Resolution (self-published)

Swim Town (self-published)